D0604817

CROUCHING VAMPIRE, HIDDEN FANG

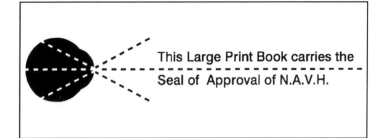

This Large Print Book carries the
Seal of Approval of N.A.V.H.

CROUCHING VAMPIRE,
HIDDEN FANG

KATIE MACALISTER

THORNDIKE PRESS

A part of Gale, Cengage Learning

GALE
CENGAGE Learning

Detroit • New York • San Francisco • New Haven, Conn • Waterville, Maine • London

GALE
CENGAGE Learning

Thorndike Press® Large Print Romance.
The text of this Large Print edition is unabridged.
Other aspects of the book may vary from the original edition.
Set in 16 pt. Plantin.
Printed on permanent paper.

LIBRARY OF CONGRESS CATALOGING-IN-PUBLICATION DATA

MacAlister, Katie.
    Crouching vampire, hidden fang : a Dark Ones novel / by Katie MacAlister.
        p. cm. — (Thorndike Press large print romance)
        ISBN-13: 978-1-4104-1982-8 (hardcover : alk. paper)
        ISBN-10: 1-4104-1982-7 (hardcover : alk. paper)
        1. Vampires—Fiction. 2. Seattle (Wash.)—Fiction. 3. Large type books. I. Title.
    PS3613.A227C76 2009
    813'.6—dc22   2009025757

Published in 2009 by arrangement with NAL Signet, a member of Penguin Group (USA) Inc.

Printed in the United States of America
1 2 3 4 5 6 7 13 12 11 10 09

DEC 1 6 2009

CROUCHING VAMPIRE, HIDDEN FANG

PROLOGUE

"He's here."

"Is he? Where? Let me see."

The air moved behind me as Magda hurried over to peer around me. "Are you sure that's him?"

I nudged aside the heavy blue tweed curtain, creating an infinitesimally small gap between curtain and window that allowed me to eye the man who stood on my front step. "It has to be. Just look at him."

"I would if you moved your hand . . . Ah." Magda had what I thought of as an opera singer's voice, rich in timbre, and with a Spanish accent that managed to be simultaneously charming and sultry. "Well, it's true he is wearing dark glasses. But lots of people wear those."

"At night?" I asked.

She pursed her lips. "He doesn't have long hair like Alec had."

"No, but he's got a widow's peak. That

screams vampire. So does the fedora he's holding."

"Bah. It's just a hat."

I pointed. "That is not just a hat. It's leather and stylish, and all the vamps I've seen have worn something similar."

"Hrmph. Lots of men wear hats like that. And long dusters."

"Oh, come on! Who do you know who dresses like something out of a European male model's agent portfolio, wears dark glasses and a hat, and positively reeks of sexy, smoldering danger?"

"Well . . ." Her face screwed up for a moment while she thought. "I just don't know. Are you sure that's the messenger?"

"Positive."

"Hmm." Magda's chin rested on my shoulder as we huddled behind the curtain. "He could be a religious person trying to convert you. Or someone who ran out of gas and needs to use your phone. Or maybe he's a spirit, and is lost, and needs you to help him find that place the spirits call heaven."

"The Icelanders call it Ostri, and he's not a spirit."

"How do you know? Are you wearing your thingie?"

I lifted my hand. A small oval moonstone

charm swung gently from a silver bracelet.

"OK, so he's not a ghost. Why don't you let him in and we'll see who he is?"

"Are you kidding?" I asked, giving her a gimlet eye. "He's a vampire! Don't you know anything? You never invite a vampire into your home. Once you do, they can come in anytime they want!"

Her lips curled. "Unlike, oh, say, a normal man?"

"You know what I mean."

"Why don't you just ask Kristoff?" she asked, moving away, her tone dismissive.

I let the curtain drop to glare across the small living room at my friend. "You know full well I haven't heard a single word from that particular man since that horrible time in Iceland when I ended up being his Beloved instead of Alec's. He hates me because I took his dead girlfriend's place. I couldn't possibly ask him, even if I knew where to find him, and I don't, so that point is completely moot."

"Don't be ridiculous," Magda said, plunking herself down on my couch, waving a hand toward the archway that led to my kitchen. "He's right here. You can ask him all you want."

My jaw dropped as a shadow detached itself from the darkness of the room beyond, and a man stepped forward into the light. Eyes the color of purest teal practically glowed at me, causing my heart to leap in my chest until I thought it would burst right out of me.

"Pia," Kristoff said in that wonderfully rich, Italian-accented voice that never failed to make me feel as if he were stroking my bare skin with velvet.

"How . . . how did you get here?" I stammered, my brain overwhelmed with the sight and scent and sound of him, right there, close enough to fling myself upon.

"You are my Beloved," he said, and took a step toward me, the light from a nearby lamp casting a golden glow on him, shadowing the sharp planes of his face and the little cleft in his chin, burnishing the short, dark chocolate curls that kissed the tips of his ears, curls that I knew were as soft as satin. And his mouth — oh, that mouth with the lush, sensitive lips that could drive me insane with desire even now had me remembering the taste of him, the slightly sweet, slightly spicy taste that was so wholly unique to Kristoff. Instantly my legs threatened to turn to mush. I clutched the back of a chair to keep from melting into a giant puddle right there on the floor in front of him. "We are bound together for all eternity, Pia. I cannot be parted from you."

"But . . ." My mind was pretty useless at this point, focused solely on remembering a million little intimate moments with him, but I forced it off those extremely pleasant memories and into some semblance of a working state. "But we *have* been parted. For almost two months."

"Kristoff did not expect you to take the steps of Joining with him," a man's voice said behind me.

The messenger who had been on my doorstep now stood in the doorway. I blinked a couple of times as I realized that I'd seen him before. "You're Andreas. You're Kristoff's brother."

"He did not expect to have a Beloved," Andreas continued, his face only slightly resembling that of the man whose memory had haunted my dreams.

"No more than I did, but you didn't see me running away," I said, turning back to Kristoff, intending to ask him why he hadn't contacted me once in the two months since I'd saved his life, inadvertently restoring his soul, but before I could say more, he slipped back into the shadows.

"You are my Beloved," he repeated as the darkness swallowed him up, the lyrical tones of his voice lingering in the air even as he disappeared from sight. "We are bound together."

"Wait —" I said, starting forward.

Andreas grabbed my arm, saying with earnest intensity, "He did not expect you to save him."

"I had to," I tried to explain, but Andreas simply shook his head and walked out the door.

"I had no choice," I said, my hands outstretched as I looked for someone to whom I could explain the situation. Magda sighed, set down her magazine, and stood up.

"Ray's calling for me. I have to go now. We'll be here soon, and then you and I can talk about it, OK?"

"You're leaving me?" I asked, a sudden sense of panic filling me as she walked toward the dark kitchen. "You're leaving me alone?"

She paused and shook her head, her lips curved in a gentle smile. "I'm not really here, Pia. It's just a dream, nothing more."

"But Kristoff was here," I said, gesturing toward the door to my bedroom. "He was right there. I saw him."

She said nothing, just gave me another little smile; then she, too, melted into nothing.

"I saw him!" I insisted to the now empty

12

room. "Kristoff, I saw you. Kristoff?"

The echo of my voice was the only sound.

I wrapped my arms around myself and sank to my knees with a sob of pure misery as my heart cried out his name. *Kristoff!*

Pia?

His voice was soft in my head, soft and intimate and warm, the feel of it flooding my senses with the memory of him. It was enough to jerk me out of the dream, hot tears leaking from the corners of my eyes as consciousness returned, and with it the profound sense of loss that seemed to be my constant companion.

As my mind fought to free itself from the muzziness of the dream, I realized what had happened. I'd called out to Kristoff from the depths of my dream, and he'd answered. Although I knew that frequently Beloveds and their Dark Ones had the ability to mind-talk to each other, our parting was sufficiently heartbreaking to keep me from trying it.

Pia?

The word resonated in my head, a sense of reluctant concern lingering long after the last echo faded away.

Yes, it's me. I'm sorry; I was asleep. I didn't mean to disturb you. The silence that filled my head wasn't made up of silence at all —

I could feel emotions flowing through him, but he was guarding himself, not allowing me to sense just what they were. Still, I wasn't going to let this opportunity slip by me. *I . . . I've been worried about you, Kristoff. Are you OK?*

Go back to sleep.

I buried my face in my pillow, trying to ignore the finality of his words, pretending I hadn't felt his mind withdraw from mine, but it was no use. Despite my nightly pledge that I would not think of him, would not dream of him, and would not wake up crying, I did just that.

At one point I thought there might be hope of a future with Kristoff. That tiny little morsel of hope shriveled up to nothing and wafted away as my body curled itself into a fetal ball, the pain of Kristoff's rejection leaving me racked with sobs as the long hours of the deep night passed into a joyless dawn.

CHAPTER 1

Crash!

"Sorry! I have a cart with a wonky wheel," I said by way of an apology to the woman whose shopping cart I had just bumped into while trying to maneuver my own out the door of the grocery store.

My victim reclaimed the package of toilet paper that bounced out of her cart at the impact, and waved away my apology with a gentle, "That happens. Light be with you."

"You called me up to tell me you have a wonky shopping cart?" An amused voice laughed softly in my ear as I swore under my breath, struggling one-handed to make my cart behave.

"No, I called you up because you left a message telling me to call you. Dammit! I'm so sorry, sir. It has a mind of its own. Are you hurt? Oh, good. I'll back up so you can get your shoe from the maw of the beastly thing."

15

A pleasant-faced young man gave me a somewhat weak smile as he knelt down to wrestle his shoe from under the wheel of the cart, his voice somewhat muffled by his position and the noise of the busy parking lot. "It's no problem. Light bless you."

"Oh, Pia." Magda laughed even more vigorously, her voice spilling out of the cell phone I clamped between my cheek and shoulder as I fought to shove the cart the few remaining feet to my car. "Only you could find such comical happenings at a grocery store."

"Well, it's partially your fault," I grumbled, giving in as the cart made a sudden swerve and seemed hell-bent on slamming into a sleek crimson Porsche sitting next to my somewhat battle-scarred Hyundai. I hauled the cart backward to my car. "The second you called the cart went wild on me, and it's impossible to control such a thing with one hand. But it is nice to hear from you."

"Likewise. And for the record, I was responding to your message when I called you. Are you stocking up on my behalf?"

"Yup. Per your request, I have purchased suitable amounts of animal flesh and seafood for my new grill. I promise you're going to go wild over my ginger-garlic scallops."

"Oh, Pia, about that . . ."

"Ma'am?" I turned at the tug on my arm. The man whose shoe my cart had tried to consume held out a bright blue package. "I think these fell out of your cart. I don't use this brand."

"My original plan was to stay with you for a week, and see my sister in Vancouver for a week, but . . ."

I made a face as I took the industrial-sized package of sanitary pads he shoved toward me. "Life seems to be bent on discomposing me today. Thank you."

He laughed. "Don't let it bother you. I have a wife, so I'm hip to all sorts of feminine products. Although I don't believe I've ever seen this particular product before. Does 'effusive flow' mean what I think it does?"

". . . and Ray managed to get away, so I thought I'd just switch to two weeks, if you don't mind . . ."

I shoved the pads into the car and tried to will away the blush that was sweeping upward. "Thank you. I think I'll just die of embarrassment now."

He laughed again and sauntered away, waving a friendly hand. "I wouldn't want to diminish any light in the world, least of all yours, so I'll be on my way."

"Pia? Pia? Are you listening to me?"

"Sorry. I was wanting a hole to open up and swallow me. . . ." I paused, looking back at the man as he hopped into a blue minivan. "Did he say what I think he said?"

"I don't know; I couldn't hear him — I was too busy telling you about the change in plans. Boy, you really *are* having a day, aren't you?" Magda's voice was choked with laughter.

"You have no idea. . . ." I thought for a moment, then shook my head. "I must have misheard. My day, as you said, has been interesting." I flung the rest of the groceries into the car, manhandled the cart over to a designated holding area, and returned to my car, cranking the air-conditioning on high as I slumped against the hot seat. "Hang on a sec while I plug in the headset . . . much better. Now, where were we? Oh! You said something about a change in plans? Don't tell me you're not coming to visit after all?"

"Would I do that to my favorite Zorya?"

I grimaced at the word. "You know full well I'm an ex-Zorya. The nearest Brotherhood group is in southern California, and I'm not about to offer my services to them."

18

"We can talk about your future when we get up there."

"We?" I pulled out of the parking lot and drove slowly through the tiny town perched high in the mountains, located about an hour's drive out of Seattle. My house, modest as it was, sat near the edge of the town, nestled between tall fir trees and a sheer rocky wall. "Who's we?"

"Ray is coming with me. If you don't mind, that is."

"Mind? No, I like him." I had to work a little to bring up my mental image of the man Magda had met on the singles' tour we'd taken some two months before. All I could really remember of him was that he was tall and rather skinny, balding, with mild eyes and an innocuous manner. To be honest, he seemed to fade to near invisibility when Magda was around, but she had that effect on a lot of people. She was full of life and color, with snapping black eyes and a joy of life that was infectious. "So you guys are still going strong, eh?"

"More than ever," she cooed. "He rearranged his schedule so that he'd have a month to spend with me before he has to go back to Denver. Isn't that sweet? So I hoped you wouldn't mind if he came with me to visit you. I swear he's housebroken, and he's promised he'll be happy to just sit and read or watch movies if we want to have some girl time together."

"Sounds perfect," I said, parking my car in the tiny carport attached to my equally tiny house. I puffed a little as I hauled all the groceries inside.

"You OK?" Magda asked when I grunted with relief as I dropped the heavy bags on the kitchen table.

"Yeah, just out of shape. And before you ask, no, I haven't found time to go to the ladies' gym like I said I was going to."

Magda giggled. "Plump is in, sweetie. I keep telling you that."

"Uh-huh. Maybe your plump is in, but mine is spilling out all over the place. Whoever said that pining for a man would make you waste away to nothing was full of bull. I've gained ten pounds since I came back from Iceland!"

"Judging by the way you and Kristoff went at it while you were there, I'd say he was a man who appreciated a woman with abundant curves, and you have nothing to worry about."

The vision rose in my mind of a midnight tryst in a barn, my body suffused with heat as I remembered the sensation of Kristoff's mouth caressing the flesh of my neck and breasts. But with that memory came another one: that of Kristoff silently withdrawing his mind from mine.

I didn't doubt that despite my physical flaws he desired me sexually . . . but a Beloved was supposed to be so much more than that.

How could I be anything to a man who didn't want me?

"Pia, you still there?"

"Yes," I said, clearing my throat and trying not to sound as if I were on the verge of tears.

Instantly, her voice was filled with sympathy. "Oh, honey, I'm sorry; I shouldn't have brought up the subject of Kristoff."

"No, it's OK. It's just that I had this strange dream this morning. That's what I was calling about. You remember the messenger I told you the vampires were going to send me? I dreamed he came, and somehow you were here, and so were Kristoff and his brother, and it seemed so real until I woke up."

"That's how dreams are."

"I know, but this was . . . well, different. Oh, hell, someone's at my door. I really don't want to see anyone." I snatched up a box of Kleenex and dabbed at my eyes as I moved through to the living room. I hesitated for a moment at the door, then scooted to the side to peek out of the window at the front porch.

"I'll go, then."

"No, it's OK. It's just a couple of religious people," I said, watching as a woman and a man slid a small pamphlet into the screen door before leaving.

"Bah. I usually tell them I'm a cannibal and they leave me alone."

"I tried that once. I told them I was an anarchist, and they just visited me every week to try to save me," I said, opening the door just enough to snatch up the religious newsletter, closing it quickly before slumping down on the couch next to the window. "So exactly how long will you and Ray be able to stay? The whole week that we planned, or will you guys want to go off on your own and make smoochy faces at each other?"

I didn't want to admit how much I'd been looking forward to Magda's visit. Although my job at a no-kill animal shelter specializing in elderly pets was satisfying, ever since I'd returned from my adventures in Iceland, life seemed to be . . . empty. It was as if a part of me were missing; something that I used to have was now gone, leaving me a shell of a person. I didn't expect Magda would change that, but she had become a very good friend, and I was cheered no end by the thought of her visit.

"No! That's the good part. Because Ray is taking a whole month off, I managed to talk my manager into giving me an extra week, so I'll have two weeks with you, and then one with my sister before we have to come back to San Francisco. That is, if you can stand us that long. Ray, hand me the basil, would you? No, the fresh stuff. Could you chop that onion for me? Sorry, Pia. We're making spaghetti."

"Sounds yummy. And stand you?" I laughed somewhat grimly. "I may never let you guys go home!"

"Oh, yes, we'll just see how long that opinion remains once Kristoff shows up and apologizes for being such a butthead." Her voice dropped suddenly. "Speaking of that . . . do you want me to tell Ray? About you being a Zorya and Kristoff and the you-know-whats and all the rest?"

I rubbed my forehead. Lately I seemed to always have a nagging, low-grade headache. "I don't think that's necessary. I'm not a Zorya anymore, and given this morning, I think I just need to face the fact that Kristoff isn't ever going to — Crap. Some-one's at the door again."

"Use the cannibal line this time. I guarantee you it'll work."

"I'm sorry, but I'm not interested," I was
saying even before I had the door all the
way open. My excuse dried up at the sight
of the man standing on the steps. "Gark."

"What?" Magda asked. "What about a
park?"

The man raised an eyebrow at me. "You
are Pia Thomason?"

"Ack!" I said, and slammed the door shut
in his face. "Oh, my God, Magda, it's him!"

"Him? Him who?"

A shivery déjà vu sensation washed over
me as I leaped over to the couch, shoving
aside the curtain on the window just enough
to peek out at the man. He knocked at the
door again.

"Him the messenger. Good Lord, we've
already done this!"

"We've done what?" Magda sounded confused.

"This, we've done this! This was the
dream I had this morning."

Muttered conversation was audible on the
phone for a moment before Magda uncov-
ered the mouthpiece and said, "Honey,
would you go down to the basement and
get me that bottle of olive oil? The Italian
one. Pia's having a crisis, and this may take

24

a few minutes."

I heard Ray say something as he moved off to do Magda's bidding.

"I'm not having a crisis," I hissed, peeking out at the man on my porch. "I'm just facing the messenger, that's all. Just a vampire come to do God knows what to me."

"Ray sends his love, by the way, and says he hopes your crisis isn't a serious one," she said in an aside before continuing. "How do you know the man is the messenger? Maybe he's someone else. Maybe he's another religious type. Or maybe he's trying to sell Girl Scout cookies."

I eyed the stranger again as he raised his hand to knock. "He's around six feet tall and is wearing a very tailored black sports coat with matching pants, a scarlet shirt that looks like it's made of raw silk, and shoes that probably cost more than my car."

"That could be anyone," Magda insisted, the sounds of chopping accompanying the words.

"And a fedora that's angled to shade his face from the sun. I covered all this in the dream! Although that messenger turned out to be Andreas, and this guy is definitely not Kristoff's brother."

Silence followed for a moment. "OK, that

description does sound like a you-know-what."

"Vampire."

"Yes. Ray, my cherub of delight, that is indeed a bottle of olive oil, but it's Greek, not Italian, and I will not put Greek olive oil in spaghetti. Would you mind . . . Thanks, love. Mwah." Magda was silent for a moment as faint sounds of footsteps fading away were audible even on the phone. "All right, he's gone again. Pia, you're going to have to let the vamp in."

"I don't want to," I said stubbornly, turning my back on the window, glaring suspiciously at the bedroom. I knew full well that Kristoff wasn't going to walk out of there, as he had in the dream, but I couldn't stop myself from looking. "My life is going really well right now. Kind of. Somewhat. Oh, hell, it's a nightmare, but that's only going to be made worse by involvement with the Moravian Council, or whatever it is the vamps call themselves."

"From what I remember of them, you're not going to have a choice. They seemed kind of pushy."

The knocking at my front door got even louder. Obviously the messenger was getting tired of waiting. "I don't care. I have to get rid of this guy. What is it vamps don't like? Garlic and holy water? I don't have any of the latter, but I have garlic bread. You think that will work?"

"Pia, sweetie . . ." Magda's voice took on a frustrated tinge as I marched out into the kitchen and dug through a bag until I found a loaf of garlic bread. "I really don't think pretending none of this exists is the answer."

The vamp on my doorstep stopped knocking and was outright pounding on my door now. "Wish me luck," I said, setting down the phone in order to peel back the wrapper on the garlic bread. I wielded it like a club as I swung open the door.

Madga's voice was faint but audible from the phone. "Pia? Pia? What are you . . . Oh, she is so silly sometimes. . . ."

"I have garlic and I'm not afraid to use it!" I shouted at the vampire, shaking the bread in his face.

He looked at it for a moment; then his gaze shifted to me, a look of stark incredulity on his face. "Bread?" he asked, his voice silky with some European accent.

"It has garlic on it," I said, pulling open the loaf to show him the tiny bits of garlic smooshed into the butter. "So just stay back!"

He reached out and touched the garlic

butter, licking the tip of his finger. "Very tasty."

"You're not . . . Garlic isn't poisonous to you?" I asked, taken aback.

He closed his eyes for a moment, a martyred expression on his face. "No, that's a fallacy created by mortals. I assume you are Pia Thomason? I am —"

"No, you don't," I said, desperately looking around as he started to enter my house. I snatched up the religious newsletter and shoved it at him.

He didn't flinch, or shriek, or run madly away at the image of something religious. He just took it and gave me a long-suffering look. " 'The Watchtower'?"

I slumped against the door. "I should have known it wouldn't work — Kristoff dragged me to a church to marry me, after all — but it was the only thing I had."

He took the garlic bread from me, and set it and the newsletter down on the table next to the door. "Pia Thomason, I am here by a directive from the Moravian Council. As you are no doubt aware, you have been ordered to appear before the council to answer questions that have arisen since the events of June this year. For matters of your safety and comfort, I will escort you to Vienna, and am authorized to meet any reasonable financial needs the journey will impose upon you. The plane leaves in four hours. Am I correct in assuming that you are not yet packed for the journey?"

I picked up the cell phone, saying into it, "It's the messenger, all right, and he's immune to both garlic and religious things. He wants me to go to Vienna."

"I heard. We can watch your house for you if you like —"

"That won't be necessary. I'll call you later." I hung up the phone and faced the vampire. Like the other males of his species, he would have been at home on a fashion show runway. I wondered if it was some rule that all vampires had to be drop-dead sexy. "I told the council when they sent me the e-mail saying you were coming that I had no intention of letting them do any sort of third degree on me. Christian Dante is the head of the council, isn't he?"

The vampire inclined his head in agreement. "He is executive director, yes."

"He was there in Iceland when all the stuff happened. Well, he was there for most of it. I told him then everything I knew, so I have nothing further to say to any of the council."

"You are a Midnight Zorya in the Brotherhood —"

"I am not," I interrupted, holding up my

hand to stop him.

He looked pointedly at the moonstone charm hanging from my wrist.

"Not anymore," I said, lowering my hand. "I gave up Zoryaing. If there were someone else I could give the stone to, I would, but there is no Brotherhood group here, for which I am profoundly grateful, if you want to know the truth. So you can just go back to your precious council and tell them that I said no."

He was silent for a moment, his dark eyes assessing me in a manner that made me very uncomfortable. Mentally, I ran over any stake-shaped objects I might have in the house. "I should tell you that my orders to bring you before the council did not take into account your wishes."

I lifted my chin, matching his intense gaze with one that I hoped did not show the fear that suddenly rolled around in my stomach. "Is that a threat?"

"No. It is merely a statement of fact. I am charged with bringing you before the council, and I will do so."

His arrogant statement was fortunately just what I needed. The fear inside me changed to anger: anger that the vampires were so high-handed, anger that the man in front of me thought I was such a pushover, and anger that I was in this position to begin with. Where was Kristoff when I needed him to protect me from the ire of his brother vampires? Why wasn't he here like he was supposed to be, suitably grateful that I got back his soul?

The anger grew hot, building and intensifying until it threatened to burst out of me.

"No!" I suddenly shouted, flinging my arms open wide. A brilliant, blinding blue-silver-white light burst forth from my hands, arcing above and below me, surrounding me in a sphere of brilliance.

The vampire yelped as the rays of the light touched him, flinging himself backward through the open door.

"I will not be used," I shouted at him, the light growing in intensity. "Not by you, your council, or anyone! Do you understand? No one!"

The vampire started to say something, but I slammed shut the door, locking it before I crumpled to the floor, face resting against the cool wood as the light surrounding me slowly faded to nothing.

CHAPTER 2

"Last One Standing Shelter, this is Pia. No, I'm sorry, our shelter is closed until the end of the month. We're having some remodeling work done to the buildings, and the animals have been moved to a temporary shelter so as not to be disturbed by the construction and such." I tapped on the keyboard and pulled up the information on the caller. She was cleared for adoption, but hadn't made up her mind yet on which dog she wanted. A couple entered the office and, after looking around for a moment, headed for my desk. I covered the mouthpiece of the phone. "I'll be with you in just a sec."

The woman smiled and nodded, and wandered over to look at the board with pictures of all the available senior pets for which the temporary shelter was currently serving as home. I gave the caller only half of my attention, watching the woman and wondering why she looked familiar.

"Yes, you can come by the dogs' temporary housing, although we won't be conducting any adoptions until the remodeling is finished. You're welcome." I hung up the phone and gave the man standing at the reception counter a bright, professional smile. "Can I help you?"

"Do you run this shelter?" he asked, looking around the office.

"No, I'm just the Internet guru and fundraising administrator. I'm afraid our office is closed. I'm just about to leave myself, actually. We're having some remodeling done, and —"

"You're Pia," the man interrupted.

"Yes," I said slowly, looking at him a little closer. Something about him was ringing a bell in my head, too. "I'm sorry. I have a horrible memory for faces. Have we met?"

"Not formally, no." He smiled. The woman came over and smiled at me, as well. I stood up slowly, suddenly wary. "We met, if you can call it that, a week ago. Outside the Safeway. Your cart bumped into my wife's, and later seemed to be attracted to my shoe —"

"Oh, yes," I said, goose bumps marching up my arm. I glanced at the stone swinging gently from the bracelet on my right wrist. It wasn't giving me any sign that the couple was anything but what they seemed, and yet the hairs on the back of my neck were standing on end. "How is it that you know my name?"

The man's smile grew larger. "A new Zorya is always celebrated, no matter where she is located."

"Oh, no," I said, backing away slowly. "You're reapers."

He bowed. "We have the honor of belonging to the Brotherhood of the Blessed Light."

"Then I did hear you right the other day at the store. And you . . ." I turned to the woman. "You said something lightish, too."

She came forward, stopping in front of me to dip an awkward curtsy. "I'm Janice Mycowski. This is Rick, my husband, and I can't tell you how thrilled we are to meet you."

"So . . . what, you're stalking me?" I asked in stark disbelief.

"Oh, no! We wouldn't do that," she said, distress visible in her muddy hazel eyes. She cast a worried glance at her husband. "We were just so excited that you were here, in our area — when word reached us that a new Zorya had been made, and that she was from Seattle, we were naturally excited. But then the governors said that you were a bit confused, and asked us to help clear some things up for you. You can imagine what a thrill and an honor it is for us to be asked to aid a Zorya."

"Um . . . all right. I'd be thrilled and honored, too, but I'm not a Zorya anymore." A bad feeling was growing in the pit of my stomach. "I hung up that hat almost two months ago. What . . . what exactly are you supposed to be helping me with?"

Janice clasped her hands together, beaming first at her husband, then at me. "The governors asked us to answer any questions you might have — Rick is very learned in Brotherhood history, and I've led more than two hundred welcome sessions, so between us, there probably isn't a question that we can't answer."

"I've made it a policy to never turn down an offer of help, but I'm afraid I'm still a bit lost. You keep mentioning governors, but I don't know exactly who you're talking about." The headache that always seemed to be hovering over me like a dark cloud intensified.

"The governing board," Rick explained.

"Governing board?" I frowned and rubbed my forehead. "I thought the Zenith ruled the Brotherhood."

"One normally does, but the last Zenith . . ." Janice sent another glance toward her husband.

He picked up where she left off. "The last Zenith was destroyed by the vampire scum she fought so valiantly against."

"Whoa, now! First of all, vampires are not scum. I know several of them, and they're perfectly nice people."

The couple wore identical shocked expressions. "You . . . *know* them?" Rick finally asked.

"Yes." I crossed my arms, daring them to say something. There was absolutely no love lost between the Brotherhood and the Dark Ones — quite the opposite, since pretty much a state of war existed between the two. But I was long past caring what the Brotherhood thought of my knowing vampires. In fact, I considered telling them I was Kristoff's Beloved. That might just guarantee that I wouldn't be involved with their group anymore.

Then again, it might also mean my demise. The Brotherhood held to a no-quarter policy when it came to vamps and their buddies.

Jan and Rick exchanged glances. "That's . . . unusual," Rick finally said. "I don't know quite what to say to that."

"Well, I have some other news that you

might be interested in. Those vampires you are blaming for the death of the Zenith are innocent. She was shot and killed by one of your own."

"No," Janice said, shaking her head. "The director of the board of governors was there. I read his report on the horrible tragedy, and he stated quite clearly that he was there trying to protect the Zenith. She was killed by a vampire. It was his gun that shot her."

I sucked my bottom lip for a moment as I moved behind the reception desk, keeping a distance between us. I didn't exactly expect them to fling themselves upon me with knives, but stranger — and deadlier — things had happened during my time in Iceland, and if nothing else, my time there had taught me a certain amount of circum-spection where members of the Brother-hood were concerned.

"I was there, too, you know," I finally said.

Surprise lit their eyes.

I nodded, a little curious by that. I had a suspicion I knew who they were talking about, although I hadn't known he was the director — Frederic Robert, a soft-spoken Frenchman who was no stranger either to power or the ability to use it. But he was in jail in Iceland, although obviously he'd had some sort of contact with the Brotherhood if he had been able to make a report. The question that tickled my mind was why he hadn't told the reapers that I was present at the same time. "I saw exactly what happened, and I can assure you that Denise was *not* shot by a vampire. But that's really a moot point, isn't it? The fact is that she's dead, and I'm no longer a Zorya, so although I'm flattered that you're so keen to see me, I'm afraid that you're bound to be disappointed. I do not intend to do any more Zoryaing."

"Unfortunately, it doesn't work that way," Rick said.

"I don't care what the procedure is to de-Zorya oneself; whatever it takes, I'll do it," I said sharply. "I will be happy to hand over this stone to whoever wants to take the job, so long as someone takes it, and soon. In fact, there's no time like the present."

Janice backed away as I walked forward, taking off the bracelet in an attempt to hand it to her. She lifted her hands as if to hold me off. "Oh, no, I couldn't take that! It's the Midnight stone!"

"Someone has to take it," I insisted. "I'm not going to hold on to it forever."

"You're the Zorya," Rick said with a decidedly stubborn set to his jaw.

"Oh, for God's sake . . ."

The door jangled as a woman entered, her presence and voice seeming to fill the room with sunshine. "Are you ready to go to lunch? Ray found the most divine diner. It's just like something out of . . . What was that show set in Alaska, Ray?"

Magda, in the doorway, turned to look back at Ray, but all I saw of him was his hand waving as he disappeared down the walk toward the street. Magda shrugged and turned back to me with a smile. "It doesn't matter, although he says the pie there is a definite must. Oh, I'm sorry; I didn't realize you were busy."

The last was addressed to Rick and Janice.

"They're from the Brotherhood," I said, my frustration at the situation making me snappish. "This is my friend Magda. She was with me in Iceland. She knows all about the vampires and you people."

"Then she must know how vital it is that you use your abilities for good, not evil," Janice started to say, but my temper was becoming more and more frayed. If it wasn't the vamps wanting me for one thing, it was the reapers wanting me to do their dirty work. I rubbed my temples, irritated at being caught in the middle of a war that was not of my own doing. "You cannot turn your back on humanity now, not when we are in such a strong position, not when we have the opportunity to eradicate the vampires once and for —"

"Just how many vampires have you met?" I shouted, startling Janice into silence.

Magda blinked at me. "Pia, I doubt if yelling at the poor woman —"

"Well, I don't doubt." I turned from Magda to Janice and pinned her back with a look that should have scared her to her toenails. "How many?"

"I . . . We . . ." Janice shot a worried look at her husband, who took her hand and answered for her.

"We haven't actually met any vampires, but we don't need to be on a friendly basis with evil to recognize it."

"Evil, schmevil!" I stormed, my hands waving around as I stomped toward them. I realized I was being rude, but I'd had as much as I could take.

To my secret enjoyment, they backed up. Magda gave me a tolerant smile as she told the couple, "The vamps really aren't that bad, you know. Some of them are very nice, in fact. I think they've probably just gotten a bad rap over the years because of the fact that they're kind of intense. Nice, but intense. And sexy as hell."

"Nice!" Janice choked on the word.

"Yes, nice. They're no more evil than you are," I said, trying to calm myself down. "No, I take that back — they're a whole lot *less* evil than you, because they don't blindly follow some dogma that requires them to hate an entire group of people based solely on their origins. Honestly, at times I think the Brotherhood is no better than the Nazis! How dare you tell me that vampires are evil when you haven't even bothered to meet one!"

"We couldn't meet one! They're murder-ous —" Janice said, but once again I cut her off.

"Oh, they are not any such thing. They may defend themselves, but they don't go out of their way to harm people. You guys have given them such a bad rap over the years that I don't think any of you really knows what they're like. Yes, it's regrettable that they've had to defend themselves, and that may result in some deaths, but if you people wouldn't attack them, there wouldn't be *any* deaths!"

"Amen," Magda said, nodding brusquely.

Janice's spine stiffened. "Oh, there wouldn't be any deaths? Those . . . *monsters* that you insist on defending attacked and killed several members of the Brotherhood in Iceland. Without cause they attacked

41

them, so you'll have to forgive me if I don't believe what you're saying."

"Are you calling me a liar?" I crossed my arms, holding firm to my temper.

Janice cast another nervous glance toward her husband. I'm not normally the type of person who gets her jollies out of intimidating someone else, but I was beginning to see the attraction of doing so with someone so misguided, so intent on refusing to face the truth. If letting her see that I didn't believe in what the Brotherhood stood for would help her understand the truth, then by heavens, I would become the scariest person around.

"No, I would never so insult a Zorya. I am certain that you have been misled —"

I took a step toward her, narrowing my eyes as I did so. "Good, because unlike you, I was present in Iceland, and I can assure you that the only reapers who were killed were a couple of guys who tried to slaughter a Dark One named Kristoff and me in cold blood. They attacked us without warning or cause and told him flat out they were going to kill us both. He simply defended us, and quite frankly, if Kristoff hadn't been there to protect me, I wouldn't be alive now."

That stopped both of them for a moment.

"Are you sure it was members of the

Brotherhood who attacked you?" Rick asked slowly after he and Janice exchanged a couple of doubtful looks. "Did the vampire tell you it was members of the Brotherhood? Perhaps he was mistaken, or you misunderstood."

"No, they were members, all right. It was confirmed for me later."

"I don't understand," Janice said, frowning. "Why would they attack a Zorya?"

I glanced at Magda, now really curious as to what Frederic had told them about the events in Iceland. He knew full well that I was a Beloved, but he didn't appear to have mentioned it.

Magda gave a tiny little shake of her head, obviously just as baffled as I was.

"That doesn't matter now. What does matter is the fact that you are blindly following the precepts of an organization without any justification."

"We're not mindless sheep, you know," Janice replied quickly. "The Brotherhood has been cleansing evil from the mortal world for almost five hundred years. It could not have done so without a need for such acts. There is precedent."

"Precedent," I scoffed. "That's the blind following the blind if I ever heard it. Tell me, do you even know *why* the Brotherhood started going after vampires?"

"Er . . . no," Rick admitted. He looked a bit shamefaced. "I've done quite a bit of research on the Brotherhood, but haven't gone that far back in the records yet. We only joined a few years ago, after Janice had a bad experience with an evil being."

"Not a vampire, I assume?" Magda asked.

"No, it was a necromancer, a woman who was trying to raise an undead army," he said in all seriousness.

Magda and I gawked at him.

"You're kidding," she said. "An undead army? Like of zombies?"

"Liches, from what I understand," Rick answered.

I blinked at Magda. She blinked back, saying, "This is so . . . so . . ."

"Hollywood bizarre," I finished for her.

"Like a B-movie scriptwriter gone insane," she agreed.

"Regardless," I said, giving myself a mental shake to remove the *Night of the Living Dead* images from my brain and focus on more important things. It was easier said than done. "Well, hell. I've forgotten my point."

"Vampires are good; Brotherhood is crazy," Magda said absently. "What exactly is a lich, do you know?"

I ignored her attempt to sidetrack me. "The point is that you have no real reason for believing that vampires are the evil undead deserving of merciless slaughter, and I for one refuse to be a part of any such organization."

"But you *are* a part of it," Janice pointed out.

"Only until I can find someone to give the Zorya stone to."

"You were a part of the incidents in Iceland," Rick said, frowning. "You were involved in all those deaths."

"I told you, there were only a couple of people killed, and they attacked us —"

"The vampires wiped out the entire Icelandic branch!" Janice interrupted. "There were at least fourteen people altogether that your *friends* slaughtered."

I stared in openmouthed surprise for a moment before saying, "They're not all dead! Two were held by the Icelandic police, although the Zenith is now dead, and it wasn't a vampire who shot her. The others are in the custody of the vamps, but they're not dead, either."

"How do you know?" she asked, and for a moment, I was speechless.

I looked at Magda. "Christian wouldn't kill the reapers, would he?"

She looked somewhat doubtful. "I don't think he would. Not without cause. Did he say anything to you about what would happen to them?"

"No," I said, frowning as I cast my mind over the events of the last couple of months. "They don't have fourteen people, though. They only caught a couple of them: Mattias and Kristjana, and those two people who Frederic brought."

"Then it would seem that we aren't the only ones who can be accused of falling victim to blind faith," Janice retorted. "You don't know that the vampires are treating the Brotherhood, your own people, well at all. You only assume they are, but you don't know for a fact what has happened to them. For all you know, they could be dead."

I wanted to protest that point, but I had an uncomfortable feeling that any explanation I made would sound just as feeble as their mindless attacks. "You're right. I don't know for certain that they're not dead, but I highly doubt that it's so."

"They didn't hesitate to kill others," Janice said, her eyes calculating. "Why should they stop at doing so to those captives?"

"I've told you several times now, they're not that way. They seek justice for the deaths of their fellow vampires, yes, but they did not start this war, nor do they want to continue it. Can you say as much about the Brotherhood?"

"If you truly mean what you say," Janice said after she and her husband traded silent glances, "then you will not mind proving it."

"How so?" I asked, wary about falling into any verbal traps.

Janice lifted her chin. "The director of the board of governors sent us to negotiate with you. Yes, that's right, negotiate."

"What, specifically?" I asked, leaning against the desk.

Magda moved to my side in a blatant show of support.

"The director told us that you would refuse to do your duty."

"I'd have thought *that* was made clear by my replies to the letters and e-mails I've been pelted with from you guys demanding I go help out with one cleansing or another."

She studied me for a second, her mouth tight and slightly pursed, as if she smelled something offensive. "The director authorized us to negotiate a way for you to end your career as a Zorya."

"Excellent." I started to take off the bracelet bearing the moonstone.

"No." Janice held up her hand to stop me.

"Removing a Zorya from the Brotherhood is not as easy as simply handing over the Midnight stone."

"Is there some sort of formal court-martial she has to go through to be stripped of her rank?" Magda asked.

"As a matter of fact, there are only two methods of removing a Zorya from the Brotherhood. The first is, naturally, death," Rick said.

"Pass," I said with a wry little smile to myself.

Janice looked like she wanted to consider that option a bit longer, but Rick, bless him, continued on. "The second is an execration."

"I said that death is out —"

"Not execution, *execration.* The modern usage of the word 'execrate' means to detest or loathe, but in centuries past it was used to mean 'to curse.' The Brotherhood has long labeled those cast out of the fold as cursed to walk the earth in darkness."

"There could be worse things than that," Magda told me.

"Like remaining in. I agree. And I agree to the execration, assuming that there is something I must do in order to get the ball rolling. Make a statement of my beliefs? Provide a witness to say I'm friendly to the enemy? Or do you need some sort of blood oath?"

"Nothing so easy, I'm afraid," Rick said with a genuine smile.

Despite the fact that he was one of the bad guys, I kind of liked him. His wife, however . . .

"The director said you would refuse to listen to reason," she said, her lips still tight.

I almost asked her why she bothered to argue with me, but let that go in favor of ending this conversation more quickly.

"So he empowered us to make a deal with you. You failed acting as Zorya in two separate instances: The first was refusing to send on a spirit who had sought help from you."

"Ulfur," I said, a pang of guilt zinging through me at the memory of him. "I didn't refuse him at all. I would have sent him on if I could have, but he opted to remain and help me."

Janice's lips tightened even more. I was surprised she could crack them to talk. "Nonetheless, you must find him and send him to Ostri, as you were meant to do."

"I have no problem with helping him," I said. "Although he said he would be fine when I left Iceland. But he must be tired of poking around with nothing to do but watch tourists. What's the second thing?"

"You must engineer the release of those Brotherhood members whose detention by the vampires you aided two months ago. If you do those two things, the director will ask the board of governors to execrate you from the Brotherhood."

"Free the reapers?" My stomach wadded up on itself when I realized just what they were asking.

"Mother Mary," Magda said under her breath, her gaze fixed on me. "The vamps aren't going to want to do that, are they?"

"What you ask is too much," I protested, my hands flailing a little as I tried to imagine me marching up to the vampires and asking them sweetly if they'd let their mortal enemies go. "Even if I knew where they were being held, there's no way I could get them released."

"Nonetheless, those are the terms of the agreement. Either you restore to the Brotherhood the four people listed here" — she handed me a card — "or you will fulfill your duties as Zorya."

"You can't make her be a Zorya," Magda said hotly.

"Actually, we can," Rick said, one side of his mouth quirking up. "I always thought it was a bit odd that a Zorya is merely a conduit to the power of the moon, but I can see why it would be useful in just such a case."

I grimaced at the idea of being used again as a tool of destruction. The very idea made me sick to my stomach. Therefore, the vampires were just going to have to play ball with me. Which meant I would have to face that silly council after all. "All right," I said slowly, looking at the card. The name Mattias had been written next to a name I recognized, followed by the word "Vienna"; Kristjana was evidently being held in Iceland, while the other two had a notation that they were being detained in Oslo.

"I doubt I can do anything for these three people," I said, pointing to Kristjana and the two flunkies Frederic had brought in. "I don't know the people in charge of them. But I do know the one keeping Mattias. I will agree to rescue him in exchange for my freedom."

Janice frowned and looked as if she were going to object, but Rick leaned in and whispered something. She answered, and they spent almost a minute in conversation before Janice finally turned back. "We will concede the rescue of the two Norwegian members, since you had no direct contact with them, but you are responsible for

Kristjana being held. Therefore, we will be satisfied if you will bring back to us the sacristan and the priestess."

"Priestess?" I was momentarily taken aback by the idea of Kristjana being some sort of a holy woman. Devout people did not scream like banshees while flinging themselves on others with the intent of gouging out flesh with their bare hands.

"It is the title given to the person in charge of each chapter," Rick explained. "It's more an honorific than anything."

"Ah." I thought for a moment, but didn't think I could get them to budge on that point. "All right, we have a deal. You can go back and tell your director that. Er . . . for the record, the director *is* Frederic, isn't it? For that matter, has another Zenith been chosen?"

"Yes, the director is Monsieur Robert," Janice answered, picking up her purse. "No Zenith has been named yet. The director and governors are meeting in Los Angeles to discuss candidates."

"Wow," Magda said, watching as Rick waved and followed Janice out without saying anything further. She raised her eyebrows as I carefully closed the door behind them. "That was . . . Frederic? The same Frederic that I met?"

"Yes," I said slowly. "Somehow he must have escaped jail in Iceland. I wonder how he did that."

"And he's the director of the governing board? Whew. No wonder you didn't like him. Are you really going to do it? Free Mattias and Kristjana, I mean?"

"I don't have a choice, do I?"

Her face screwed up in thought. "Nope. Can't see any other way out of it."

"Me either." I turned off the computer equipment and the lights, preparing to lock up the office.

"Boy, I'd give just about anything to see that delicious Christian's face when you walk up to his door and ask him for the reapers. You have to take me with you — I can't possibly miss something that's going to be so very entertaining."

"Oh, yes, it'll be a laugh riot, all right." My stomach felt like lead, my spirits dampened and drooping like soggy feathers.

She giggled, but watched me closely as I gathered up my things and stuffed them into the leather satchel that I used as a briefcase. I stood her scrutiny for as long as I could before turning to her with an irritated, "What?"

She nodded toward the door. "You were impressive with that woman, you know? It was a side of you I hadn't seen before."

"Needs must and all that crap." I set down the bag and slumped into a nearby armchair. "I just hate it when someone pulls the rug out from under me. It makes me feel so irritable. And now I have two separate groups pulling two separate rugs, and I don't know how on earth I'm going to do everything they want me to do."

"Suck it up, buttercup."

I glanced at her in surprise.

She laughed and gave my shoulder a little squeeze. "That's what my dad always used to say to me. I know you don't particularly want to have anything more to do with the vampires, but this may turn out to be a good thing."

"In no way will my further involvement with the vamps be considered anything but potentially disastrous," I complained, rubbing my temples. "Dammit, Magda! This isn't fair!"

"It's called life, and it sucks at times." She looked up as Ray opened the door and stuck his head in, asking if we were almost ready to go. She told him we'd be right there. "Then again, there are times when it really is very nice." She sighed happily as she watched him through the window.

"Christian is holding Mattias prisoner,

which means I'm going to have to try to reason with him. You know what that means, don't you?" I said glumly to my hands. "He'll make me go talk to their council. And you and I both know what they want to talk about."

"A certain incredibly gorgeous vampire, so handsome he makes your eyes hurt, and we won't even go into that sexy, sexy Italian accent? Oh, yeah. And I can't say I blame them. I'd want to talk about him, as well. *Mrrowr.* I mean that, of course, in the strictest of platonic ways."

"It wouldn't matter if you didn't," I said, sighing heavily before picking up my satchel and purse. "It's not like Kristoff wants me."

"Bah. You just need to have a little quality time with him." Amusement was rich in her voice as she walked out the door. "Besides, I've never been to Vienna. I bet it's very pretty this time of year!"

I locked the door behind us, giving her a little shake of my head. "You can't possibly be serious about wanting to go with me."

"Of course I am," she said, whapping me on the arm. "We're here to spend two weeks with you, aren't we? So if you go to Vienna to meet with the vampires, and then pop over to Iceland to pick up Kristjana and Ulfur, we'll go with you. We'll be your entourage! It'll be fun!"

Fun. For some reason, that was the last word that came to my mind.

CHAPTER 3

"Well, that looks . . ."

"Ominous," I said, pausing next to Magda as we emerged from customs at the Vienna International Airport. Three men stood waiting at the end of the hallway for us. All three were tall, clad in black or midnight blue, and each wore the same identical suspicious expression. Two were dark-haired, one blond. All three were gorgeous enough that more than one woman's gaze lingered on them.

"They look familiar," Magda whispered to me as we walked toward them.

"They should. The one on the left with the scowl is Andreas, Kristoff's brother. The middle one is their cousin Rowan. And the guy on the left is named Sebastian. I don't know what his connection is to everyone else, but he seems just as unflinching as the others."

"Oy," Magda said under her breath.

I thought for a moment of turning and running back to the plane to demand that I be taken back to safety, but I had a feeling that Julian, the messenger, would grab me before I took more than a few steps. "You're the one who begged to come with me," I reminded Magda in an equally soft voice.

"I didn't beg. I just had you suggest to your watchdog that if he ponied up tickets for Ray and me, you would be less inclined to smite him with that blinding light you can summon up. And you have to admit he didn't really protest much once you told him you changed your mind."

I glanced behind us. Ray walked alongside the messenger, the former chattering happily and looking about with bright, interested eyes, while the latter stared at me in stony silence.

"I just wish we didn't have to involve an innocent bystander in all this. You're sure Ray is OK with the whole vampire thing?" I asked Magda.

"He is, rather surprisingly. He said he always suspected there was more going on around him than people were willing to admit, and who am I to pooh-pooh general paranoia? To be honest, he's dying to see them, since he's a big Joss Whedon fan. He was a bit disappointed when I told him they don't change their appearance at all, but he'll survive."

My gaze moved to our reception committee. "The question is, will I?"

"They do look awfully grim, don't they?" Magda agreed.

"Hello, gentlemen. I expect you remember my friend Magda," I said as the three men stepped forward to greet us. I gestured to Ray, who stopped on Magda's other side. "This is Ray Victor. He's a friend of Magda's who has kindly consented to accompany us."

"Pleasure to meet you," Ray said, sticking out his hand. After a moment's slight hesitation, Andreas shook it. "Can't tell you how grateful I am you let Mags and me come along. I've been a big fan of *Angel* ever since the show came out, and it's a real thrill to meet a vampire in person."

The three men introduced themselves briefly to him before turning back to me. I was a bit puzzled by the cold reception we were getting — although I hadn't parted on the very best of terms with the Dark Ones, we weren't enemies, either. In fact, Christian had gone to great trouble to ensure that I was not blamed for the murder of an innocent woman, handing over to the police the person to blame. I knew how much that had cost him, and was duly appreciative, a fact about which Christian was aware. So why was I now getting the icy treatment?

"Hello, Andreas. How's your brother?"

Andreas had blue eyes, as did Kristoff, but where the latter had eyes of the purest teal, Andreas's were darker, a midnight blue that considered me now without the slightest bit of warmth. "You will find out soon enough," was all he said before he turned around and started walking out.

The two remaining vampires fell into place behind us as we were escorted out of the airport to a waiting limousine.

"Your vampire friends sure know how to travel," Ray said in a hushed voice as we filed in to occupy the backseat of the limo. Andreas and Rowan sat facing us, while Julian and Sebastian took up positions in the front of the car. "This is very nice. Are we going to the hotel first? I'd like to get my camera out of my bag so I can get some pictures for my travel album."

"I assume so," I said, puzzling over Andreas's comment. I leaned forward a smidgen. "Is Kristoff here? In Vienna?"

Andreas ignored me, turning to look out of the tinted windows.

I switched my attention to Rowan. "I realize there's no love lost between us, but I would appreciate it if you could overcome your natural aversion to me and answer my question."

Rowan had reddish brown hair and grey-green eyes. His face was not as angular as his cousin's, and had hints of laugh lines around the mouth and eyes. There was no evidence of any form of amusement on his face now, however. He simply looked at me as if I were a bug before answering, "He is here."

I sat back, my heart beating wildly all of a sudden. Kristoff was here, in Vienna. I was going to see him.

Magda touched my hand and mouthed, *I told you so.*

I shook my head at that — if Kristoff had suddenly been possessed by a change of heart regarding me, he would have told me, not had the council summon me with grim faces and a pronounced air of suffering. Still, he was in Vienna. That meant something. Didn't it?

To my surprise, we weren't taken to a hotel. Instead, we stopped at a large pale pink stone house that sat at the end of a row of connected tall, narrow cream-and-yellow houses in the fringes of Josefstadt, a section of downtown Vienna.

"This house belongs to the Moravian

61

Council," Julian said, showing us into a room on the top floor. "The administrative offices are below us. The top three floors are set aside for residents and guests."

"Nice," I panted as I dropped my bag and tried very hard not to collapse on the floor. "Sixth . . . floor . . . Nice . . . view."

"Sweet Mother Mary." Magda gasped as she, too, staggered into the room. Ray propped her up on one side, his own breathing a bit frantic as he leaned against the wall. "Couldn't you people put in an elevator? Or at least install a bench halfway up?"

"Your room is across the hall," Julian said, a somewhat martyred look on his face as he opened the door in question.

Magda shot him a narrow-eyed look, but followed him out to the other room. I looked around while I caught my breath, admiring the clean blue-and-white decor of the room. It was rather sparsely furnished, but the bed, bureau, and small writing desk and chair were all antiques.

"Do you wish to change your clothes?" Julian asked as he returned to my room, eyeing me in a manner that had me tugging self-consciously at the collar of my blouse.

"That would be nice." It hadn't occurred to me that I would want to change as soon as I got here, but seeing the coolly elegant vampires made me feel sticky, sweaty, and decidedly unattractive. I might not be able to do much about the last item on that list, but at least I could greet the council looking a little less unkempt.

Julian gave a short nod. "I will tell the council you will be ready to meet with them in a quarter of an hour."

"Can you make it half an hour?" Magda called from the room given over to her and Ray. "I'd really like to take a quick shower. I had no idea Vienna got this hot in the summer."

Julian paused on his way downstairs, frowning slightly. "Your presence will not be required."

"Now, wait a minute," Magda said. I stopped digging through my suitcase for something that wouldn't leave me looking like a rumpled tourist, and went to my own door. "You guys agreed that we could come with Pia. I was there when she talked to you, remember? You said that it would be fine if we accompanied her."

"To Vienna," Julian said, glancing over at me. "The council agreed to the Zorya's terms because they had no other option, but only she will be permitted in their presence."

Magda looked at me. "What do you think?

We can leave if you're not comfortable with the idea of bearding the lions by yourself."

"The Zorya already agreed —" Julian started to protest.

I raised a hand to stop him. "I'll be OK by myself."

"You sure you don't want someone with you when you tell them you want . . . you know." She cast a glance toward Julian.

He raised his eyebrows at her.

"I don't think you can help me there, but thank you," I answered.

"All right, but I'm willing to make a fuss if you need me." Magda's face, normally filled with sunny good humor, was clouded with worry.

I gave her a little smile. "I'm still technically a Zorya. I think Christian knows the sort of power I can wield if anyone gets out of line."

Julian took an involuntary step backward.

"You have a point," Magda agreed, watching him. "All right, but if you need us, just yell."

It didn't take me long to get cleaned up and presentable. I spent a few minutes shaking out my clothes, trying to decide between a pair of linen harem pants that were flattering to my figure, or a gauzy peach sundress with a matching shrug, eventually going with the latter. Although I knew the vamps would not have forgotten the fateful evening in Iceland — or, more to the point, my role in it — I figured it couldn't hurt to emphasize the fact that I was a woman.

"If men insist on being chauvinists," I muttered to myself as I slipped on the thin shrug and tied it beneath my breasts, adjusting so it exposed a smidgen more cleavage, "then they can't complain when it's used against them."

Julian was waiting outside my door when I emerged. He said nothing, just gestured toward the stairs. I caught him wrinkling his nose, though, as I passed.

"Is something wrong?" I asked, pausing on the landing.

"No. Why do you ask?" He looked surprised at my question.

"You made a face when I walked by you. I'm sorry if you don't like my perfume. I didn't use much of it because I know some people are sensitive, but I hate going out without a little dab of something."

An oddly embarrassed look flitted across his face as he gestured again toward the stairs. "It's not that. It's . . . er . . . you are a Beloved."

"Technically, yes."

"Has no one told you what that means?"

he asked, marching down the stairs beside me.

I met the frankly curious glance he slid my way. "Not really, other than the fact that I evidently gave Kristoff back his soul or something along those lines."

"It's a bit more complicated than that," he said slowly. I continued down the stairs, grateful we were going down, not up, so I wouldn't arrive before the all-important council sweaty and out of breath. "Once Joined, a Dark One can't exist without his Beloved."

"I hate to doubt you, since you must know your people much better than I do, but I'm pretty much a contradiction to that statement. I haven't seen Kristoff since the night he got his soul back. So obviously Dark Ones can get along just fine without their womenfolk."

He didn't look surprised, just gave a little shake of his head. "You will judge for yourself how well Kristoff has been without you."

I stopped at the bottom of the stairs and looked at him, a sudden stab of fear piercing my heart. "Is something wrong with him? Is he sick?"

Julian just waved toward a hallway. We were on the second floor, at one end of a long hallway that ran the length of the house. "As a Beloved, you must know the mental, physical, and emotional state of the one mated to you."

I laughed a grim little laugh. Julian's prim, chiding manner somewhat reassured me that nothing serious was wrong with Kristoff. Surely if he had been injured, someone would have told me? "June Cleaver I'm not. Besides, communication is a two-way street, and thus far Kristoff has refused to venture down that particular avenue."

"I find that difficult to believe." Julian paused, his hand on one handle of twin doors. "He could not stop himself if he wanted to, and I can't imagine why he would want to do so. His state makes it obvious that one or both of you is trying to deceive us. I will warn you not to speak such obvious lies to the council. They take a dim view of people who attempt to mislead them."

"Lie!" I stopped him as he was about to open the door, anger at being so clearly wronged doing much to drown out my concern and nervousness at the thought of seeing Kristoff again. "Me? I haven't lied to any of you vampires, and I'm certainly not deceiving anyone. I'm sorry you don't believe me when I say that Kristoff won't answer me when I try to talk to him, but it's the truth. I tried just a couple of days ago, as a matter of fact, and he shut me down quickly enough."

Julian frowned at me for a moment, his gaze searching my face. I had a feeling he was trying to judge whether or not I spoke the truth.

"Why would he do that?" he finally asked, evidently realizing I was speaking with absolute honesty.

"I have no idea. If he's saying I'm refusing to talk with him, he's either delusional or . . . well, *he's* lying, but I don't think that's very likely. He didn't seem like the sort of man who lies."

"He has proven himself a master of deception," Julian said simply, dumbfounding me as he flung open the twin doors. He indicated the room beyond. "That much has been demonstrated during the last month. The council awaits you."

It took me a moment to gather my scattered wits, so shaken was I by Julian's statement. Kristoff, a master of deception? What on earth was he talking about?

I entered the room, my gaze quickly searching it for any signs of the man who haunted my nightly dreams. There were four people standing together, three men and a woman, the latter speaking as I came in.

"... might have at least warned me she was coming so I could make her comfortable. Honest to God, Christian, you may be nine hundred years old, but sometimes you act like a caveman! That poor woman is probably as confused as all get-out, and you're not helping — Oh, hello."

The woman who was, to my utter amazement, chewing out the very frightening Christian Dante turned and limped over to me with a friendly smile and outstretched hands. "I'm so sorry about this. You're Pia, aren't you? I'm Allie, Christian's wife. You'll have to forgive him for simply dumping you in the attic like you were a bundle of old laundry. I didn't have a chance to check your room first to make sure you're comfortable up there, but I'll do so just as soon as we're done here."

"There's no need; my room is lovely," I reassured her, momentarily nonplussed by the fact that her eyes were mismatched — one was very pale grey, almost white, while the other was an odd sort of mottled brown.

Her smile took a wry twist as she gestured toward her eyes. "They're a bit freaky, aren't they?"

"They are not freaky in the least," Christian corrected, frowning at his wife as he moved over to stand next to her. Behind him, the other two men — Sebastian and Rowan — stood silent and watchful. "They are charming and unique."

She made a face at him before turning back to me. "I tried contacts, but I'm allergic to them or something, so I just have to live with what I have. Josef! No! We do not bite guests!"

I spun around, looking in surprise at the toddler who had crept up behind me. He, too, had eyes that didn't match, one being green, the other brown, but the difference was not nearly so pronounced as in the woman I assumed was his mother.

Allie scooped up the boy and told him to say hello.

"Hello, Josef," I said, smiling.

He bared his teeth at me. I was stunned to see that he had fangs.

"No!" the boy said, pointing at me. "Bad!"

"Not bad, pumpkin. She's a Beloved, like Mommy," Allie corrected. "I'm so sorry, Pia. He just got his fangs, and we're in the process of weaning him off mortal food and onto a blood diet. It makes him a bit fractious sometimes, and he tends to want to bite people."

"Allegra," Christian said, a warning in his voice as he moved to stand protectively between us, as if I posed some threat.

"Oh, stop it! I don't for one moment believe anything you lot have been wringing your hands about," she answered back in a tone that I wouldn't even dream of taking with the head vampire.

His frown grew darker. "We are Dark Ones! We do not wring our hands!"

"You know what I mean! You guys have your panties in a bunch over nothing."

Christian made a quick, angry gesture. "Allegra, your irreverence is out of place here."

Behind him, the two vampires nodded.

"Bah!" She snorted, glaring back at her husband. "I'm not going to let you railroad someone just because it assuages your conscience."

Christian took a deep breath. I backed up, not wanting to be near him if he exploded. "Your arguments have already been heard, and your presence is therefore not required at this hearing. You may take Josef to the park if the sun has set."

"Oh, don't even think of trying to get rid of me, Fang Boy," she snapped back, handing over the boy to a middle-aged woman who bustled into the room. "Edith, I think he's hungry. Can you find something for him?"

"Fang Boy!" Christian said, outraged. Rowan snickered. Sebastian gave Christian a sympathetic look. Christian glared at his wife, his hands on his hips. "I have told you before that you are not to refer to me by such names. It is an especially appalling breach when conducted in front of outsiders!"

"Hungry," Josef said, burying his face against the woman's chest in the manner of a child suddenly turned shy.

"She's not an outsider," Allie said, waving toward me. "She's a Beloved!"

"She's also a Zorya!"

"I'll go see if we have any fresh meat," the woman named Edith murmured, taking the little boy away. He looked like he was about two or three, grinning and waving at me over his nanny's shoulder.

"Now look what you've done," Christian said, gesturing toward the door as it closed behind the pair. "He's *waving* at her! I will not have my son endangered —"

"Oh, blow it out your piehole." Allie snorted, stomping over to a long table. Four chairs had been set along one side of it, a single chair on the opposite side. She grabbed one of the four and hauled it over to the other side, sitting down with sublime indifference to the fact that her husband looked as if he were going to blow his top.

"Allie, my dear, a lady never refers to a gentleman's hole, pie or otherwise, not even if that gentleman is her husband," a disembodied voice said.

I spun around in a circle, trying to pinpoint it. A small glimmer of light at the far end of the room grew brighter, cohering into the unmistakable image of a short, dumpy female ghost. She beamed at me as Allie answered, "You have to admit that sometimes he has it coming."

"No matter how trying a gentleman may be," the ghost answered, switching her smile to Christian, who was now wearing an odd, martyred sort of expression, "and heaven knows dear Christian could never be considered trying, references such as that are inappropriate. How do you do. I'm Esme. Have you seen Mr. Wuggums?"

"I don't think so," I said hesitantly.

"Mr. Wuggums is Esme's cat," Allie said from her chair. "Esme, as you can see, is a ghost. I had several others, but she's the only one who's remained. Other than Antonio, that is, but Christian and he have an ongoing war, so Antonio only comes out when the coast is clear. And you can stop swearing at me under your breath, Christian. Just because I don't understand Czech

doesn't mean I don't know what you're saying."

Christian sputtered but, with immense
control, managed to get a grip on his emotions.

"Allie, my dear," Esme started to say, but
Allie stopped her by holding up a prohibi-
tive hand.

"Another time, please. Right now I'm
more concerned with keeping Pia from being bullied than maintaining proper deco-
rum."

Esme pursed her lips but said nothing.

"No one is bullying anyone," Sebastian
said, moving over to stand next to Christian. "We simply wish to get the facts of the
situation."

"If you will take a seat, we can begin the
hearing," Christian said, gesturing me to
the chair next to Allie. He shot his wife a
look that she met with raised chin and
crossed arms.

"Yes, I will, but . . . um . . . this might be
out of line, but are you by any chance looking for Ostri?" I asked Esme, who was humming softly to herself.

"Ostri?" she asked, looking surprised for a
moment. "I'm afraid I don't know him. Is
he a friend of yours? I do love it when we
have visitors."

"Ostri is kind of like heaven," I said, at a bit of a loss to explain it to a ghost. "I'm a Zorya, you see. It's my job to take people to wherever it is they're supposed to go."

"Oh! You're just like Allie! Only I've never heard of Ostri."

I glanced in surprise at the woman sitting in the chair, currently engaged in glaring at her husband. "You're a Zorya, too?"

"Hmm? Oh, no. I'm a Summoner."

I stared at her in blank incomprehension.

"We Summon ghosts. We can also Release them. That's sending them on their way to the next plane of existence. From what I've heard from Christian, it's very similar to what you do as a Zorya."

"You are nothing like a Zorya," Christian said emphatically. He held out my chair, obviously waiting for me to sit in it.

I did so, not wanting to irritate him any more than he already was.

"We'll talk about it later," Allie said in a confidential tone.

"You will do nothing of the kind," Christian declared, taking up his spot on the other side of the table. Sebastian and Rowan flanked him on either side, the three of them making an intimidating presence.

"Pfft," Allie said, leaning toward me. "Don't let them scare you. They're really not that bad when you get to know them. Just as soon as we get this business cleared up, you'll see that underneath all that bluster there are some really nice men. But I expect you've found that out with Kristoff."

"This business?" I asked. "What business, exactly?"

Allie gaped at me for a moment before turning her stunned gaze on her husband. "You didn't bother to tell her?"

"That is what this hearing is for," he said with a faint air of discomfiture.

Allie stared at him for a couple of seconds before saying, "I'm going to have a few things to say to you when this is over, you know."

"I know," Christian said, looking grim.

Allie snorted to herself, but gave me a supportive pat on the hand. "Don't worry about anything, Pia. I'm sure it's all just a big mistake. And I apologize right now for you being brought here without having the slightest idea why."

"To be honest, I came because I have my own agenda," I admitted, meeting Christian's gaze with what I hoped was composure.

"I have no doubt of that," Rowan said, speaking up for the first time since I'd seen him in the car. His voice was carefully neutral, but I sensed hostility from him that I hadn't felt in Iceland. I wondered if Kristoff had bad-mouthed me to his brother and cousin, but almost immediately dismissed the idea — Kristoff might not want me in the place of his dead girlfriend, but he wasn't the sort of man who would indulge in a smear campaign.

"Why did you want to see the council?" Allie asked, obviously curious. Esme perched on the edge of the table until Christian shot her a look. She drifted over to the wall, where a couple of satin-covered armchairs sat in a cozy arrangement.

"I . . . er . . . I want to talk to Christian about Mattias and Kristjana."

She looked surprised. "The two reapers? One of them is here. The woman is still in Iceland, though. Christian said something about it being more trouble to move her than was worth the effort. Did you want to see Mattias? I'm sure he'd be happy to see you. He's been a bit vocal about wanting someone, anyone to visit him. I think he's suffering from a touch of cabin fever, if you want to know the truth."

"They're all right, aren't they?" I asked her, since she seemed to be much more forthcoming with information.

"Of course they are." She smiled and glanced at the frowning Christian for a few seconds. "Honestly, Pia, these guys may look like badasses, but they don't hurt people without a really good reason."

"Our asses are as bad as they come," Christian insisted. He stopped himself, closed his eyes for a second, then opened them and said, "This conversation is not to the purpose of the meeting at hand. If we might start?"

"We'd better let him. He gets a wee bit cranky if he doesn't get to do things properly," Allie whispered.

"I heard that, woman!"

"I'm sorry. I didn't mean to sidetrack anyone. I just wanted to make sure that the Brotherhood people are all right."

Sebastian's eyes narrowed on me. "Why is it that I don't find it surprising that you are concerned with the welfare of the people who tried so hard to kill us?"

"Probably for the same reason I'm not surprised you would ask that," I heard myself say, somewhat to my horror. "You didn't like me back in Iceland, and it's clear you're still of the opinion that I'm the devil incarnate. Given that you obviously have your mind made up about me, I guess it's clear that whatever this hearing is about, it will not be unbiased."

"Brava, Pia," Allie said, applauding.

Sebastian, who had sat down after speaking to me, leaped to his feet again.

"Outbursts will not be tolerated," Christian said smoothly, shooting his friend a warning glance.

With a sharp look at me, Sebastian sat down again.

"That's the pot calling the kettle black," Allie said under her breath to me, a little chuckle following the observation.

"Nor will interruptions be allowed," Christian continued with a pointed look at his wife.

To my surprise, she blew him a kiss and sat back with a smile.

Christian eyed me for a moment before saying, "You are concerned about the welfare of the prisoners. As my Beloved says, the woman Kristjana is detained in Iceland. Would you like to see the sacristan?"

"Yes, I would. I don't believe you would deliberately harm either of them without cause, but at the same time, I can't help but feel somewhat responsible for their welfare."

Christian nodded to Rowan. "Have the prisoner brought in."

Rowan slid him a questioning glance, but Christian sat with calm assurance, his gaze flickering from me to his wife.

No one spoke for the next few minutes. Despite that, I had an odd sense that Christian and Allie were holding a mental conversation, for every now and then a frown would flicker across his face, and once I heard her laugh to herself.

The door opened at last, and behind it marched a familiar man, tall and blond, with an open, friendly face, and a manner to go with it.

"Wife!" Mattias said, taking a step toward me as if he were going to rush me.

Sebastian leaped from his chair, causing Mattias to flinch backward, yelling, "The evil one will torture me!"

"We haven't harmed you yet," Sebastian said with obvious lack of patience as he pushed Mattias into a chair along the wall. Esme drifted over to sit next to him. "Tempting as it is to fulfill your opinion of us, you will notice that we have thus far refrained."

"Hello, Mattias," I said politely. "You look well."

"You have come back for me," Mattias said, nodding. He was as handsome as ever, an obvious throwback to his Viking ancestors, but he left me feeling as cold as a dead flounder. "It is only right that you do so, wife."

I grimaced at the last word, not wishing to be reminded that in the eyes of the Brotherhood, we were legally married.

"You will tell these vermin to release me," Mattias continued, his incarceration obviously doing nothing to eliminate some of the hatred he felt for the vampires. "I have endured their company long enough."

"Oh, my," Esme said, her cheerful face suddenly turning dark as she glared at him. "You are a very rude young man to speak of dear Christian and the others in such a manner."

Mattias's expression of surprise as Esme chastised him was comical. "I . . . Who . . . You're a spirit?"

"Yes, I am, and I am very fond of Christian and Josef. *Very* fond of them! If I weren't a lady, I'd take you out back and give you the thrashing you deserve for referring to the Dark Ones as you have." Her large grey curls bobbed angrily as she spoke.

Mattias's eyes widened at the threat.

"That's enough, Esme," Allie said, pulling out a little yarn bobble, the kind found on the tips of winter hats. "Bobble time."

"I have not yet finished giving this young

man a piece of my mind," the ghost answered.

"Yes, you have." Allie held her other hand over the bobble and mumbled a few words. To my amazement, Esme dissolved into nothing.

"How did you do that?" I asked, profoundly curious.

"I'll show you later, if you like. It's the best thing I ever learned." She smiled at her husband. "Well, almost the best."

He looked distracted for a moment before he recalled himself and turned to me. "As you can see, the reaper has not been starved or tortured."

"Yes, and I'm very gratef—"

The door opened again, and Rowan and Andreas appeared with another person slumped between them. They hauled the man in and let him fall to the floor.

The words dried up on my lips as the crumpled heap of man raised his head.

"Pia," a familiar voice croaked.

I was on my feet and running toward him before the word could even form in my mind . . . *Kristoff.*

CHAPTER 4

"What happened to him?" I cradled Kristoff's head against my chest protectively as I hastily searched his upper torso for signs of injury.

Kristoff made a plaintive noise. It resonated within me, bringing to the surface all sorts of emotions that I had no idea lurked beneath. I wanted to protect him, shake him, demand he speak to me, give him comfort, and tear off all his clothes and have my wanton way with him.

It was an effort, but I managed to tamp down the wave of emotions. "Dear God, what happened to you?"

Eyes that I knew could shine a brilliant teal were now dulled with pain. Waves of anguish rolled off him, suffering etched in every line of his now horribly gaunt face.

"Pia, don't," he groaned, trying to push back out of my embrace. "I can't fight it if you touch me."

"Fight what? Good Lord, Kristoff, you look like death warmed over. Haven't you been eating at all?"

He closed his eyes, his face a mask of pain as he again struggled to get away from me. I wrapped my arms tighter around him.

"Animal blood."

"That obviously isn't doing you much good. Why didn't you tell me you needed some blood?" I asked.

He shook his head and wouldn't answer.

"Why did you bring him here?" Mattias demanded of Rowan. He gestured toward where I sat. "That one seduced my wife!"

"Oh, be quiet, Mattias," I said, brushing the hair back from Kristoff's brow.

"I gave you the benefit of the doubt once," Christian said, strolling up behind me. "I will not be so foolish as to do so again. You may cease playacting."

"Playacting?" I asked, suddenly furious. Couldn't they see that something was horribly wrong with Kristoff? He looked terrible, his flesh grey and clammy, his body emaciated, racked with waves of pain so strong even I could feel them. "What the hell is going on here? Why aren't you doing anything to help him?"

"They deserve no help," Mattias muttered. "They are evil. You should have destroyed them. You should have wiped them from the earth, as you were supposed to do."

"Knock it off," I snapped at Mattias.

His expression grew darker, but at a menacing gesture from Andreas, he slumped back in his chair.

"I do not like to be deceived, Pia. I would have thought you'd recognize that fact." Christian stopped next to me, his eyes distrustful.

Julian, standing in the open doorway, shook his head. "I told you the council would not welcome lies."

"What lies?" I yelled, wanting to scream at them.

Julian said nothing more, just closed the door.

I twisted my head around to glare up at Kristoff's brother. "You're his brother! Why aren't you doing anything to help him?"

"His plan has been discovered," Andreas said in cold tones that sent a little shiver down my back. "His plan . . . and yours."

Mattias burst into laughter. I wanted nothing so much as to smack him right at that moment, but reminded myself that Kristoff needed my attention more.

"You're all insane," I said, looking around for help. Kristoff shuddered in my arms, his knees pulling up as he fought an almost overwhelming wave of purest agony.

"Please." He gasped. "I can't stand your being here much longer."

"Well, life is full of trials," I snapped at him, too overwhelmed with anger and pain at his insult to temper my words. "I'm sorry to burden you with my presence, but no one here is making any sense!"

"Christian," Allie said, limping slowly over to us.

"Stay out of this," her husband said without taking his eyes from us.

"It is not too late, wife," Mattias called out. "There are two of us here — we could perform the ceremony for you to end that pathetic one's life."

"So help me God, if you don't shut up, I'm going to call down the light and smite you with it!" I bellowed at him.

My threat echoed around the suddenly quiet room.

Mattias's eyes grew round. "You are Zorya. I am sacristan. You cannot harm me."

"You want to bet?" I growled, my attention returning to Kristoff as another wave hit him.

"Leave me," he begged, his body convulsing so tightly I wondered how his muscles could stand the strain.

"I'll be happy to, just as soon as I figure out what's going on. Much as you despise my presence, I'm not leaving you until I know why you're in so much pain."

"Despise you?" His eyes opened up for a moment, burning me with a feverish light.

"I think you're all wrong," Allie said, taking her husband's hand. "Just look at them. This isn't right, Christian."

"She is an actress, nothing more," Sebastian said.

Another wave of red pain roared over Kristoff, catching me in its wake. I gasped for breath as he fought it, my own body suddenly racked with an intense, desperate need.

"Help them," Allie said, tugging on Christian's hand. "Can't you see this is real?"

"It is of their own doing," Andreas said slowly. His face was impassive. I hated him at that moment, hated them all for standing around watching Kristoff die. For that was what I was sure was happening — no one could endure such agony, such soul-searing torment, and survive it.

"Christian!" Allie said louder, and to my surprise and relief Christian nodded.

"Feed him," he ordered.

"What?" I asked as the pain ebbed away. My mind felt bruised, every atom of my body aching and screaming with horror.

"No! I refuse to allow you to feed that monster," Mattias yelled.

"Take him out," Christian ordered, waving a hand toward Mattias.

"You must not let them enthrall you," Mattias yelled over his shoulder as Rowan and Andreas bundled him out of the room. "You must listen to me and allow me to guide you!"

"Feed . . ." The word sank into my head as I looked down at Kristoff, and I realized the truth, realized why he was in this condition. He hadn't eaten *anything,* not even the animal blood he mentioned, since we'd been parted.

I cradled his head to my chest, awkwardly trying to press some part of my anatomy to his mouth, but he tightened his lips and turned his face away from me.

"Please, Kristoff," I said softly, uncomfortable at being pressed into such an intimate act in front of others. "I really don't want you to die."

"It's better than the alternative," he said, his voice weak and hoarse.

Pain lanced me, but I ignored it. "Do you hate me so much that you'd rather die than drink my blood?" I whispered into his ear.

His eyes opened again, confusion in their

88

depths. "I don't hate you. It is for you that I am willing to give up my life."

"Me? I just told you I don't want you to die."

"Come on, boys. Let's give them a little privacy." I glanced up as Allie dragged her vampire out the door, Sebastian reluctantly following them. "You can stop looking so suspicious, Sebastian — it's clear that Kristoff isn't in any sort of condition to escape, even if he wanted to."

"I don't think we should leave them alone," he said stubbornly.

Allie paused in the doorway. "Oh, really? Does Belle like it when others watch you feed?"

Sebastian looked thoughtful and, without another word, closed the door, leaving me alone with my dying vampire.

I looked down at him, meeting his gaze. "I have no idea why you are so hell-bent on martyring yourself, but I assure you it's not necessary. They're all gone, so you can go ahead and eat."

A little moan slipped out of his lips as I bent over him, allowing him access to my neck.

"I'm sorry to be so clichéd, but this is easiest," I told him as I tipped my head slightly to the side.

He groaned, his breath hot on my neck, the stubble from his few days' growth of beard sending little tingles of electricity across my skin.

"For God's sake, stop fighting it and just —"

Pain pierced my neck, hot and fast and over so quickly I hardly remembered it in the rush of sensation that followed. I held Kristoff tight as his body welcomed the life-giving blood from mine, the pleasurable feel of it as it flowed into him so great that I shared it as well. I held him, allowing him to drink from me, satiating the overwhelming need that had driven him so close to death, holding his head for what seemed to be hours, days, even, but I knew that in reality only a few minutes had passed.

"Dio," he swore at last, his tongue as hot as a flame as it caressed the wound on my neck.

I pulled back enough to look at him. I remembered well from past experiences that the act of feeding was a very sensual one, making us both prone to thoughts of a sexual nature. I assumed that with Kristoff so close to death, neither one of us would find this time anything but a purely lifesaving act, but as I looked down into his face, I was suddenly overwhelmed with desire.

He must have shared my thought, for a ghost of a smile flickered across his lips. "I'm afraid I would disappoint you if we tried. At least, not until my body has had time to process the blood."

I eased him off my lap, discomfited that he could read my interest so clearly. Instead I examined him, noting with relief that the grey tinge to his skin was fading, and the lines on his face, while still stark and harsh, were softened a bit. "You look a smidgen better."

He eased himself to a sitting position against the wall, saying, "Thanks to you."

"You're welcome."

He waited a moment, then shook his head. "If you only knew what you have done."

"Saved your life, you mean? I'm a woman, Kristoff. I tend to be a nurturer. As little as you like me, you certainly can't expect that I'd be so heartless as to let you die when it was within my power to help you."

He frowned, not an uncommon expression for him. "Why do you keep saying that? I thought we had that out months ago."

"Had what out?" I got to my feet, re-arranging my dress. My entire body hummed as if it were filled with electricity, the sensation itching along my skin in an oddly pleasant fashion.

"You insist on pretending that I dislike you. I've told you before that that's not true."

"I can't tell you how relieved I am to hear that you don't actively loathe me," I said lightly, not wanting to get into a discussion of our respective emotions. "But I think we both know that you're not exactly yipping for joy that I'm your Beloved."

"No more than you are," he said, his eyes narrowing on me. "You thought you were Alec's Beloved."

An unspoken accusation hung heavily on the air. I turned away, wandering over to the window, pulling aside a gauzy curtain to look out at Vienna. The sun was setting, lights starting to come on up and down the street as people, normal people, hurried to their homes and loved ones. For a moment a yearning so strong it hurt swept through me. I wanted to be one of those people. I wanted the loving husband, and happy children, and a home that radiated happiness and contentment.

But I wasn't normal. With a sigh I let the curtain drop. I wasn't a normal person anymore, and the one man I might be able to love could never give me his heart. "So here we are, bound together for all eternity, you mourning your dead girlfriend, and me having lost Alec because I'm tied to you, not him. Sometimes you have to admit that life really is the pits, but I guess there's nothing we can do about that. I take it you'll be popping in on me for a quick bite to eat whenever you're tired of dieting or drinking animal blood?"

Kristoff was silent for a moment before he rose somewhat unsteadily to his feet. I took a step forward, ready to help him if he needed it, but he kept a firm grip on the back of the chair. The blood was evidently doing its job, because he looked stronger with each passing minute. "You truly do not know what has happened, do you? You fed me, Pia."

"So? You've fed off me before."

His face was carefully devoid of emotion, but he wasn't able to stop it from burning brightly in his eyes. "I told you before that a Dark One can only feed from his Beloved."

"Which is obviously not exactly true, since you've existed without me," I pointed out.

His lips thinned. "That I was able to do so was simply because you had not fed me after the Joining was complete. Now that you have, my body won't tolerate any blood but yours. My existence now depends on you. There will be no popping in on you. From this time forward, we cannot be separated for more than a few days without the direst of repercussions for me."

I stared at him as comprehension dawned in my slow-witted mind, my heart sinking with the knowledge of what I'd just set into motion. "Hell," I said, speaking more literally than figuratively. My life was hell — as hard as it had been to not have contact with Kristoff for the last two months, at least I had managed to have some sort of a semblance of a life. Oh, he haunted my dreams, and I was prone to a strange depression when I wasn't thinking of him, but all that, I was confident, would fade with time. But now . . . Dear God, how was I to cope with having him in my life every day?

I glanced at him. His gaze was on his hands; he was looking, I thought, at the ring on the middle finger of his left hand. I'd seen it before, but thought nothing of it — it was just a simple silver band, a strange, sinuous design etched on the face of the ring, but with a sudden flash of horror I realized the significance of it — it was a ring marking his commitment to his deceased girlfriend. Not a wedding ring per se, but something so similar as to make little difference.

My shoulders slumped as pain stabbed through my heart, but before I could apologize to him, the door opened and Andreas entered, followed almost immediately by Rowan, Christian, and Sebastian.

"Don't even think of trying to keep me out," Allie said, hurrying in through the door with a glare at Sebastian. "And don't tell me you weren't, because I heard you telling Christian he ought to have better control over me. If there's one thing I hate, it's someone assuming I'm a frail little Beloved who doesn't have a mind of her own."

Sebastian looked somewhat abashed as he said, "I thought you would be tending to your child."

"Oh, please," Allie said with a snort, taking the hand Christian held out to her. "Josef is happily scarfing down the blood squeezed from a steak, and that always makes me a bit queasy to watch. Besides, someone has to keep an eye out for Pia and Kristoff, since you guys are so determined to be blind to the truth and condemn them without the slightest concern whether or not they're guilty."

Sebastian shot Christian an irritated look. "Are you going to tolerate this? Ysabelle would never speak with such brashness to me."

"Get over yourself, Vlad," Allie said with a

roll of her eyes.

Christian, to my surprise, defended his wife. "Allegra has always been free to speak her mind, and will continue to do so. I will not have you attempting to control her."

Sebastian looked surprised for a moment at the undertone of threat in Christian's voice before making a cold little bow in his direction. "I would not dream of correcting your Beloved. I simply objected to accusations she felt comfortable flinging at us."

"That sounds like a guilty conscience talking," Allie said.

"This council has always been interested in seeing justice done," Christian said calmly, holding out a chair for his wife. "It will do us no harm to examine our behavior to ensure that it continues to do so."

Sebastian shot him a thin-lipped look.

"You wouldn't know it, but these two are actually very old friends," Allie told me. "As close as brothers, to be honest." Her gaze slid over to where Andreas stood in stony silence, watching Kristoff with suspicious eyes. "Closer, even," she amended.

Christian, who had been eyeing Kristoff, merely said, "You look better. I take it there was no trouble with the feeding?"

"Trouble as in I might have refused to save his life?" I shook my head, confused as to why everyone suddenly thought I had turned into a cold, heartless bitch. "I'm his Beloved. I can't do that, can I?"

"No, of course you can't," Allie answered quickly, elbowing Christian. "It would be impossible. No Beloved in the world would ever torment her man that way. Right, my little love squash?"

Christian turned an expression of horror on her. She giggled.

"Love squash?" Sebastian asked, looking equally appalled. "First Vlad, and now love squash? Christian!"

"It's better than Fang Boy," Christian murmured, glaring at Allie as she stood on tiptoe to kiss the end of his nose.

"When I have a Beloved, she will speak to me in the proper manner, and will at all times be respectful and obedient," Rowan suddenly said.

Christian and Sebastian burst into immediate laughter.

"Obedient," the latter said, shaking his head.

"Respectful," Christian said, his voice rich with amusement as he brushed back a strand of hair from Allie's face. "I look forward to the day when I see an obedient and respectful Beloved."

I glanced at Kristoff to see what he

thought of this wholly unexpected byplay, but he had the most curious expression on his face.

"But 'love squash,' Christian!" Rowan said. "That is beyond inappropriate."

"It's a love name, and Christian knows that full well," Allie said with a private little smile to her husband. "I won't say that he didn't used to kick up a fuss when I used pet names for him, but he's long since learned that the affection behind them is very genuine."

I thought for a moment that Christian was going to kiss her, but he evidently remembered where he was, and simply said, after clearing his throat, "Quite."

"Ysabelle calls me her little cabbage," Sebastian said with a heavy sigh. "Only in private, I would point out, never in front of others. But I believe it is something inherent in Beloveds to use such terms. I've asked her to stop, but that just made her switch to 'sweet potato pie of my dreams' for two weeks, until I begged her to go back to cabbage."

Allie grinned. "Good for Belle. What do you call Kristoff, Pia?"

Startled, I looked at the man in question. His face was now oddly devoid of any emotion. "Er . . . Kristoff."

She blinked for a moment. "Oh. Sorry. That was . . . Never mind."

I sighed again and, with limbs that felt like they were made of lead, brushed past Kristoff and walked over to the chair I had occupied previously. "I seem to be at a loss in that I don't have the slightest idea why Andreas and Rowan are acting the way they are to Kristoff, any more than I know what it is you all are talking about. What am I supposed to be guilty of doing? Why did you drag Kristoff in as if he were a prisoner? Why did you let him starve, not even giving him animal blood if he couldn't eat human blood? And why, exactly, have I been called before this council when I haven't done anything to harm any of you?"

Rowan sat down next to Sebastian. Christian, rather than answering me, glanced at Andreas. "You do not sit with the council?"

"No." Andreas's gaze flickered over to where his brother still stood, holding on to the chair.

Christian pursed his lips. "Do you stand with Kristoff?"

Andreas's gaze brushed me briefly. "No. I wish to remain neutral."

"I see." Christian nodded toward Rowan. "You do not suffer the same doubts?"

"I've seen the evidence with my own

eyes," the latter answered with stony condemnation. "I stand with the council."

"So be it," Christian said, then gestured wearily toward the chair next to me. "Sit down before you fall down, Kristoff. Despite your Beloved's obvious belief otherwise, we are not barbarians. You are weak still, and do not look that far from collapsing."

I held my tongue. I didn't exactly believe they were barbarians, but something was going on; some negative emotion was running rampant through all of the vampires that hadn't been there when we parted ways in Iceland. Why were the vampires upset with Kristoff? Why were his brother and cousin treating him this way?

Kristoff sank heavily into the chair next to me. I was very aware of his leg just a few scant inches away from me, aware of the heat of his body, of his scent that teased my nose and made me want to run my hands over his bare flesh. . . .

Kristoff glanced at me, his eyes strangely alight.

"To answer your questions, Pia, you and Kristoff have been brought here to answer a number of charges for crimes that have recently come to light, beginning with the disappearance of Alec Darwin," Christian said, his voice carefully neutral.

I gawked at him. I outright gawked at him. *"What?"*

"In addition to that," he continued, glancing at a piece of paper in front of him, "you are also charged with the death of the Zorya known as Anniki Belvoir, and lastly, Kristoff is charged with embezzlement of several million pounds of funds rightfully belonging to the heirs of the Dark Ones destroyed by the Brotherhood."

My jaw sagged as I looked from Christian to Kristoff. The words spun around in my head in a horrible mixture of confusion and disbelief. We were charged with killing Anniki, the previous Zorya? With doing something to Alec? With stealing money?

Kristoff sat impassive, his face inscrutable, but I could sense anger and frustration rolling around inside him.

"How do you answer these charges?" Christian asked.

I shook my head, so stunned I found it hard to put words together in a coherent manner. "This is all obscenely wrong," I said finally. "I haven't killed anyone, certainly not Anniki. And as for Alec . . . you were there that night when he walked away from me. You said yourself that he and Kristoff had left Iceland without a word to me."

"I was, and I did," Christian said, and again his voice was carefully stripped of all emotion. "But proof has come to light that indicates you had subsequent . . . er . . . *dealings* with Alec, and that he disappeared shortly after his most recent visit to you."

My brain had a hard time dealing with the astonishing things he was saying to me.

I glanced at Kristoff. He watched me with eyes that were several shades paler than normal. "It is no use to deny the charges," Kristoff told me. "I have done so for two weeks, but they will not listen."

"They think I was having an affair with Alec," I said, unable to get past that point. "They think that even after we found out I was your Beloved, I'd continue on with Alec."

Kristoff just looked at me. Horror crawled up my skin as I realized the truth. "You think so, too."

"You've made it clear that you prefer him to me," he said softly.

I opened my mouth to protest that I might be many things, but I was not the sort of woman who would have two lovers at the same time. Before I could, however, Christian stopped me.

"You deny all the charges, then?" he asked mildly, making a note on a piece of paper.

I looked from him to the faces of the others in the room. Allie looked sympathetic. The vampires regarded us with expressions ranging from Christian's apparent mild indifference to Sebastian's outright hostility, Rowan's uneasiness at meeting my eye, and Andreas's stony countenance that gave nothing away.

My eyes moved to Kristoff, sitting so still next to me, obviously having gone through great personal torment in the last few months, and just as obviously too pigheaded and stubborn to bother asking me for help.

Anger boiled up inside me, anger at the stupidity of men, anger at the vampires who were either gullible or fools, and anger at myself for trying to hide away for the last two months. I'd wanted to give Kristoff the space he needed to come to grips with our situation, but all I'd done was leave him believing I was coldly indifferent to him.

Well, that time was over. "I most certainly do deny them!" I said, getting to my feet, slamming my hand down on the table to emphasize my outrage. "I don't know what this proof is that you claim you have showing we've done anything wrong, but I can assure you that I will not sit here and let you railroad me! Kristoff might be content playing at being a martyr, but I'm sure as hell not!"

"I am not playing at being a martyr," Kristoff objected, leaping up to glare at me.

"No? What do you call letting yourself starve nearly to death, huh?"

His jaw worked for a moment. "I told you — once we were Joined, if I took any of your blood, we would be bound together for the rest of our lives."

"And that's so awful you just couldn't stand the thought of it?"

"The matter really isn't —" Christian started to say.

"No!" Kristoff shouted back at me. "I was thinking of you, dammit! You wanted Alec."

"Oh, really?" I took a step closer to him until we were almost touching. "What about you?" I asked, poking him in the chest.

"If we could please stick to the point at hand," Christian said.

We both ignored him. Kristoff grabbed my fingers as they poked him again. "What about me?"

"You're the one so madly in love with your dead girlfriend that you can barely stand to be around me. Oh, yes, the incredibly hot sex is fine and well to take the edge off now and again, but when it comes to a little thing like being grateful to me for saving your soul, not to mention your life, then it's a

104

whole other story, isn't it?"

"I don't know about anyone else, but I, for one, don't underestimate the value of incredibly hot sex," Allie said mildly.

"You're not helping," Christian growled.

Kristoff's eyes all but spit blue sparks at me. "You told me you disliked me."

"You told me you wanted to kill me!" I countered.

"You made it very obvious it was Alec's attentions you wanted."

"That is so patently false!" I said, outraged and incredibly aroused at the same time. I just wanted to grab his head and kiss the breath right out of him.

Christian took another stab at regaining control. "Your relationship questions aside —"

"You let him touch you, right there in front of me!" Kristoff yelled, his hands gesturing wildly as he spoke. His Italian accent became more pronounced, which for some reason just aroused me all that much more.

"I *what?*" I asked, momentarily taken aback by his accusation.

Silence followed. Everyone in the room turned a speculative eye on me.

"Well, now," Allie said. "That's rather interesting."

"When did I let him touch me?" I asked Kristoff.

"That morning when we were in the restaurant, he touched you, touched your hand and your knee, and pulled you close to him, and you said nothing!"

My own hands did a little waving about. "Trust you to remember that and ignore the important stuff!"

"What important stuff?"

"Important things like the fact that I told him we had just slept together! I thought that was a pretty definitive statement!" I shot back.

His eyes burned, his breath hot on my face as he leaned in to me. Once again, the scent of him made a heady aphrodisiac. "You said that just so I couldn't!"

"I said it so he'd know he wasn't the man I was interested in!" I yelled.

An odd look crossed Kristoff's face. "You didn't want him?"

"No!"

"Then who . . ." His eyes narrowed suddenly, his words coming out with a hiss. "The sacristan . . ."

"Oh, for God's sake." I gave in to my desires and twined my fingers through the soft, silky curls on his head and pulled his mouth down to mine. I was well aware we had an audience, but at that moment, nothing mattered but showing Kristoff that he occupied a place in my heart, not Alec.

"Awww. That really is sweet, in an odd sort of way," I heard Allie say over the wild beating of my heart. I didn't pay much attention to her words, my mind and body wholly focused on the man who was kissing me with a fever that left my brain reeling and my heart soaring.

"Much as I regret interrupting this fascinating, if somewhat confusing scene, we do have a hearing to conduct." Christian's voice cut across my thoughts.

Kristoff's lips moved on mine, his tongue gently probing and tasting, his body hard as he pulled me closer, his fingers biting into my hips. I wanted to capture that moment and hold it, unchanging, forever, a perfect state where passion mingled with desire and need and the beginnings of something I really didn't want to name. How on earth could Kristoff believe I preferred Alec to him? How could he not understand?

You said you were his Beloved. You wanted to see him, not me. How could I think otherwise?

CHAPTER 5

You talked to me!

"I don't know, Christian. They've been apart for two whole months. I think they deserve a little reacquaintance time."

You did the mind thing!

"I'm not disputing their need for time together, my love. I simply would prefer that we finish up here before they indulge in acts better suited to a more private situation."

Of your own free will you mind-thinged me!

"Might I point out that you are the one who detained Kristoff? Personally, if I were Pia, I'd jump his bones right in front of you just to make a point, but she appears to have more dignity than I do. That really must be one humdinger of a kiss, though. I haven't seen them stop even once to breathe."

Kristoff's sigh was a mental one, brushing around in my mind with a disturbing sense of intimacy.

Why did you not tell me you didn't want Alec?

I broke off the kiss, moving back a few steps, my fingers touching my still-burning lips. He might be easier in his mind now that he knew I wasn't secretly pining for Alec, but that hadn't really changed anything between us. He was still mourning the loss of his love, and there wasn't anything I could do to change that.

"I'm sorry," I said, turning around to apologize to the vampires. Allie grinned at me. The others had less pleasant expressions.

"If you're quite through?" Christian inquired politely, his eyebrows raised in gentle chastisement.

"We haven't seen each other in a while," I said lamely, waving a vague hand toward Kristoff. "Obviously, there are some issues we still have to work through."

"Ones I trust you will discuss at another time," he said with a pointed look at Kristoff.

"Assuming you allow Pia the opportunity to visit me while you have me incarcerated, certainly," Kristoff answered with no little sense of irony.

"Nice one," Allie said, nodding approvingly, adding, "What?" when her husband turned a frown on her. "I can root for both sides, you know."

"You're supposed to be on my side," he said with a touch of indignation.

"Only when you're right, my little mashed potato of love," she answered.

Christian's expression bore an uncanny resemblance to the one I'd seen on Kristoff's face, but it slipped away quickly enough when he glanced back toward us, eyeing me a moment before saying, "Your argument, albeit out of place, was regardless convincing. I admit to finding it confusing as well."

"Confusing how?" I asked, waving toward Kristoff. "He was sitting right next to me when I told Alec that he and I had spent the night together —"

"You can't possibly blame me for thinking that you only did that to steal my thunder, not that I was going to tell Alec," Kristoff interrupted me.

I rounded on him. "How was I supposed to know that? You told me you were dumping me on Alec, and that I was his problem!"

"You just had to set that off, didn't you, Mr. Troublemaker?" Allie said, laughing at her husband.

Christian sighed and, before Kristoff could protest, said quickly, "If we could refrain from continuing the 'I said, you said' argument and stick to the facts."

"You know, you guys sound just like Christian and me on a bad day," Allie said in a confidential tone.

Christian took exception to that. "They do not! We never argue!"

"In your dreams we don't! What about last week, when I wanted to send Josef to a nursery school for some socialization, and you had that great big scene where you ranted and raved about him mingling with mortals?"

Sebastian snickered. It distracted Christian from the retort he was clearly about to make, but it didn't stop him from sending his wife an annoyed glance. "We have strayed from the point again."

"I've told you I'm innocent of your ridiculous charges," I said — somewhat snappishly, it was true, but I was beginning to feel the effects of jet lag. "I don't know anything about Kristoff's financial status, but I'm just about willing to guarantee he hasn't done any embezzling."

" 'Just about'?" the man of my dreams asked, obviously outraged.

"We haven't known each other very long," I said in a soothing voice before turning back to Christian. "Just exactly what proof do you have that either one of us committed such atrocities?"

"There are financial records," Christian said, gesturing toward a file folder lying on the table.

"I've seen them. They're clearly false," Kristoff said. At a nod from Christian, I shuffled through the paperwork. Most of it was financial statements and transaction logs, showing sums of money in various currencies being moved from one account to another. "Easily created, but not so easily proven."

"There is the matter of your own personal account," Christian said as Sebastian held out a single sheet of paper.

"What about it?" Kristoff asked, his brows pulling together. "I gave you the access information for my account so you could see for yourself that I do not have an inordinate amount of money."

"I printed this balance statement for your account this morning," Sebastian said, offering Kristoff a sheet of paper.

He took it with a swift intake of breath. I peered over his shoulder to read it, my eyes widening as I did a swift mental exchange-rate calculation. "Holy moly. It's too bad we really aren't married — you could really keep me in style with that metric butt-ton of money."

"Pia, my dear, I may not have known you for long, but as you are a friend of Allie's, I feel I can offer a little morsel of advice — a lady never refers to a gentleman's holdings except in the most obscure terms, and never as a metric butt-ton," Esme chided.

"Sorry," I said, amused.

"That isn't mine," Kristoff protested, shoving the paper back. "I don't have anywhere near as much money as that."

"And yet, the money was transferred to your account two weeks ago, just about the time that Alec disappeared," Sebastian said. "You'll notice that the amounts deposited over a five-day period correspond exactly with the funds withdrawn from the trusts set up to provide for the families of those slain by the reapers."

"It's not mine," Kristoff repeated with stubborn finality.

"You know, it doesn't take a rocket scientist to figure out how to transfer money to someone else's account. Someone is setting Kristoff up." I felt obliged to point that out, since it obviously hadn't occurred to anyone else.

"Why would anyone want to do that?" Rowan asked. "The money has gone to him. No one else would benefit from that."

"Oh, I don't know," I said in a tone lighter than the way I felt. I held his gaze firmly. "I can see someone who hated Kristoff going to all sorts of lengths to get revenge. Someone he thought of as close, but who turned out to be a traitor."

Rowan leaped to his feet and was over the table before the last word left my mouth. Instantly Kristoff was between us, his hands fisted as he scowled at his cousin.

"Oh, my!" Esme said, clutching the belt of her tattered bathrobe. "Fisticuffs!"

"Your Beloved is ill advised to speak thusly to me," Rowan spit.

"And you dare much to threaten her, *cousin*," Kristoff answered, making me look at him in surprise. His lovely lyrical, Italian-accented voice was thick with anger. It warmed me that he'd be so protective, even when his heart wasn't touched by our bond.

"Sit down, both of you," Christian said, sounding weary. "What the Zorya says is true."

"My name is Pia," I said somewhat forlornly as I sat back down in my chair. "I really hate being called the Zorya."

"It is what you are," Sebastian pointed out.

"Not for long it isn't."

"Zoryas cannot be unmade," he answered

with a curl of his lip.

I smiled. "They can if you approach it the right way. But before I discuss that, I'd like to deal with the rest of the ridiculous charges against us."

"It's so nice to see another Beloved who refuses to be a doormat," Allie said with a happy sigh. "Remind me to introduce you to Nell. You'll love her. She doesn't take any crap, either."

"Nell is perfectly charming and has exquisite manners," Esme agreed, with a look at me that told me she found mine lacking.

"The charges against you were not brought without ample proof, I assure you," Christian said after giving his wife a long look. "Nor do we make them lightly."

"You sure could have fooled me. So far all I've seen is a bunch of confusing paperwork that anyone could have faked," I said. "You might find that compelling, but I certainly don't. And while we're on the subject of this council, can we discuss the fact that you're all so very quick to turn on Kristoff? I'd think you would be acquainted with him well enough to know he isn't the sort of man to embezzle. I mean, really! You've all known him for what? Three hundred years? Four?" Without intending to do so, I found myself on my feet again as I expostulated.

"What sort of friends are you that you are so willing to believe the worst about someone who you've known that long? Don't you have any concept of what loyalty means, what it means to call someone a friend?"

"Pia, dear —" Esme started to say.

I ignored her. "From where I'm standing, you guys are nothing more than a bunch of hypocrites, talking big, but when it comes right down to standing up for a friend in a time of need, you're all nothing but lame-asses. Yes, you heard me! Lame-asses! Of the . . . er . . . lamest kind!"

I sat down with a *hrmph*. Silence fell heavily in the room. It was at that moment that I realized just who I was yelling at — a roomful of vampires who had made it their life's calling to rid the world of Zoryas.

"I really like you," Allie said, applauding. She met the look her husband was sending her way with one of her own. "Oh, don't look at me that way. I told you all along that I never believed Kristoff would do any of the things you guys believe he's done."

"Tsk," Esme said sadly, shaking her head. "Women these days just have no idea about the subtle art of persuasion. One never shouts, dear. And one certainly never refers to those in a superior position as asses of any kind, no matter whether or not they deserve it."

Christian shot Esme a look of surprise.

She smiled a little regretfully at him. "I'm sorry, dear Christian, but I do believe that in this case, the ladies are right and you gentlemen are the teensiest bit mistaken. Kristoff has been nothing but polite and a true gentleman when I pay my daily call on him, and, as you know, a gentleman would never steal money from others."

"Thank you, Esme," I said with a curt little nod at Christian.

"I am willing to concede that perhaps we have been overhasty with regards to the proof of the financial issue, although I find myself most curious as to how such a sum of money could have found its way into Kristoff's personal account without his knowing. Regardless . . ." He held up a hand to stop me when I was about to protest. "I agree that it would be relatively easy for someone to arrange for him to look guilty, so I am willing to dismiss those charges, pending, of course, a further investigation into the matter."

"One down, two to go," I muttered to Kristoff.

"It matters not," he grumbled.

I patted his hand before I could stop myself. His eyes darkened as my fingers lingered on the backs of his, capturing them in a gesture that made me flush to the tips of my toes.

"However . . ." Christian continued in a louder voice. I dragged my attention off of Kristoff and onto him. "However, two charges do remain."

"Yes, let's talk about that," I said agreeably, trying not to let the feel of Kristoff's thumb stroking the back of my hand distract me. "I don't know where you got the idea that I killed Anniki, but I certainly did not. In fact, it was because of her that I got involved in the first place. If she hadn't been mere seconds from death when I discovered her, I never would have agreed to become a Zorya."

"Exactly," Rowan said, sitting back in his chair, his fingers tapping ever so lightly on the table.

"What sort of a comment is that?" I asked a bit testily.

"He means that they all believe you wished to become a Zorya, and you simply took the most expedient method to do so," Kristoff explained, his thumb still stroking my hand.

"They're nuts, then," I said, giving them all an astounded look. "I'm doing everything I can to *stop* being a Zorya."

"Indeed." Christian pursed his lips slightly. "And what, if you do not mind me asking, would that entail?"

I opened my mouth to answer, but thought better of it, taking my time before I finally said, "We'll come to that, but after we've taken care of your stuff first."

"I have a foreboding suspicion that your issue is very much connected with ours," he answered dryly.

"You bet your —" I glanced over to where Esme watched with bright, interested eyes, and an air of being about to impart some of her homey advice. "Er . . . you bet."

"Very well. As for the situation with the Zorya, she was found in your bathroom, a dagger stabbed into her heart. Locating and charging her killer is obviously beyond the mortal police; therefore, the crime falls under our jurisdiction. We have reviewed the facts, and can come to only one conclusion."

"An erroneous conclusion," Kristoff scoffed. "Pia said she didn't kill the Zorya. I was hesitant to believe her at first, but I know now that she would not be capable of such an act."

"Thank you," I told him with a little smile that had his eyes darkening.

"Then who did kill her?" Sebastian asked.

"You've stated that you didn't. If it's not you or the Zorya, who did?"

I hated to dwell on this, but now was not the time to worry about niceties. "I wasn't alone that night."

"Mercy!" Esme gasped.

Kristoff's fingers tightened around mine.

I'm sorry. I'm not trying to rub it in.

He said nothing.

"We are aware that Alec was with you." Christian inclined his head in an acknowledgment of what I was hesitant to say right out. "But he left shortly after two a.m., and the Zorya did not arrive until approximately three hours after that, whereupon she asked the desk clerk for your room number. He refused to give it to her, and she apparently left but, in reality, entered the hotel by a secluded side entrance, after which she was seen entering your room."

I blinked at him a couple of times. "How on earth do you know all that? Even the police didn't know what she'd been doing before she died."

Kristoff's fingers tightened again. "I was watching your room," he admitted.

"You were watching me?" I asked, turning an incredulous look on him. "Why?"

"You are a Zorya. We had to know where you were at all times."

My astonishment fizzled into irritation. "You mean you and Alec *both* spied on me?"

"It is our job . . ." He glanced toward the other vampires. "It *was* my job to be aware of all movements of the reapers, you included. It was not until I realized that you were different that I ceased surveillance."

"You surveyed me," I asked, outraged. "Like I was a criminal? Before or after we slept together?"

He had the grace to look embarrassed. "Mostly before."

I punched him in the arm. "*Mostly* before? Do you have the *balls* to sit there and tell me that you followed me around *after* we spent the night together?"

"Dear, a gentleman's personal accoutrements are never mentioned in polite —"

"I had no choice. Alec was busy trying to find another reaper, and I had no idea if you were just using me or —"

"If we might continue," Christian said in a mild tone.

"Using you!" I was surprised to find myself on my feet. I was even more surprised at the fact that I was yelling at Kristoff. He sat before me, still gaunt, but with color in his face now, and his eyes burning with a cool blue heat. "If our marriage had been legal, I would divorce you

121

right now!"

"Please —" Christian said, but he didn't stand a chance.

Kristoff jumped to his feet. "Our marriage *is* legal, and you can hardly blame me for suspecting that you might be manipulating me, since you had made it clear you preferred Alec to me, and yet there you were in *my* bed."

"It wasn't a bed. It was a bunch of moldy straw, and don't you dare try to make yourself out to be the victim! I'm the one whose trust was abused!"

"I never abused your trust," Kristoff said with a grim note to his normally sensual voice. "I didn't believe you were actively working against us, but I knew that the reapers could use you without you being aware of it. I was simply trying to protect you and us at the same time."

"You were?" I asked, surprised. *You really believed me?*

Yes.

Oh. I . . . oh. Thank you.

"Enough!" bellowed Christian.

We both turned to look at him.

"Still think they're putting on an act?" Allie asked him.

A flicker of irritation was momentarily visible in his face before his mouth relaxed. "I am beginning to see your point."

"It takes them a while sometimes," Allie said with a fond smile at her husband before turning to me. "But they usually get there in the end."

"The fact remains that the Zorya was killed in your bathroom."

"That means nothing," Kristoff answered abruptly, warming me with his quick defense. "Anyone could have gotten into her room. The door to her balcony was open, and the bathroom connected to the room next door."

"The room containing the same woman who accompanied you here," Christian said, looking thoughtful.

"Magda had nothing more to do with Anniki's death than I did," I said.

He continued looking thoughtful. "No one else was seen entering your room."

"Exactly. No one was seen entering. But much as the idea gives me the willies, it doesn't mean someone didn't enter." I turned to Kristoff. "Where were you watching?"

"Outside, in the garden beneath your window."

"That means you couldn't see who was coming or going."

He shook his head. "I could see both hotel

entrances that were still unlocked, and your door through the window. No one entered after Alec left."

I thought for a moment. It was true my room had been at the end of the building, but there was more than one way into it. "Then someone must have come through Magda's room. She had a balcony, too."

"It's possible, of course," Christian said. "But likely? Why would anyone but you wish to kill the Zorya?"

"Why don't you ask some of the other vampires you seem to have granted the right to kill Brotherhood members?" I asked somewhat snappishly.

"Ooh, she has you there, love muffin," Allie said.

His mouth tightened. "Despite what you may think, we do not encourage our people to murder reapers without a reason. We imprison, yes, but that is only for the safety of our people, and as you see, our captives are treated humanely."

"I will grant you that, but I'd just like to know how we're supposed to prove we didn't do something."

"In mystery books, that would be motivation for finding the killer yourself," Kristoff said.

That astounded me. "You know how to

find a killer?"

"Yes. But not in this situation. There were only so many people who had access to your room. One of them must have done it."

I thought over the list. Magda and Ray had been asleep in the room next to mine, the one that shared the bathroom. But neither of them would have a reason to kill a woman they didn't know. That left Alec and Kristoff, but I couldn't believe they had done it.

Thank you for the vote of confidence in my moral base.

Oh, I don't mean you wouldn't have done it — I think under the right circumstance, you'd be perfectly capable of killing a woman like Anniki. I just don't think you did.

"I really think you're going to have to go with a verdict of death by a person or persons unknown," Esme suddenly piped up. "Like they say in those fascinating police shows you like to watch when no one is around."

"I do not watch television," Christian said sternly. "That is a mortal pursuit."

"Uh-huh. Think I didn't discover your secret stash of those British homicide DVDs that are so conveniently hidden in your study?" Allie asked.

"Very well," Christian said, obviously

ignoring the teasing tone in his wife's voice. "I am willing to withdraw the charge of unauthorized murder against the Zorya pending further evidence. But the last charge will not be so easily dismissed."

"I don't see how you can think Alec going to ground has something to do with us," I said, wishing Kristoff would hold my hand again, but lacking the nerve to just take his.

His fingers curled around mine, warm and strong and bringing me untold comfort. I slid a quick glance at him, but his face was impassive, his attention on Christian as the latter reiterated the charges.

"I have not seen Alec since he left Iceland. Neither has Pia," Kristoff said firmly.

"We have evidence to the contrary," Sebastian said with a smug little smile.

"Evidence? What evidence?" I asked, suddenly worried. What if someone had gone to the trouble of manufacturing evidence against us the way they had against Kristoff?

Christian nodded to Rowan, who rose and left the room. "We will bring in our proof."

I gnawed my lip a moment as I considered Kristoff. "Alec hasn't been in contact with you at all?"

He shook his head. "I haven't seen him since that night in Iceland. He said he was returning to his home in California."

"Where do you live?" I asked, somewhat surprised to hear that the very urbane Alec made his home in California.

"Outside of Firenze."

"That's Florence, isn't it? In Italy?"

He nodded as the door opened and Rowan reappeared with Mattias.

"First you put me in the cell. Then you take me out and taunt me with the sight of my wife. Then you put me back in, and now you bring me here again. Your methods to break me are most cruel, but I will never give in to you. Never!" Mattias said in a dramatic fashion. "Wife! Have you convinced them yet to set me free?"

"She's my wife, not yours," Kristoff grumbled as Rowan shoved Mattias into a chair. "I married her first."

"She's a Zorya, and I am the sacristan. A Zorya must be wed to a sacristan in order to have full access to her powers, and since we've all seen proof that she has those, it is the marriage to me that is valid," Mattias retorted.

"I'm afraid he has a point," I murmured.

Kristoff's glower turned even darker.

"The discussion of your release hinges, as you have repeatedly been told, on your cooperation," Christian told Mattias in mild chastisement.

My ears perked up. Christian was considering releasing Mattias? Perhaps it wouldn't be as hard as I thought to get him to see reason.

"You will repeat what you told us earlier."

Mattias's pale blue eyes rested with consideration on me. "I will speak only to my wife."

Sebastian made an impatient gesture. "We can force you to speak."

"You may torture me all you like — I will speak only to Pia!" Mattias yelled.

I began to see a way to present my case. "Am I to understand that Mattias has said something that connects us with the disappearance of Alec?" I asked the council members.

"He stated . . ." Christian shuffled a few papers until he found one he liked. "He stated that he knew how you and Kristoff were involved in engineering the disappearance of Alec, and where he was now. He refused to say any more when pressed."

"Tortured!" Mattias shouted. "I was tortured."

"You look just fine to me," I told him. And he did; he was practically radiating health, whereas poor Kristoff had nearly wasted away. "I'm afraid you've been had. Mattias is either confused or lying."

"Wife!" Mattias sputtered.

Kristoff glared at him.

"That eventuality crossed my mind, which is why we asked you here," Christian answered smoothly.

Allie snorted but said nothing.

"You know . . ." I looked at Mattias with what I hoped appeared as innocent speculation. "If you were to release him to my custody, I'm sure I'd be able to get from him everything he knows."

Both of Christian's eyebrows went up at such a bold suggestion. Sebastian scowled and said in a voice rife with scorn, "Although we have not done so, despite what the reaper says, we are not above using force to extract the information we need. I doubt if you could bring yourself to do so."

"Ah, but I have two points in my favor," I said, smiling my most winning smile.

"And those are?" Sebastian asked.

I held up two fingers and ticked them off. "First, you guys may talk the talk, but I don't seriously think you're going to torture Mattias and Kristjana, although I don't think I'd blame you where the latter is concerned. She definitely has more than one bat loose in her belfry. But cold-blooded torture?" I considered the vampires before me for a moment, shaking my head. "No.

129

You guys aren't that way, not really."

"Brava," Allie said, nodding.

Sebastian looked disgruntled for a moment before asking, "And the second point?"

I tossed a little more charm into my smile. "I am the Zorya. Mattias has to do exactly what I tell him. So if I tell him to spill everything, by the laws of the Brotherhood, he has to spill. But I'm not going to do that unless he's in my custody."

"Impossible," Sebastian pronounced.

Christian, to my surprise, said nothing. He looked thoughtful, though, which gave me hope.

"To have you and the sacristan running free . . . it is impossible," Sebastian repeated.

"What exactly are you holding Mattias for?" I asked, curious.

"Exactly what I have asked them myself, wife!" Mattias said, shooting an outraged look at Rowan. "I have done nothing wrong."

"You are a sacristan," Rowan answered.

"Yes, but he hasn't actually committed any crime against you guys," I pointed out. "He wasn't even present at the ceremony where Frederic and the others tried to use me to hurt Kristoff and Alec. You guys had nabbed both him and Kristjana before that.

So I really don't see that you have any grounds to continue to hold them. And as I am willing to guarantee their good conduct, I don't see a reason you shouldn't turn them over to me."

Sebastian sputtered and grumbled at the idea. Christian continued to look thoughtful, finally saying, "You seek to have them released. That is why you agreed to meet with the council."

I slid a look at Kristoff. He was watching me with an impassive expression. "Well . . . yes. But not because I didn't want to help Kristoff. I had no idea he was in this state, or I would have come weeks ago. But yes, I have been asked to facilitate the release of Mattias and Kristjana."

"I knew it!" Mattias said gloatingly. He smiled at Kristoff. "I knew you truly wanted me and not that one there, the one you had carnal relations with right in front of me. I knew it must be a mistake."

Allie's eyebrows went up as she gave me a long look.

"It wasn't at all like that," I told her, my blasted genes kicking in with a blush that was hot enough to fry bacon. "Mattias wasn't actually right there with Kristoff and me. We were locked in a cell. By ourselves. In the dark, actually. And Kristoff was handcuffed —"

"Pia," Kristoff interrupted me, his lips twisting a little. "I don't think anyone wishes to know about our time imprisoned in the Brotherhood house."

"Sorry," I said hastily, the blush cranking up another notch. "I just want to say right here and now that I've never had sex in front of an audience."

"Well, then, there you go," Allie said cheerfully.

"Er . . ." Christian looked a bit dazed. "Where were we? Ah, yes. I assume there is a reason other than altruism that you wish us to release the two reapers into your custody?"

"Yes. It's a means to an end — mine. Or, rather, my career as a Zorya. If I can convince you to release Mattias and Kristjana, the Brotherhood will revoke my permit to be Zorya, or something along those lines. The end result would be that I would no longer have any special powers against vampires."

"No!" Mattias gasped. "An execration? You cannot mean that! You cannot give up!"

Everyone ignored him.

"Sounds like a smart plan to me," Allie said, nodding at me. "I approve."

"Well, I do not!" Sebastian snapped. "Nor

will any other member of the council tolerate such an idiotic idea. Is that not right, Rowan?"

Kristoff's cousin shook his head slowly. "I do not think it would be wise for the Zorya and the sacristan to be together. We have no guarantee that the reapers will do as they have promised her."

"Agreed. Andreas?" Sebastian looked to the man who'd been standing so silent, it was easy to overlook his presence.

Andreas roused himself from what appeared to be a deep meditation. His face gave none of his thoughts away. "I object to the release of reapers on general principles. There is no reason to believe they will not later harm our own people."

Mattias sneered.

"You are not helping," I told him. His sneer faded away to a pout.

"Christian?" Sebastian asked.

Christian was even slower to reply than Andreas. "We have held reapers before who have not been directly responsible for harm. Since Kristjana and the sacristan are both members of an active chapter, a chapter that we know has made several attacks against both Kristoff and Alec, we are within our right to continue to hold the two of them, regardless of whether or not they themselves participated in the attempts to harm Dark Ones."

My heart sank. So much for doing this the easy way.

"There is also the possibility that they do, in fact, have information regarding Alec's whereabouts," he added.

"That, at least, I think we can clear up." I turned my attention on Mattias. Beside me, Kristoff stiffened. "Mattias, you told me once that since I was a Zorya, you were obliged by Brotherhood laws to honor any demands I made of you. You will now answer me truthfully — do you know anything about Alec's disappearance?"

Mattias's normally sunny expression turned petulant. "It is not right for you to ask me such in front of the evil ones."

"Do you know anything about Alec?" I repeated.

His expression was sullen for a good minute. "No."

I relaxed. "Then why did you tell the vampires you knew Kristoff and I were responsible for Alec disappearing?"

I thought for a moment that he wasn't going to answer, but he finally did. "The evil ones would not bring you to me as I asked!" he answered, waving his hands around in expressive unhappiness. "I knew that you would come to rescue me if they would allow you in. Therefore, I said what needed to be said in order for them to summon you to me."

Kristoff muttered a rude word under his breath, exchanging glares with Mattias when the latter heard it.

I looked back at Christian. "I rest my case."

"This proves nothing," Sebastian said, waving away Mattias's confession. "They are working together to confuse us."

"I believe," Christian said slowly, with deliberation, "the charges against you precipitated by the sacristan's original statement will require further investigation."

I found a little smile. "That means you'll let Kristoff go."

"No."

My spirits, which had been frolicking around happily, stumbled to a stop. "What?"

Christian shook his head. "We will investigate further. Once we know the truth of the situation, then we'll act."

"That is not acceptable!" I said, slamming my hand down on the table. "I'm not going to let you do this to us!"

"You're a Zorya," Mattias said with a gleam in his eye. "Use the power of the light to smite them."

Sebastian rounded the table to stand near me, obviously prepared to spring if necessary.

Kristoff growled deep in his chest and leaped to his feet.

I jumped up to stop him from doing anything rash. *That was impressive. Can you bark, too?*

The look he gave me should have dropped me dead on the spot, but for some reason, I just found it amusing.

"I would be very unhappy if you smote Christian," Allie said calmly, her hand on her husband's arm. "Tempted though I am to see you use this mysterious moon power. But it's probably best if you don't."

She's not the only one who's tempted, I told Kristoff. *I don't suppose if I distracted everyone, you could grab Mattias and escape?*

No.

Too bad. I have a horrible feeling we're going to have to do something drastic to get out of here. I just wish I knew what happened to Alec, whether the Brotherhood really has him, or if he's off doing something covert. He said nothing to you after that night?

He said a few things, but they are not worth repeating, Kristoff answered, reluctance evident in the brush of his mind against mine.

136

He was your friend, wasn't he? I mean, he wouldn't knowingly leave you in a situation like this?

We have an extensive history, and yes, I've considered him my friend.

Then why are you suddenly worried? I turned to face him, peering deep into his eyes. *You're hiding something,* I said with a sudden realization. *I can feel it. You're holding something back, hiding it from me. Is that why you refused to speak to me this way?*

Everyone has things they wish to keep private, he said stiffly, and gently but firmly pushed me out of his mind.

I was shaken to my very soul by a sudden, horrible fear that the man I thought I'd known never really existed.

"As I see it, there are two choices we can make," Christian said, nodding toward us.

I took a step closer to Kristoff. *Stop looking at me like that. I can't help it if it makes me feel better standing next to you. Safety in numbers and all that.*

Kristoff made an inarticulate noise of disagreement, but he reached out, wrapped an arm around my waist, and hauled me up until I was pressed against him, a defiant look on his face as he eyed the other vampires.

Allie beamed at us.

"Our first option is to incarcerate both of you until such time as one of you three — Pia, Kristoff, or the sacristan — decides to be forthcoming with information regarding the whereabouts of Alec, at which point due justice will be meted out."

"They will torture you just as they will me!" Mattias shouted. "You see what this has come to, wife? It is the end!"

"Oh, stop it!" I snapped, at my wit's end with him. "You're not hurt at all, so you can just stop your belly-aching! No one has tortured you, although right now, I certainly wouldn't blame them if they did."

Mattias's eyes opened wide. "Wife!"

"And stop calling me that!" I was so frustrated, I could have screamed.

"Why don't you simply light-bind him if you're tired of his constant whining?" Rowan asked.

Mattias gasped. "She wouldn't!"

"Light-bind?" I asked, confused by his use of the term. "What's that?"

"You're a Zorya. He's a sacristan," Rowan said, just as if that explained everything.

"Er . . ." I looked at Kristoff for help. He avoided my eye.

"Do not listen to them, wife," Mattias said hastily, his eye fixed sternly upon me. "They do not know of what they speak. There is no way you can enslave my mind. That is an old wives' tale, nothing more."

I pursed my lips as I looked at him. "There's a way to enslave his mind? Would that make him shut up about being tortured?"

"Of course," Christian answered with a shrug.

"Do not listen to the evil ones, Pia. They are trying to confuse you, and to divide our joined strength."

"How do I do it?" I asked, my gaze still speculatively on Mattias.

He tried to get to his feet, but Rowan pushed him back down in the chair before answering. "You are a Zorya, yes? You wield light. The light is what dazzles reapers, bemusing their minds and leaving them open to your command."

"Wow. How come Summoners don't get some sort of brainwashing skill like that?" Allie asked, looking a bit disgruntled. "I think I went into the wrong line of work."

"Wife, I insist that you cease listening to these devils," Mattias said with an arrogance that was the last straw.

I summoned up a ball of light and held it for a moment, imagining it bending Mattias to my will before tossing it at him. The ball exploded around his head, swirling slowly around it in a corona of glittering, silver light. It glowed as it slowly revolved, fading away after a few seconds until all that was left was a vague look in Mattias's blue eyes.

"Mattias?" I asked, concerned that I might have done some harm to his vision.

"Yes?"

"Are you all right?"

"I'm quite fine, thank you."

He looked at peace, a mild expression on his face.

"The vampires are going to torture you now, all right?" I asked, seeing if he really was bedazzled, as they claimed he would be.

"That's fine. Or would you prefer I torture myself?"

"Er . . . no. You don't need to do that," I said, a little taken aback. "You don't mind if they set your hair on fire, do you?"

"No, that's fine," he answered, uncharacteristically agreeable. "Unless, of course, it's any trouble to you, in which case I would be happy to do it myself. Which would you prefer?"

"I'll get back to you on that." I turned to Christian, demanding, "Why the hell didn't anyone tell me about this before?"

He shrugged again. "I assumed you knew. You are, after all, a Zorya."

"One who hasn't been around the Brotherhood block," I pointed out, watching Mattias. He was humming softly to himself, his body language relaxed and happy. "How long will he stay like that?"

"Him? Probably a couple of hours," Rowan said with a disgusted look. "The weaker the mind, the easier it is to lightbind."

"Glory hallelujah," I murmured, trying to wrap my brain around the idea of such a thing. "Can I do that to anyone?"

Allie laughed. "I was just wondering the same thing."

Christian hesitated for a second before admitting, "I understand you can, although reapers, as worshipers of the light you wield, are supposedly more susceptible. I assume it has a much shorter duration on someone who is not a reaper, or one who has a very strong presence of mind. And as you can see, the effect on someone who already has a tie to you can be quite . . . profound."

Mattias made odd little whistling chirrups until I looked at him, at which point he simpered and said, "Pia, Pia, Pia!"

"More like drunk than bedazzled," I said, somewhat startled by his change in behavior.

"It has been likened to that, yes," Christian agreed.

"Do you need a hug?" Mattias asked, his face scrunched up with worry. "You're frowning. I should hug you. And then take off all your clothes and lick —"

"No! No hugs! Or anything else. In fact, I'd like for you to just sit there quietly and not mention anything about torture or hugging. And stop doing that."

A rapt look came over his face as he stopped making loud kissing noises. He clasped his hands together as he answered, "I will lick you later."

I blinked at the offer. "Er . . . OK."

Kristoff shot me a look.

"That is to say, no, thank you. Um . . . where were we?"

"I love you," Mattias told me.

Everyone ignored him.

"Christian was just saying that he could toss everyone in jail, but he's not going to do that because it's patently obvious that Pia and Kristoff haven't been separated as part of a big, elaborate plan to not only siphon away funds from widows and orphans, but also to kidnap and hide Kristoff's oldest and dearest friend, not to mention killing off an innocent woman who hadn't even taken up the job of Zorya, because instead of archcriminals, they are instead victims of what seems to be a really nasty twist of fate," Allie said, smiling at her husband. "So instead of damning them for something that was not their doing, you're going to let them go on their way so they can try to live happily ever after, not that living with a Dark One is easy by any stretch of the imagination. Isn't that right, snuggles?"

"Our second option," Christian said, trying to look stern, but I could have sworn his lips twitched a smidgen, "is to allow one of you to prove the innocence you so vehemently claim."

"One of us?" I asked, my stomach feeling as if it were made of lead. "Just one?"

"How do you expect us to prove that?" Kristoff asked at the same time, his eyes narrowed in suspicion.

"I believe in this instance my usage of pronouns is confusing," Christian answered. "My apologies. My intention is to allow *Pia* to prove both your and her innocence."

"All right," I said without hesitating. "If it will end all of this nonsense, I'm willing to do whatever it takes."

"Good." Christian glanced at the other two vampires at his table. "Then it is the decision of this council to postpone the hearing until such time as Pia has located and freed Alec, and identified the person behind his abduction."

"What?" I almost shrieked. "Wait a second! How am I supposed to do that?"

"You are a Zorya," Sebastian said. "You are a member of the Brotherhood no matter if you decry them or not."

"That doesn't mean they're going to tell me anything if I march up and ask where they keep the captive vampires!"

I could swear I heard Kristoff snicker, but when I glanced at him, his face was without expression.

"You stand a better chance of gaining information from them than any of us do — without, that is, the use of those practices that you find objectionable."

"You do know what you are asking me to do, right? Here I am trying my darnedest to get out of the Brotherhood, and you guys want me to stay in so I can be some sort of super-secret double agent for you."

No one said anything for a moment. Even Allie looked a bit nonplussed.

I turned to Kristoff. *I don't have a choice, do I?*

If there is another way, I don't see it, he admitted.

Great. Now I have to find Alec, when I have no idea where he is or what he's doing. Guilt stabbed at me at the memory of Alec's stricken expression when he realized I was Kristoff's Beloved, not his.

Kristoff, did Alec . . . That night, Alec was upset, wasn't he?

Again I sensed Kristoff's reluctance to speak to me. His presence in my head was tentative and hesitant, and I felt once again a darkness within him, something he shielded me from seeing.

That worried me more than anything.

Yes.

Do you think he would have done anything stupid?

Suicidal, you mean? Kristoff turned that thought over a few times. *I don't believe he would. If you had turned out to be his Beloved and you were taken from him, he might, but not otherwise.*

Pain twisted inside me at his casual words. Alec might have felt despair at the thought of losing his Beloved, but Kristoff had managed quite well on his own for two whole months.

Yes, nearly dying of starvation was my master plan all along.

I stared at him, startled by both the amusement and the self-loathing in his mind.

"Do you agree to our terms?" Christian

145

asked, pulling my train of thought back to the present.

I was torn. Part of me wanted nothing more than to figure out the mess that was my conflicted emotions toward Kristoff, but there were other things at stake. If I could find a way to locate Alec before I was de-Zoryaed for freeing Mattias and Kristjana, then everyone would be happy. The question was, could I pull off both tasks? "Yes, I agree," I said at last, my shoulders slumping as I leaned into Kristoff, drawing comfort despite the horrible situation. "But only on the condition that Kristoff help me find Alec, and that you release Mattias and Kristjana to my custody."

"My first inclination would be to refuse both demands, but since Allegra would take issue with keeping Kristoff from his Beloved, we will accede to the first."

"If you expect me to get anything out of the Brotherhood people without having Mattias and Kristjana released —" I started to say.

Christian gave me an odd look. "I expect you to do whatever is necessary to achieve your goal. I cannot authorize the release of the two reapers, however. You will have to find another way."

"There is no other way," I protested. "I

have to have Mattias and Kristjana."

"You may have me," Mattias said, opening his arms. "I'm all yours. Take me!"

"You cannot infiltrate the Brotherhood as our 'super-secret double agent' if you are no longer a Zorya," Christian said with a hint of a smile.

"But —"

"It is too dangerous," Sebastian said, getting to his feet when Christian rose and offered Allie a hand. "The sacristan must be held in custody. To have the two of you together and unattended is too risky."

"But if he's this way, he's not dangerous at all," I said, gesturing toward Mattias.

He blew me a kiss and waggled his eyebrows.

Kristoff rolled his eyes.

"As he is now? No. But what guarantee do we have that you will not lift the light-binding, or order him to do some act harmful to Dark Ones?" Sebastian countered.

"You *really* don't like me, do you?" I said, my hands on my hips as I faced him. Mattias got to his feet and mimicked me, his hands on his hips as he glared at Sebastian. "What have I ever done to you?"

Sebastian blinked in surprise, his expression disconcerted. "You are a Zorya."

"Move past that," I said, too tired and jet-lagged to listen to the voice of reason warning me against an outburst. "Is it something about me personally you don't like? Every time I come near you, you make a face like you smelled something bad!"

"You make a face," Mattias accused. "You do not want to lick the beauteous Pia!"

Sebastian stammered out a nonanswer as Allie laughed. She came around the table, taking my arm. "Come on; I'll go up to your room with you to make sure you guys will be comfy there. And while we're on our way, I'll explain to you about Dark Ones and this really obnoxious thing they have about Beloveds who aren't their own smelling like roadkill."

"I will come with you," Mattias said happily, batting his eyelashes at me. "Pia, Pia, Pia."

"*Dio,* he's worse than he was before," Kristoff muttered, elbowing Mattias aside when he tried to crowd me.

Mattias blew Kristoff a kiss, causing the latter to look in horror at him.

"Mattias, calm down and behave yourself," I told him. "Rowan is going to take you to your room. I want you to be very nice to him and do as he says."

"I will be very nice to him," Mattias repeated, beaming at Rowan. "He is pretty, too. Should I kiss him?"

Rowan recoiled.

"No kissing. Just go to sleep. No, not here. Sleep in your room."

Mattias left, waving madly as Rowan led him away.

"It's not going to cause his brain permanent damage to be like that, is it?" I asked, worried about Mattias's extreme change in personality.

"How could you tell if it did?" Kristoff muttered.

"It will wear off in time," Christian said, laughing. "Then it will be up to you whether or not you re-light-bind him, or let him return to his normal state."

Allie grinned. "I don't know; I think he's kind of cute this way. He reminds me of Antonio when he doesn't have someone to lust after."

Christian heaved a martyred sigh and said to Kristoff, "I would like a word or two, if you don't mind."

"Roadkill?" I asked Allie as she pulled me toward the door, glancing over my shoulder to Kristoff. "You're joking."

His eyes glittered with a light I found hard to understand.

"I wish I were. There's a lot you have to learn about vampires, Pia. Take it from someone who went into her relationship kicking and screaming all the way — the learning curve may be steep, but it's also a whole lot of fun."

CHAPTER 6

". . . and then the spirit is bound to the item you picked to be the keeper, and voilà! Instant way to transport them when they can't get around themselves."

I eyed the small blob of yarn on Allie's palm as we entered my room. It had a slight glow to it, a little shimmer that warned it was not all that it seemed. "That is very handy, I admit. But my spirits don't seem to have any problem traveling around. That is, they can get in a car with me if they want. That sort of thing."

Allie nodded and tweaked the satin eiderdown on the bed. "Christian might have given you a larger room, but I suppose there's nothing wrong with being cozy. Especially since you and Kristoff have been separated for so long."

"You're going to have to forgive me, but I'm curious — why did you believe that we're innocent when everyone else didn't?"

Before Allie could say anything, the door to a corner closet was flung open as a small child burst out, a towel tied around his neck in the form of a cape, his hands curved into claws, his fangs bared as he yelled, "I am Dwacula!"

"You'll have to forgive Josef. He likes springing out at people," Allie said with a motherly smile. He jumped around the room making various gargling noises that I imagined he believed were terror-inspiring. "He and Esme watched one of the old Dracula movies, and he decided that he wants to be a vampire when he grows up."

"Wise up, childwen of the night!" the boy shouted as he climbed onto a tapestry-backed chair, leaping off with a triumphant yell.

I gave Allie a startled glance. She laughed. "That was my first response, too. Christian was less amused, but you know how the Dark Ones are — they may look modern and sound modern, but they are far too medieval for words sometimes. You should hear him rant when I let Joe watch *Buffy*. You are innocent, aren't you?"

"Of the charges laid at my doorstep? Yes," I said, somewhat taken aback by the quick change of subject.

Josef climbed onto my bed and started

bouncing on it until his mother plucked him off with a warning.

"I thought so." She herded the boy back into the closet, telling him, "Go see to your dungeons, pumpkin. I think Van Helsing is in there."

"Van Helsing!" Josef's face lit up as he struggled with the knot on the towel.

Allie patiently untied it, tossing the towel on the chair as the boy disappeared into the closet, pulling the door closed after him. "He also wants to be Van Helsing. I can't say I blame him after seeing Hugh Jackman in the movie, although they had the vampires all wrong in it, but that happens a lot. Where were we?"

"Um . . . Kristoff and I are innocent?" Exhaustion swept over me. I plopped down on the bed.

"That's right." She considered me for a moment. I found it vaguely disconcerting having those odd eyes scrutinizing me so intently, although I had to admit that I liked Allie. There was a sense of down-to-earth straightforwardness to her that I found refreshing. "I know what it's like to have life out of your control, and I don't like being manipulated any more than I can see you do. If you were guilty, you wouldn't be quite so angry, if you know what I mean."

I nodded. "It just irritates me that everyone can suddenly think the worst of me after what happened. I saved Kristoff's life!"

She toyed with a small vase on the bureau for a moment. "Well, you have to remember that it's not just a matter of whether or not they like you. I think Christian does. He spoke quite well of you when he came home from Iceland."

"Sebastian doesn't," I said, making a little face.

"He's . . . he's a bit scarred yet. He went through some hard times and only recently found his Beloved. But he's Christian's oldest friend, and he is actually a very nice man once you get to know him. He's just a bit suspicious of people at first. Given his history, it's understandable."

"Do we really smell horrible?" I asked, sidetracked for a moment.

She laughed. "So they say, but I think it's a matter of the man in question. Christian says they get used to it, and he doesn't think of it anymore."

"It's just rather disconcerting knowing I smell like a pile of garbage," I answered. "I feel like bathing in perfume or something."

"Kristoff certainly didn't look like he found you offensive," she said, a teasing note in her voice.

I looked down at my hands for a moment, not really wanting to discuss the issue of a relationship with Kristoff.

"I'm sorry," Allie said quietly, her odd eyes seeing far more than I was comfortable with. "I didn't mean to get personal."

"It's all right," I lied. "It's just that . . ."

"You still have some things to work out."

"Yes."

"Who doesn't?" She smiled. "You should have seen Christian and me when we first met."

My curiosity got the better of me again. "How did you find each other? I'm kind of amazed that they ever find a Beloved at all, since there's only one for each vampire."

"Well, there is and there isn't," she said with a little laugh. "You'd have to ask a woman named Joy about that, but that's just going to confuse you, so we'll move on. The first time I laid eyes on Christian, he was lying naked and covered in blood from a hundred cuts all over his body. It was the most romantic thing ever."

I stared in horror at her.

She laughed again. "We had a rocky start. Christian was determined to have me admit I was his Beloved, and I wanted nothing to do with him."

My gaze dropped again. "That's not quite

155

the problem between Kristoff and me," I said, my heart wincing in pain at the memory of Kristoff looking at his ring.

"I'm sure you'll work out whatever is giving you grief. These guys may seem overbearing and arrogant as sin, but you have to admit there's something to be said for the fact that out of all the women in the world, you're the only one for him."

I said nothing, not wishing to dwell on it. A change of subject was called for. "Do you think there's any chance that if I worked on Christian, he'd let Mattias and Kristjana go?"

"Well . . ." She slid me an odd look. "Christian is the head of the Moravian Council. That position has a lot of responsibility with it."

She waited a moment, obviously expecting me to understand something that wasn't at all clear.

"I'm afraid that I don't see what one has to do with the other," I admitted.

She sighed and thought for a moment. "He doesn't break rules. He can't, not in his position. And what you're asking for would mean he'd have to do just that. So no, I don't think there's anything you can do that will get him to release Kristjana and Mattias."

There was an odd emphasis on the word "release" that I didn't quite understand. My brain chased around a hundred different thoughts, all of them ending with the same sad conclusion: If Christian wouldn't let them go, I was going to be damned to Zoryahood for the rest of my life.

"I think you and Kristoff will be comfy here," Allie said, looking around the room. "I'm sure you'll have him up to speed in no time. He was already looking a hundred times better after dining at Casa Pia."

I frowned at the thought of Kristoff being held prisoner, starved so callously. "He does look better, but I doubt if he's back to full strength."

"Probably not." Allie paused a moment. "Despite what you may think, he wasn't mistreated any more than the two reapers were. Kristoff was offered blood — he just refused to take it. We didn't try to starve him, Pia. You have to understand that for a Dark One to be separated from his Beloved for a short while is bearable. It's not comfortable in the least, not for either person, but it's bearable. But to go two months . . ." She shook her head. "I can only imagine the pain Kristoff must have suffered, being deprived of you. And I'm sure you didn't have a grand old time."

I looked down at myself and immediately sat up straighter to lessen the resemblance between me and a Buddha statue. "Unfortunately, I've managed to eat just fine during our separation."

"That's not quite what I meant," she answered. "When Christian is gone for more than a couple of days, I start getting headaches. Nothing truly horrible, but a low-grade headache that persists no matter what I take."

I thought of the headaches I'd been prone to during the last few months. They were so constant, I'd gone to both my optometrist and a doctor to see if I was starting to have migraines. "I've had headaches a lot lately," I admitted.

"But worse than that is a sense of . . ." She hesitated, her hands making a vague gesture. "Oh, I don't know quite how to describe it. It's a sense of being . . . incomplete. As if some part of me were missing. Things just don't seem right, if you know what I mean."

"I think I do," I said slowly, noticing for the first time that the vaguely empty feeling inside me seemed to be gone. "It's as if you were hollow inside."

"Hollow, that's it exactly. And if you're concerned about your other husband's well-being, you're welcome to talk to him. He's confined to a room on the second floor. We don't let him leave unattended — there are wards on the door — but we do take him out for little jaunts about the garden to get a bit of fresh air. He's not mistreated in any way, and I'm sure that goes for the other reaper, as well."

"A ward?" I asked. "What exactly is that?"

"It's basically a magical symbol that's drawn in the air or on an item. We find it works better than mundane things like locks. The ward allows people to pass through the door to enter the room, but not leave by it." She got to her feet, opening the door to the closet. "Come out, Van Helsing. There's a vampire downstairs who needs seeing to."

"Vampiwe!" Josef emerged from the closet with an old-fashioned wooden shoe form. He held it by the long metal skewer that poked into the wooden foot, waving it about as if it were a crossbow. "Shoot the vampiwe!"

"That's right, snuggles. Go shoot Daddy."

The boy ran out of the room, yelling about vampires. Allie followed more slowly, pausing at the door. "If you need anything, just give me a holler."

"I will," I said, still distracted by the idea

that I could be so affected by the loss of Kristoff. Just in time I remembered the question I had wanted to ask. "Oh, can I do the keeper thing with any spirit?"

"So long as they're not bound to someone else, you should be able to. Although your ghosts sound like the grounded kind. The kind I summon are unbound."

"Unbound? I'm not sure I understand."

"Well, yours can make themselves seen and heard, and can interact with our reality. There are other spirits out there who have to be Summoned to that state. Those are the ones I deal with."

"How do they get that way?" I asked, thinking of the ghosts who'd been waiting for me in Iceland.

She shrugged. "All we know is that there are several types of spirits. Some bound, some unbound, some present who refuse to be Summoned. Still others, like Esme, refuse to be Released."

"Sent on, you mean?"

"Yep."

"I know one of those," I said, thinking fondly of Ulfur and his ghostly horse. "He would have gone on to Ostri, but he stayed to help me."

"Bind him to a keeper and take him places with you," she said with a little shrug. "Assuming he wants to go, that is. Keepers are a great way to let them travel and keep them safe. Not to mention out of your hair for those times when you want a little privacy."

I smiled in response to her sudden grin, and was about to thank her when Christian appeared in the doorway. He held his son on one hip, the small metal skewer that I recognized coming from the antique shoe form sprouting out of his stomach. The glare he gave his wife would have scared me to death if it had been directed at me. "Allegra, would it be asking too much for you to *not* encourage my son to stake me at every available opportunity?"

"He was being Van Helsing. That's what Van Helsing does. And I didn't tell him to go for your heart," she answered, patting her boy on the head. "Besides, I thought he was going to shoot you with his pretend crossbow. What a clever little boy you are to make a stake out of the shoe form."

Christian's expression turned into one of sheer martyrdom as he plucked the metal skewer out of his belly. "That's it. I am destroying your *Buffy* DVDs. Kristoff, if you ever have children, I would advise you to ban any and all DVDs from your home. Come, Beloved. There are a few things I have to say to Josef, and I believe they will benefit you, as well."

Kristoff, who had been standing behind him, watched with a horrified expression as Christian tossed the stake onto a hall table before taking his wife's hand. Allie winked at me as she left with him, leaving Kristoff and me alone.

"Pia, are you back?" The door opposite me opened. Magda appeared, rosy and smelling of perfumed bath salts. "That *was* you I heard. I see you found Kristoff. Hello again. I don't know if you remember me. I'm Pia's friend Madga."

"Magda and her boyfriend, Raymond, kindly offered to come with me to Vienna," I explained.

Kristoff made her a little bow, but said nothing.

"Well . . ." Magda examined Kristoff for a moment, then indulged in a little eyebrow semaphore with me. "Ray's having a quick shower, but he wanted to go out and see the sights. I assume you two prefer to take a rain check on doing the tourist thing?"

I glanced at Kristoff. He didn't look even remotely as horrible as when I first saw him, but his face was still much too gaunt, and more important, I sensed a gnawing hunger in him that had yet to be fully appeased. "I think a rain check will be best."

"Gotcha. How did the meeting with the fanged ones go?"

I dredged up a somewhat weak smile. "It was . . . interesting. I'll tell you about it tomorrow, OK?"

"All right, but I'm going to hold you to that. Nice to see you again, Kristoff."

Magda withdrew into her room with a pointed look at me that warned she would, indeed, expect full disclosure.

I looked at Kristoff. Kristoff looked at me.

"Awkward?" he asked.

"Well . . . yes. Kind of."

"If you would prefer I do not share a room with you —"

"Don't be ridiculous," I said, grabbing him by the shirt and hauling him into the room after me. "It's not like we haven't slept together before. If you're worried I'm going to demand sex from you —"

"Christ, woman, is that all you think about?" Kristoff exploded suddenly, one hand running through his lovely brown curls.

"Sex?" I asked, my stomach contracting at his mistaken belief. I started to protest, but he cut me off.

"No!" He stormed forward, his hands clamping down on my shoulders as I tried to back away. "Why do you persist in deluding yourself that I don't desire you?"

My jaw dropped for a moment before I snapped back, "Why? Maybe the fact that you ran away from me has something to do with it."

"I explained that," he said grimly, but there was a heat building in his eyes that immediately made all sorts of hidden parts of me sit up and take notice. "You said you wanted Alec. I was simply giving you what you wanted."

"What I wanted?" I bit back the scream of frustration that threatened to burst free, saying instead, "Putting my wishes aside for a moment, why on earth would you think that Alec and I had a future? You knew I was your Beloved, not his."

He released me. I took a step backward, simultaneously wanting to climb all over him and not wanting to be so close to him. The sense and scent and nearness of him were almost overwhelming. My body and mind were fighting a huge war to decide whether I was going to yell at him or jump his bones.

"We were Joined, but hadn't, for lack of a better word, consummated the relationship. Alec might not have been able to feed off you, but if you had set your minds on being together, you could have a life with him with relative comfort."

"But you couldn't survive for long without me, could you?"

His eyes flickered to the window. "Probably not. But a Beloved can survive the loss of a Dark One. Even if I died, you and Alec could have had a future."

I was silent for a moment, dozens of thoughts spinning around in my head. Foremost among them was the knowledge that such a noble gesture was made hollow by the fact that he had no burning desire to be with me. He was willing to die to remain true to his long-lost love.

Tears burned my eyes for a moment. I turned away and made myself busy by fussing with the blankets and pillows on the bed. "Well, what's done is done," I said, ever the pragmatist. I wanted badly to tell him exactly how I felt, but I had already told him I didn't want Alec, and he had responded as I knew he would — a polite refusal to address the issue of any feelings between us beyond those of mere physical compatibility.

"Yes, it's done." There was a thread of something intangible in his voice. I felt him behind me, not touching me, but near enough that the heat from his body made my back tingle. "Speaking of that night, I

have been remiss in thanking you for returning my soul. I apologize for such an over-
sight. Having a soul again certainly wasn't
anything I ever thought would happen."

"Again?" I asked, curiosity making me
turn around to face him. "You had one
before?"

His face smoothed out into a mask of
indifference that I was coming to recognize
meant he was hiding his true feelings.
"There are two types of Dark Ones: those
born to an unredeemed father, and those
who were made."

"And you were one of the latter?"

"Yes." He walked over to the closet that
Josef had been hiding in and pulled off his
shirt, neatly hanging it on an empty hanger.
"I was human once."

"I had no idea. So, you and Andreas and
your cousin were all human, but were all
turned into vampires?"

"No." He pulled off his shoes and socks,
casting me an unreadable glance. "Andreas
and I share the same mother, but we have
different fathers. His father is a Dark One."

"Is? He's still around?"

A rueful smile quirked his lips. "Dark
Ones don't die easily. Usually it requires an
act of carnage. Yes, his father is still living.
In Bavaria, I believe. Andreas does not

speak of him much — they are not very close."

"And your mom?"

"She was human. She died centuries ago," he said, turning away as he unbuckled his belt.

I spent a moment admiring the lovely muscles of his back before his pants dropped to the floor. I stared at him, my breath catching in my throat at the sight of all that sculpted, delectable flesh.

He hung his pants in the closet and turned around, about to say something, but stopped when he caught me gawking. "What's the matter with you?"

"Nothing." The word came out rough and ragged. I cleared my throat and tried again. "Nothing at all."

He put his hands on his hips. I greatly enjoyed the ripple of muscles across his chest as he did so. "You have seen me naked before."

I shook my head, still staring. I couldn't seem to stop. "No, I haven't. The times we made love were in the dark. I've never actually seen you before."

"There's nothing unique about me to warrant such an examination. I look like any other man."

"Hardly," I managed to get out.

He crossed his arms over his chest. "You're going to insist on staring your fill at me, aren't you?"

"Oh, yes," I breathed, my eyes huge as I tried to drink all of him in. Kristoff in clothing was mind-numbingly gorgeous. Those silky reddish brown curls begged to be touched. His eyes drew me in and made me want to dive into their glittering teal depths. The cleft in his chin drove me wild with the need to dip my tongue into it. And his mouth was a symphony waiting to be played, but without his clothing, he was . . .

"Breathtaking," I said, letting my gaze play over all of him, starting at his beautiful feet, moving up along well-muscled calves to thighs that had my fingers itching to touch. His penis held my attention for a few minutes, but there was more of him to see. His stomach I remembered as having a tiny little softness to it, but that was gone now. I frowned.

"Why are you frowning at my belly?" he asked, looking down at it.

"It was nicer before. You've lost some weight," I said slowly.

His lips pursed. "I was a bit out of shape. Too much of the easy life."

"I liked you soft."

His eyebrows rose.

I blushed, unable to keep from glancing at his nether regions. Although he wasn't fully aroused, it was obvious that my visual examination of him had stirred some interest. "I meant that I preferred you with the tiny little smidgen of softness around your stomach. I love men's stomachs. And sides. There's a part of the flank that drives me . . . Never mind," I finished, disconcerted by the odd look he was giving me.

"Are you finished?" he asked politely after a moment.

I nodded, wishing I could turn away from him, but unable to.

He eyed me.

"I'm not taking off my clothes," I said quickly, tugging my shrug a bit tighter around me.

His face hardened. "I told you that I would be happy to find another room —"

"Now who's perpetuating misunderstandings?" I asked, waving a hand toward the bed. "I have no problem whatsoever with sleeping with you. I'd add, 'assuming you wanted to sleep with me,' but if I did, you'd probably just yell at me, so I won't."

"Are you going to always be like this?" he asked, a curious expression flickering across his face.

"Like what?"

"Driving me insane? You are, aren't you? You're going to make me spend the rest of my life reassuring you that I want you."

Unbidden, my eyes went back to his penis. It was showing more than a little interest now. "I never doubted that you enjoyed the times we slept together," I said carefully. "But there is more to life than sex."

"Indeed there is. Why won't you take off your clothes?"

My gaze flashed up to his, the blush that I knew was waiting for a chance to blossom doing just that. "I should think that's obvious."

His eyes narrowed. "You think wrong. What is obvious?"

I looked at the bed. I looked at Kristoff. I looked at the lamps on either side of the bed, assessing how badly I wanted to see him naked against my need to keep him from doing likewise.

An expression of sheer male arrogance filled his eyes. "You're not going to try to make me believe that you're too modest?"

"I am, as a matter of fact, a very modest person," I said, lifting my chin and trying to look down my nose at him. It wasn't easy, considering he was at least a good foot taller than me. "And you can just stop making that face at me. Yes, we've slept together.

Yes, you've felt my body, but that's not the same thing as seeing it."

"For the love of the saints . . ." Kristoff marched over to me. I squeaked and tried to get away, but he had me backed up against the wall before I could take two steps. "You are not fat."

"I —"

"No," he said, pressing me against the wall. His body was hot and hard and felt so good I just wanted to weep with the rightness of the feeling of him against me. His breath was just as hot on my lips, his hands sliding around me to grab my behind, pulling me even tighter against him. "You are as you are, Pia. And I do not find you physically repulsive, or repellent, or any of the other unpleasant images you believe I foster. I would have thought the opposite, in fact, was quite evident."

"Men have those sorts of reactions regardless of whether or not they like the body in question," I protested.

His eyes narrowed. "Who told you that?"

I freed a hand enough to make a vague gesture. "Everyone knows that. Men are ruled by their penises. Women are different. There's a huge market of relationship books that explain the ins and outs of it. So to speak."

"That's one of the most unfounded and insulting things I've ever heard you say, but I am willing to overlook it if you will forget such a ridiculous idea. Men aren't just sex machines, Pia. We have feelings, too."

"I never meant to imply you didn't —"

"Yes, you did." He paused a moment, his mouth so close to mine I had to literally curl my fingers into a fist to keep from grabbing his head. "There may be some people who enjoy sex for sex's sake — both men and women — but I assure you that I am not included in their number. I like the way you look. I like your body. I very much wish to make love to you."

I searched his eyes, looking for any sign of deceit.

Such a nice image you have of me. I am not lying to you. I couldn't, even if I wanted to, and I don't.

You couldn't? I asked, my toes curling with the sensation of intimacy that speaking thus brought with it.

No. You are my Beloved. I can't harm you, lie to you, or deceive you in any manner. So you can believe me when I say that I do not find you anything but physically appealing.

"Then you must be a truly exceptional man," I couldn't help saying.

He said nothing, just released my butt in

order to strip the shrug from my shoulders. He stared at the front of the sundress for a moment before unbuttoning the bodice, his long fingers brushing gently against my flesh.

I shivered, but not with cold.

"I can assure you that no man would find your breasts anything but magnificent," he murmured, deftly unhooking the front of my bra to release my boobs.

I clutched his shoulders and moaned as his hot breath swept into the valley between them.

"The memory of them has remained with me the last two months," he murmured, his mouth closing on one suddenly aching nipple.

"It has?" I asked, gasping as his tongue made a long, slow swipe. "Oh, dear God, do that again."

He did, releasing my breast to kiss a hot, steaming path over to where my other boob waited impatiently for its turn. "They haunted my sleep. I could taste them, feel them, feel the silky softness of them and the warmth of them in my hands."

The slight stubble of an evening growth of beard was pleasantly abrasive on my now highly sensitized flesh. I shivered as he rubbed his cheek along the underside of my breast before catching the tip gently in between his teeth.

I moaned again, my fingers digging deeper into his shoulders, my mind filled with the sensations his mouth was generating.

"I do not normally like perfume on my woman, but this one pleases me," he murmured against my flesh.

"It's not really a perfume. It's an amber oil called Love Me," I answered, sliding my hands down his back, letting my fingers dance down the swells of muscle.

"Is the name a command or a desire?"

"Whichever you want," I said, dipping my head to nibble on his shoulder. "I got it in a sample pack."

"I will get you more," he said, his mouth moving upward as his fingers continued to unbutton the front of my dress.

I made a noise of protest, uncomfortable despite his assurances, but my objection was short-lived as he leaned into me, his hands sliding my dress down over my hips. I melted, I positively melted against him, shivering from the feeling of his chest rubbing against mine.

I gasped as he suddenly grabbed the backs of both of my thighs, hoisting me up and pulling my legs around him in one move. His mouth closed on mine as he pushed me against the wall, the coldness of the wall contrasting with the heat of his body. He groaned when I suckled the tongue that was twining itself around mine, a deep groan that started in his chest and reverberated out until it thrummed through me.

He moved sinuously against me, his chest hair teasing and tormenting my breasts. I slid my hands up his back and around to his sides.

Touch me, he begged, and for a moment I was flooded with images and sensations that I recognized as coming from him, not me. They stopped almost immediately, leaving me dazed, feeling as if I'd been locked into a dark room, away from a source of blinding light.

I slid down his body until I was standing again, my hands tracing a tantalizing path around to his belly. *You've lost too much weight,* I murmured to him. *I liked you better before.*

Some things haven't changed, he answered, willing my hands lower.

I smiled to myself as I stroked a path downward, my fingers wrapping around his erection. At the touch he groaned again into my mind. I had the faintest hint of his feelings, but felt deprived, locked away in the dark when he was enjoying the light.

Share, I demanded as I let my fingers dance down the length of him.

His eyes burned down into mine.

I tipped my head back and nipped the lovely curve of his lower lip, wanting more, wanting all of him, needing him to touch me. *Share with me, Kristoff. I want to know what you're feeling.*

He hesitated for a moment, and I caught a whisper of thought, of a name.

She's not here. I am, I said, pushing down hard on the little spike of pain that accompanied his thought. *Please, I want to know what you're feeling. I want to know just how my boobs haunt you. We're going to have to spend the rest of our lives together. I want to know you.*

He groaned again as I found a rhythm he liked, his eyes burning so hot I felt as if they were lighting my skin on fire.

I need more than just sex, I said with a little mental sob, my heart suddenly feeling as if it would shatter. *I need you.*

And suddenly, the floodgate was opened. I gasped as his emotions, tangled with sensations he was feeling as I stroked him, filled me with a lightness that burned through to my soul. There was sexual desire there, almost indiscernible from the always burning urges of the hunter. I reveled in the

176

sensations, accepting his feelings and giving him everything I had.

His teeth pierced my shoulder, the pain an exquisite moment that lit bright in my mind as he filled me with thoughts that were both carnal and profound, a strange mixture of bodily needs and emotional desire.

Now do you believe me? he asked, his voice just as silky and beautiful when it was spoken only in my head. *You cannot doubt any longer that I desire you.*

I kissed a path over to his earlobe. His entire body jerked as I bit down on his ear, his head pulling back from me for a moment, an explosion of shock and rapture and sexual need swamping both of us.

His eyes flashed at me for a second before I found myself once more hoisted against the wall, his fingers biting hard into my thighs as I wrapped them around his hips. He growled low in his chest, his teeth piercing the skin of my neck at the same time he thrust hard into my body.

I went into sensory overload, my mind reeling from our shared sensations. His need just fed my own, which in turn drove him harder until we both seemed to spin out of control, my body moving of its own accord against him, straining now not just for my own moment of completion, but for his as well. And when that moment arrived, it pushed me over the edge to the single most profound moment in my life. I exploded in a nova of joint rapture, my mind a whirl of sensation and thought and feelings. Out of the confusing mass came one stark thought that shook me to my very core.

There was no question of having a life without Kristoff. He held my heart just as surely as I held him in my arms. I loved him, with every inch of my being I loved him, and nothing would ever change that.

Without realizing it, I'd slowly shut him out of my mind, not wanting him to see the truth. It was too new a realization, too raw to examine closely.

As his tongue swept over the bite mark, I let my legs drop down, my muscles trembling with the strength of our shared orgasm.

I stared at him silently as he gazed at me, my feminine ego pleased by the somewhat dazed glint in his eyes, but another part wept tears of purest sorrow. I would spend the rest of my life loving a man who might feel a certain amount of affection for me — he was not the sort of man who could make love to a woman as he had without feeling some sort of affection — but I would never wholly hold his heart.

"Dio," he said, but it was more a reverential statement than an oath.

I looked away. It hurt too much to look at his bright eyes.

His fingers turned my chin back to make me face him. "What is it?"

"What is what?" I held on to his shoulders, my legs still too shaky to support me.

With a little noise of annoyance he picked me up and carried me over to the bed. I stifled yet another moment of amazement that he could heft me without so much as a grunt.

"What is it you are hiding?"

His mind probed at mine, seeking to penetrate its depths. Just as he had done earlier, I locked away a secret little part of me, the part that acknowledged my love. Despite my desire to shout it from the balcony, to tell everyone I knew that I was madly, insanely, body-and-soul in love with him, I knew that would only bring more grief.

"Everyone has secrets," I said, paraphrasing what he had said to me earlier.

You are my Beloved. You should not have secrets from me. He followed me down to the bed, his body leaning over mine as he continued to peer into my eyes.

"You and I both know that we're not the

ideal couple," I said, pushing gently into his mind. Quickly he erected a guard over some part of himself. *You see? There are parts of you that you don't want to share.*

You have not lived the life I have, he answered slowly. *You have lived a blameless life. Your soul is not stained as mine is.*

I stared at him in surprise, unable to keep from touching him. I rubbed my thumb over the tiny little frown lines between his sleek chocolaty brows until they eased. "What have you done to stain your soul?"

His head dipped down as he claimed me in another toe-curling kiss, his body draped over mine. His tongue was as sweet as ever, dancing around my mouth, letting me reciprocate for a few moments before taking charge again. Kristoff, I noted to myself, liked to be the aggressive one. I didn't really mind that, although I expected that I would have to show him the joys of being on the receiving end.

The events of the past are just that — long gone. They do not matter now.

I thought, but didn't share with him, that they must be important, or he wouldn't feel so compelled to keep them secret.

What does matter is the fact that I've taken too much of your blood. You should have stopped me.

I laughed into his head even as a tiny part of my heart was breaking. "I don't think anything could have stopped either one of us, short of a nuclear explosion, and frankly, I doubt if even that would have done it."

"Nonetheless, you must rest," he said, tucking me under the blankets. He flipped off the light and slid into bed next to me. "You must eat extra food in the morning. You will need to replenish the blood I've taken from you."

"The last thing in the world I need is more food. You're fussing for nothing — I feel fine. You're the one who has to eat more. You're still skin and bones."

He said nothing, but rolled on his side, pulling me up against him and tossing a leg over me in a protective manner that left me melting like a big puddle of jelly.

I was embraced in a cocoon of warmth, one that smelled like a slightly tangy, sweet Kristoff and the lingering earthier scent of our recent activities.

I felt the change in him. He had accepted me in his life, acknowledged that we were bound together. I did not sense any resentment over that fact, just a recognition of what we both were, and his adjustment to the fact that he now had me to think of, as well as himself. I knew I should be grateful for that, happy that he would no longer be fighting the fact that we were together, but that little dark, hidden spot inside him ate away my pleasure.

That he hid the true depths of his feelings for his dead love said much for his consideration for me. That he held so tightly on to it boded ill for the future.

CHAPTER 7

"I've been thinking."

A slight snore ruffled my hair.

"Kristoff." I shoved his chest. He rolled over onto his back, giving a little grunt, followed immediately by another brief snore.

"Kristoff!" I clicked on the small bedside lamp, propping myself up on one elbow, and prodded him in the side until one of his eyes cracked open.

"Hruh?"

"You're snoring."

He blinked sleepily at me. "Wha'?"

"Vampires do not snore. Everyone knows that." I laid my hand on his chest, a little frisson of happiness skittering inside me at the nearness of him. "Were you sleeping?"

He was fully awake now, and the muzzy look was gone, replaced by a slight frown. "What sort of question is that? You just said I was snoring."

"It was a courtesy question, intended to

give you time to wake up so you can speak coherently."

His frown turned to a suspicious scowl. "You're one of those women who likes to talk after sex, aren't you?"

"All women like to talk after sex. It cements a feeling of intimacy and allows us to feel that our partners, frequently notorious for their 'wham, bam, thank you, ma'am' policy, are interested in more than just physical satisf — Hey! Stop going back to sleep; this is important!"

"Nothing is more important to a man after sex than getting eight or nine hours of uninterrupted sleep," he said, closing his eyes.

"You're a vampire," I felt obligated to point out. "You're not a normal man."

"I'm male. The same principle applies," he insisted, his eyes refusing to open.

"Oh, really." I thought for a moment, then shoved back the blanket, taking his now-relaxed penis in my hands.

His eyes shot open.

"Aha!" I said, shoving aside one of his legs so I could kneel between them. "I knew it."

Interest was chased by irritation in his lovely teal eyes. "Dammit, woman, I may be immortal, but there are limits to my abilities. I'm not an incubus who can satisfy your

184

lustful desires all . . . Hrnng."

I smiled at the way his eyes rolled back in his head as I bent down to take the very tip of him into my mouth. I let my tongue swish around the underside for a bit before looking up. "Now that I have your attention . . ."

His head snapped up from where it had lolled back onto the pillow. "You're stopping?"

"I just wanted to wake you up enough to talk," I said, resting my hand on his thighs.

He glared at me. "There's a word for what you're doing, you know, and it's not very nice."

"I didn't say I wasn't going to finish; I just wanted to talk to you before I do, because if the speed with which you fell asleep a short while ago is anything to go by, you're not going to want to talk to me after I finish up with you."

I could see he wanted to protest the point, but he knew he hadn't a leg to stand on. Grudgingly, he said, "What is so important you have to stop?"

"Two things, really," I said, tapping the fingers of one hand on his thigh. "The first is something that bothered me a bit at the time, but I couldn't tell why. Allie put a special emphasis on the fact that Christian was not going to authorize the release of

Mattias and Kristjana, and yet she went out of her way to tell me where they were."

He snorted and flopped back onto the pillows, his eyes closed again. "I don't see what's confusing about that. Christian made himself quite clear."

"Clear that he wasn't going to release the two reapers?"

A slow frown creased the spot between his silky brown eyebrows. "No. Clear that his hands were tied, but he fully expected us to use our own resources to achieve the goal."

I gawked at him a minute. He opened his eyes enough to give first his penis, then me a pointed look. "You're not going to continue?"

"Not until I'm through being flabbergasted. Are you trying to tell me that Christian . . . what, he mind-talked to you? Told you to go ahead and take Mattias and Kristjana?"

"We don't have that sort of a mental link."

"Then how . . . ?"

"It was clear that what he wasn't saying was what he wanted us to do."

"It wasn't at all clear to me. I thought Allie was telling me to break them out, not Christian."

He grunted and looked rather hopefully at his privates.

I patted his penis, still distracted by this new avenue of thought. "OK, I get that Christian wants us to take Mattias and make a break for it. And presumably then go to Iceland and do the same for Kristjana, which is fine, because I have to go there for Ulfur anyway. But why does Christian want that? He said himself that if I weren't a Zorya, I wouldn't be able to pump the Brotherhood for information about Alec."

Kristoff was silent for a moment. "There is a traitor amongst Dark Ones, someone working for the council who is betraying our interests to the reapers. We have known about this for a year. Christian clearly expects us to uncover who this mole is in the process of discovering Alec's whereabouts."

"You think the two things are connected?" I asked, gently stroking his thighs.

"Possibly," Kristoff admitted, his eyes darkening. "Although, as you pointed out to the council, it wouldn't necessarily have to be a Dark One who set me up. But they no doubt believe it is the same person."

"So we take Mattias and Kristjana, and what? Use them as something to barter for Alec?"

"That thought had crossed my mind,"

Kristoff said, his breathing quickening as I dragged my nails gently up his thighs. "There's no real other use for the two of them."

"Oh, I don't know. Mattias might know something. If nothing else, I can play the wife card. That seems to hold a lot of meaning for him."

Kristoff's body tensed. He glared down the length of it to me. "You are *not* his wife."

I sighed. "We went over this that night in Iceland. In order to receive the powers of a Zorya, I have to be married to a sacristan. Mattias is the sacristan. I have powers. Thus our marriage, the one between you and me, such as it was, was obviously not the legal one."

His jaw worked for a moment.

"Trust me, I don't like it any more than you do, but obviously Mattias places a lot of value on the whole marriage, so we might as well use that to our advantage."

He ground his teeth. His hands fisted into the sheets.

"Oh, stop acting like a big, scary, pointy-toothed, jealous baby, and start thinking up an escape plan."

"I am *not* jealous," he growled, his eyes lighting from within. He grabbed my hips and hoisted me upward until my breasts were smashed against his face. He took one nipple in his mouth and flicked his tongue across the tip. *And he is not your husband.*

I clutched his shoulders, my entire body suddenly turning into one gigantic erogenous zone. *My mistake. Would you please . . . Oh, yes.*

His hands slid down my hips, around my backside, and down into depths that he had so recently plumbed. I bucked against his hands, trying desperately to hold on to my thoughts.

Do not fight your passion. Embrace it; don't deny it, he murmured into my head.

I can't help it. I know where this is going to end — more mind-blowingly fabulous sex, and given my jet lag and your insistence that you're the same as any other male, we'll both fall asleep afterward. We have to think of a plan, Kristoff. We have to think of a way out of here.

His mouth was hot and wet as he licked a path over to my other breast. I curled my fingers into his hair, nibbling his neck, sucking on his earlobe, my mind giving up the battle as the desire he stirred within me swelled upward.

I have a plan, he answered, opening his mind to me. I bit gently on a cord in his neck, the feeling of which drove me — drove him — nearly past the breaking point.

I slid backward, down his body, kissing a line down his belly. His muscles contracted tightly as I moved downward, soft little groans of pleasure filling my head. I paused for a moment when I got to his penis, smiling to myself at the sensations he was sharing.

Your plan involves a blow job. I meant we need to have a plan for escaping here with Mattias, finding Kristjana, and rescuing Ulfur.

Blow job first, then escape, he answered, a note of hopefulness lingering in the back of his mind.

I laughed at him, dipping my head down to take him into my mouth. *I'll give it a shot, but I don't know if I'm any good at it.*

His body stiffened for a moment, every muscle as hard as steel, and then suddenly I was lifted high over him, my knees straddling his hips, his penis poised to pierce me.

You're good.

Kristoff, wait! I yelled, desperately trying to squirm my hips away from the ecstasy that I knew stood one thrust away.

Hunger had burst into being hot and deep in him, rising until it threatened to snap the thin shred of control he held.

I won't drink from you, he said, a note of desperation evident in his thoughts.

No, it's not that. I'm a big girl; I have lots of blood — you're welcome to it.

Then why in the name of the saints are you stopping me when I know you want this as much as I do?

I almost sobbed, so desperate was I to feel the completion that I knew awaited me. "The plan! We can't wait until morning to figure out what to do. We have to do something tonight, while people are asleep."

He snarled a mental oath, then thought at me, images of us climbing down from the second-story window with Mattias, of guards distracted by Magda and Raymond, of us using the money he was supposed to have stolen to charter a plane to take us to California.

"No, we have to get Kristjana and Ulfur first. We'll have to go to Iceland."

The image altered to that of a fjord.

"And what about Magda and Raymond? I can't leave them here by themselves to face Christian and Sebastian —"

Hurriedly, he shoved Magda and Ray in front of the fjord.

"What about —"

With a wordless roar he plunged me downward. All my protests vanished instantly, as I knew they would. Every fiber of my body was focused on his pleasure, my own driving it as he urged me on faster. He sat up, teeth flashing for a second before they pierced the skin of my shoulder, my blood flowing down his throat like the sweetest nectar, soaking into parched cells that had too long been starved. My fingers curled into the thick muscles of his back as the combined sensation of his climax and mine sent my spirit flying.

It took a long, long while for me to drift back down to my body, but I did so with the echo of Kristoff's thought tolling in my head.

My wife, not his.

"Mile-high club?"

"Hmm?" I stopped as I passed where Magda was sitting in a center aisle row of the plane. Raymond was next to her, sound asleep, his head having slid to the side, with airline earphones still stuck in his ears, his mouth ajar as he snored. Magda had tucked a napkin under his chin.

"He's a drooler," she said softly, smiling fondly at him.

"If that's the worst of his sins, you don't have much to complain about," I said, taking the empty seat next to her. Kristoff, who had been behind me, continued on to our seats in the back section of the first-class area. I was thankful the flight from Austria to Frankfurt was only half-booked, which meant there was more than the usual amount of free space on the plane.

"Absolutely. How's your sleeping beauty?"

"Thoroughly out of it, thank God. I thought Kristoff was going to punch Mattias if he tried to kiss me once more. I don't know why being light-bound has made him so amorous, but at least it's better than antagonistic."

"Much better, by the sounds of it. And I asked you if you'd joined the mile-high club, not that it's really any of my business, although I've always wanted to try it. But those bathrooms are so darned small."

"Oh, that." A little blush warmed my cheeks. "No, we didn't do that. Kristoff was hungry and was going to wait for the plane to land before eating, but I figured this would save us time."

"Uh-huh. So that would explain the lipstick all over his chin and neck?"

My blush cranked up a couple of notches.

Magda laughed and gave my arm a friendly squeeze. "I was just teasing you, silly."

"I know. It's just that feeding Kristoff . . . Well, sometimes we get a bit carried away. But you can take it from me that the bathrooms on the plane are, in fact, too small to do anything beyond a little necking."

She shook her head. "Sometimes it just hits me — he's a vampire. A real vampire. And he can only exist by drinking *your* blood?"

"That's the story. And given his appearance in Vienna, I can't deny it."

"He was pretty ragged-looking. He appears to be feeling much better now."

"I think so." I resisted the urge to glance behind me at where he was sitting. I took enormous pleasure in just gazing at him, marveling once again at the odd twist of fate that had landed the most handsome man I'd ever met smack-dab in my life. He'd caught me watching him as he dozed just an hour before.

What's wrong? he'd asked as he sat up, glancing quickly around to find whatever threat was imminent.

Nothing's wrong.

Then why are you staring at me?

Maybe I like looking at you.

He shot me a look filled with disbelief.

On my other side, with his face plastered against the plane window, Mattias snored away. I made sure he was still asleep before turning back to Kristoff. *Oh, come now. Unlike the vampires in stories, you have a reflec-*

tion, so I know you've seen yourself in a mirror, not to mention you've lived a good five hundred or so years. Surely you've noticed women going gaga over you?

I've never had a problem with them, no, he said with a mental shrug. *But you put too much emphasis on appearances. Something I believe I've had cause to point out to you before.*

That was in reference to my *appearance. And don't even think of going there again — I'm willing to admit that perhaps you are different from most men and don't mind a woman who is on the abundant side of things rather than the anorexic, but we weren't talking about me. You are really very handsome, Kristoff. More than handsome — drop-dead gorgeous. What do you think of that?*

He gave another mental shrug. *What do you expect me to think of it? There's little I can do to change how I look.*

For God's sake, man! I whomped him on the arm. *I'm telling you I think you're sexy as hell! That you make my mouth water just looking at you! That you not only start my engine — you rev it up to the point where . . . where . . . oh, I don't know any car analogies! You just make me want to fling myself on you!*

I knew that already, he replied with maddening rationality. *I feel your arousal just as you feel mine.*

Argh! I yelled at him.

He had the nerve to look surprised. *I am not belittling your physical attraction to me in any way, Pia. It pleases me to know that you are as pleased with my body as I am with yours.*

"Oh, you are impossible in this reasonable mood," I muttered, getting up and stepping over his legs.

He grabbed my arm and pulled me down onto his lap, his eyes glittering with a deep light that had my body tingling in anticipation. *I think you underestimate just how pleasing I find you,* he said, tracing my jawline with his thumb.

A little shiver went down my back. I leaned forward until my mouth was a millimeter from his. *I want a love name.*

His eyes widened. *A love name?*

Yes. Allie has several, it appears, for Christian, although they all seemed aimed more at irritating him than being a pet name. Even that obnoxious Sebastian said his Beloved called him her little cabbage.

Kristoff made a face. His breath was warm on my mouth as I softly — oh, so softly — brushed my lips along his.

I want something like that for you. Somehow

the usual ones — "honey," "sweetie," and the like — don't seem suitable. So give me something I can call you.

Kristoff wouldn't do?

A nickname. I want a nickname.

I have one already. Alec calls me Kris some-times.

I bit his lower lip.

He groaned into my mind, shifting me slightly on his lap. Since we were in the last row in our section of the plane, few people came back to see me sitting on his lap. Regardless, I didn't want to start anything we couldn't continue, so I didn't explore the reason he moved me a smidgen down his legs.

Baby? I asked.

That's hardly a term suitable for a male.

Hmm. Punkin?

One sable eyebrow rose. I kissed it.

OK, then, you suggest a name. What about something in German?

German isn't a language that lends itself easily to love names.

Italian, then?

He thought for a moment. *There's* caro.

That's like what? "Dear"?

Yes.

What else?

He looked thoughtful. *I don't know. I don't*

usually have call to find pet names for men.

Well, how about if we do it this way — if you were going to call me something, what would it be?

Beloved.

Something a little more meaningful than that.

Heat shimmered in his eyes. *There is nothing more meaningful to a Dark One than that.*

I kissed the corner of his mouth. It was just a little kiss, but it was enough to start the slumbering fire within me. *If I were a normal human woman . . . what would you call me then?*

Tesorina mia.

Which means?

My little treasure.

Treasure, hmm? Is there a male version?

Tesoro.

I rolled it around my mind a few times. *That's pretty good. Nothing else?*

He hesitated a moment. Amore.

Ah. My gaze dropped to his mouth. I didn't need help translating that word. Tempted as I was to use it, I didn't want to put him in the position that he had to acknowledge that my growing emotions were more or less unrequited. Tesoro *it is, then.*

I got off his lap and went to visit the bathroom, my body burning for him while my mind yelled at me for wanting something that he couldn't give.

"Pia?"

Magda's voice interrupted my trip down memory lane.

"Yes?"

"You haven't heard a word I said, have you? You looked like you were a million miles away."

"Sorry. Just wondering if this little jaunt to Germany is going to give the vampires the slip."

The look she gave me was part exasperation, part affection. "That's exactly what I was asking you about."

"You didn't have to come —" I started to say, feeling guilty once again that their vacation was turning into an endurance bout of globe-hopping.

"Oh, hush, we had that out last night. Since Mattias is now evidently your love puppy, with the emphasis on the 'puppy,' then I figured we'd be going to Iceland next."

"Yes. Except I think Kristoff might want you guys to act as a decoy."

"Decoy? Oh, to lead the vamps off your trail?"

"Exactly. Although they have to know we'd go to Iceland. Maybe we should talk to Kristoff. I don't really remember all he said. I was kind of busy flashing light at Mattias."

"We'll let Ray have his beauty sleep," Magda said, getting to her feet. "Let's confab with the man."

"Sounds good. It'll give me a chance to try out the new pet name I have for him."

"You found one?"

"Yes. It's Italian," I said rather smugly. "I haven't used it yet, but this would be a good opportunity to see how it feels."

"Italian! How exotic. I should have something like that for Ray."

I nudged her with my elbow. "You're Hispanic, silly! Surely there are oodles of Spanish love names."

"Bah. Spanish isn't nearly as exotic as Italian is. OK, you're up. Let's hear this great endearment."

"We've come to talk game plan . . . er . . . Kristoff." My sentence trailed away lamely as he lowered the magazine he was reading so I could crawl over his legs to my seat.

Magda sat on the arm of the seat opposite him, shaking her head. "Chicken."

My shoulders slumped.

Kristoff gave me an odd look. "What is it you are accused of being afraid of?"

"It's the pet name you gave me. Well, not

gave me, but gave me to use for you. I can't do it. It just doesn't feel right."

"Ah," he said, clearly not bothered in the least.

"Maybe you should forgo exotic and stick to something you're more comfortable with," Magda suggested. "Did you try plain old 'honey'?"

We both looked at Kristoff. He rolled his eyes. "No," I said at the same time Magda shook her head.

"Agreed. He's not the 'honey' type. How about . . ." She tapped a finger to her chin. " 'Angel'?"

"Definitely not," Kristoff said, going back to his magazine.

"He's not really an 'angel' type, either," I admitted.

"You may have something. Let's see . . . 'sweet pea'?"

"Christ, no," Kristoff said.

"Hush, you," I said, concentrating. " 'Sugar pie'?"

He shuddered.

"I suppose 'snuggle bunny' is out," Magda said thoughtfully. " 'Sugar lips'?"

"Ohh, now that's not bad —"

Kristoff leveled a glare at me. "Don't even think about it."

"Party pooper," I muttered, flicking his

magazine in an annoyed manner. He just grunted and buried himself in it again.

" 'Pooh bear'? I had a boyfriend I used to call my cuddly little Pooh bear. He was a dream," Magda said, sighing happily at the memory. "Then he met a masseuse, and last I heard they have five kids and are really happy. Oh! I know! 'Poochikins'!"

I looked at Kristoff and giggled. He glared at the magazine. "I don't think so, Magda, but thanks for the suggestion. I'll just have to find something else."

" 'Sugarplum'?"

"Nooo," I said slowly, regretfully setting the name aside.

" 'Sweet cheeks'?"

You do, and you'll live to regret it.

I laughed out loud. "Pass. But I think I thought of something."

"You did? What?" she asked.

Do I want to know? Kristoff asked at the same time.

"I think I'll hold off on saying it out loud for a bit," I told Magda with a smile.

You'll find out soon enough, Boo.

He looked at me, the oddest expression on his face. *Boo?*

Magda grinned back at me. "I totally understand. Now, about Iceland."

I thought it was appropriate. You scared me

silly the first time I saw you. Well, not the first time, but right after that. You know, when you tried to strangle me.

Pia, if I wanted to strangle you, you would have been dead, he answered, looking slightly disconcerted.

What's wrong? You don't like 'Boo'? I think it has kind of a nice ring to it. It's short and snappy, but not overly syrupy or otherwise embarrassing.

No, it's not too embarrassing, he said hesitantly. I could feel him shielding something from me.

What is it, then? If you don't want me to use it, I'll just have to find something else —

I shudder to think what else you will come up with. If you feel the need to use a nickname for me, and you refuse to use Kris, then I suppose I can live with Boo.

"Pia said you might want Ray and me to go somewhere else."

But you don't like it?

"Yes. Andreas and Rowan will expect us to try to shake them, but they will also expect us to head to Italy as soon as possible."

"Why's that?" she asked.

"There is a group of reapers in Rome."

"Gotcha."

Kristoff?

Reluctance filled my mind. *I suppose I'll have to tell you. Before I was changed, my mother called me* Bärchen. *It's German for "little bear." Your name reminded me of that.*

I laughed. *I'll never wrap my tongue around German words, so I'll go with Boo. Besides, it really is appropriate. You can be very scary when you want to be.*

"We go to Rome while you guys go to Iceland to pick up the other reaper and Ulfur the friendly ghost," Magda said. "I'll tell Ray when he wakes up. He's always wanted to go to Rome."

I smiled, the memory of a laughing young man, handsome and rugged, clad in clothing of more than a hundred years ago, rising to my mind.

"If his damned horse tries to eat my jacket again, there will be hell to pay," Kristoff said, turning the page of his magazine.

"I kind of liked his horse. . . . Oh, Ray's awake. I'll go tell him the good news."

She toddled off as Kristoff heaved a mental sigh. *Only you two would consider having to create false trails in order to throw off Dark Ones, all the while rescuing a hundred-year-old ghost and a murderous reaper, as "good news."*

CHAPTER 8

"Remind me . . ." I hit the floor with a *whump,* dazed for a moment despite the soft padding Kristoff had assured me would break my fall. Even with that, it took me a moment before I felt my wits returning. "Remind me next time to take a plane instead of a portal."

Hands grabbed my arms, hauling me to my feet. I leaned against the warm, hard body attached to the hands, breathing in his delicious scent.

"You wanted to use a portal." Kristoff's voice rumbled deep in his chest. I let out a sigh of sheer happiness and managed to take a step back from him, just in time to see a body suddenly appear in midair, twisting like a cat as it, too, hit the floor.

"Yeah, I know. I thought it would be quicker and easier to get out of Germany that way, but I've changed my mind. Ow." I rubbed my butt as I eyed the body on the floor next to us.

"Have your light ready," Kristoff warned as he released me in order to grab Mattias by the back of his collar.

I nodded, gathering up another small handful of light. Kristoff had warned me that traveling through a portal could well remove the effect of the light-binding on Mattias. "Just one more reason to take a plane."

Mattias shook his head for a moment, squinting until his eyes focused on me. "Wife!" he said.

That was all I needed to hear. I tossed the light at his head, watching with some amazement as it wrapped itself around him, slowly dissipating into nothing.

The frown that Mattias had donned upon seeing me melted away into a happy grin. "Pia-pooh!"

"Ugh. I had hoped he had forgotten that. Mattias, we're in Iceland. I want you to do exactly as Kristoff says."

"I love Iceland!" he cried, delighted. "I love Pia! I love Kristoff!"

"If he tries to hug me again, I'm going to —"

Kristoff didn't get to finish his threat before Mattias, who was as big as Kristoff, shouted, "Hug time!" and enveloped both of us in a bear hug.

"You just had to say the word, didn't you?" I said, extricating myself from Mattias's grip. "Mattias, remember what I said before about inappropriate shows of affection?"

Mattias released Kristoff, a pensive look on his face. "I'm not to kiss you anymore because Kristoff doesn't like it."

"That's right. And?" I prompted.

"And I can't lick you when he's looking because it makes you squirm."

Kristoff eyed me.

"No," I said hastily. "You can't lick me at any time because it's wrong."

He sighed. "I can't lick sweet, adorable Pia because it's wrong. How about him?" He pointed at Kristoff.

"He can lick me if he wants. But that's neither here nor there."

"Can I lick her?"

I looked over to my shoulder to where an employee of the portal company we'd used to transport ourselves from Berlin to Reykjavik stood waiting for us. "Judging by the expression on her face, I don't think she'd enjoy that, no."

"I want to lick someone," he said forlornly.

"I know you do," I said, taking his arm and propelling him toward the door. "I'll get you an ice-cream cone or a puppy or something lickable later. Right now we have to get going before certain vampires figure out we're not with Magda and Raymond."

"They should follow them to Rome before they realize we aren't with them," Kristoff said as a form of reassurance as we exited the tiny office that was the portal service in Reykjavik. "You can stop worrying, Pia. I know my brother's mind."

"I just hope so. I'm not going to under-estimate him again, though. Not after he was waiting for us in Frankfurt. We barely made that train to Berlin. You're sure he didn't read your mind to know what we were doing?"

"I'm sure. We do not have a sympathetic connection like that."

"Hmm. How's your nose?"

Kristoff's shoulder twitched. I took his hand, enjoying once again the feeling of his fingers twining through mine. "I told you it wasn't broken. Andreas wasn't trying to hurt me, just stop us."

Mattias, walking behind us on the narrow sidewalk, nudged the back of my shoulder. I ignored him. "I don't care. I think that was pretty underhanded of him to sock you on the nose just because I roasted his toes a bit."

Mattias nudged me again, making an unhappy, lost-puppy noise. Exasperated, I stopped.

He held out his hand.

"Oh, for God's . . . Fine." I took his hand as well. He beamed at me. "Just so you know, I feel like I'm three years old and being escorted across the road."

Kristoff, who had been glaring across me to Mattias, donned a familiar martyred expression. "I can't decide if I would rather have him as he normally is, or this human version of a puppy demanding constant petting."

"Hugs?" Mattias asked.

"No!" I said quickly, ignoring the looks we were getting as we strolled through town to a nearby car rental agency. "Behave yourself, or you'll have to take another long nap like you did on the plane."

"I will behave," he promised solemnly.

Are you absolutely certain the reapers want him back? Kristoff asked as we entered the car rental place. *We could just drop him off somewhere and make our escape.*

Kristoff! We can't do that! He's like a child in this state, very suggestible and clueless. Anyone could take advantage of him and make him do the most heinous acts without him being aware of it. They could even make him throw himself off the top of one of the fjords.

Only if we're very lucky.

I gave him a mental glare. He actually smiled into my mind, a warm, tickling sensation that left me silently bemused, watching him as he arranged for a car.

"Ulfur first," I told him once he had possession of the keys.

"Reaper first, then your spirit."

"Ulfur has been left alone, and is probably bored out of his mind —"

"And the Dark Ones guarding the reaper could be alerted at any moment that we are in the vicinity."

I made a little face. He had a point. "All right, but if Ulfur yells at me because we got Kristjana first, I'm totally blaming you."

Fifteen minutes later we were beetling out of Reykjavik to a town about half an hour away, where the Brotherhood folk had said Kristjana was being held. I looked up from the GPS unit and over to the man who sat beside me, and decided the time had come to get to know him better.

How come you know terms like "blow job"? "Turn left at the next cross street, then a right onto the highway."

Kristoff shot me a quick glance before returning his gaze to the road. *Why shouldn't*

I know what a blow job is?

"Pia, Pia, Pia," Mattias said happily from the backseat.

I sighed. "Nap time, Mattias! You're tired. Very tired. Go to sleep until I wake you up."

"All right. I will sleep. You will wake me up. Smoochie?"

Because you were born during the Renaissance, weren't you? "I'm going to give Magda hell for ever using that word in front of you. No, you do not need a good-night smooch. Go to sleep."

Yes. Kristoff smiled. *That doesn't mean I hadn't had a blow job before I met you.*

No, of course not, I answered, pushing down a nasty sting of jealousy at the thought of him being so pleasured by any other woman.

The smile deepened.

But it's an awfully modern term for you to be bandying about. I mean, didn't you have some other name for it back then? Something euphemistic and romantic?

A soft "Pia, Pia, Pia," drifted up from the backseat, where Mattias, still firmly in the grip of the mind-altering light-binding, lay with his eyes closed. I felt a momentary pang of guilt at keeping the spell on him, but a memory of his antagonistic tendencies had me brushing away the concern.

Well, there was one phrase I recall being used.

Oh, good. What was it?

The whore's kiss.

I shot him a glare.

His lips curled a smidgen more. *Why did you want to know?*

If we're going to spend the rest of our lives together, I thought it would be nice if we got to know each other better. I'm boring, but you've lived centuries. I can only imagine the sorts of things you must have seen.

All I remember is death, disease, and lots of fleas.

I sat back in my seat, disgruntled.

Oh, and one exceptionally talented prostitute in Rome. She had the most amazing muscle control. You would not believe what she could do with a hard-boiled egg.

You know, I'm willing to bet I can guess.

Silence filled the car as we drove through the night. It was starting to get dark now in Iceland during the nights, the endless sun of summer beginning its journey into early fall. I looked out into the darkness, wondering at how much my life had changed since I had first been here.

What is the mortal expression — "penny for your thoughts"?

Oh, come, now — you may be immortal, but

you've been around us lesser folk long enough to pick up phrases like "blow job." I couldn't help but smile a little at his attempt at mental coyness.

I guarantee you that every male, no matter what form he takes, knows every colloquial phrase for oral sex. Some of us, however, have little to do with the mortal world.

I slid him a glance. "That must make it a bit difficult. Surely you had to interact with humans in order to eat."

"I seldom fed from mortals. They complicated things too much."

My heart, as usual, contracted at the oblique reference to his deceased love.

"When I did, I tried to keep the contact at a minimum. It was better for everyone's sake."

"Did you . . . er . . . did you . . . you know . . . have sex with everyone you drank from?" I asked, driven by a horrible spurt of jealousy I badly wanted to pretend wasn't there.

His lips softened into a slight curve. "I told you once before that feeding, to a Dark One, is an intimate act that sometimes involves other aspects of intimacy. It is seldom planned, but sometimes happens."

Damn him. I ground my teeth a little as we approached the town, trying to cope with my unreasonable need to demand to know just how many times he'd given in to that particular impulse.

You're jealous, he said with a hint of surprise.

Shut up, I muttered, glaring out of the window at the blackness. *I've had boyfriends, too, you know.*

I know.

Startled, I looked at him.

Alec would have mentioned it if you'd been a virgin.

My mouth dropped open in horror. "You talked to Alec about me? About . . . sex with me?"

"He brought it up," he answered, negotiating an exit into the town, consulting the GPS unit briefly before taking the appropriate turn.

"You talked about me?" Heat washed upward from my chest. I felt perilously close to tears or a nervous breakdown. I just couldn't decide which.

"He told me about spending the night with you." He glanced at me, frowning slightly as we came into a street filled with people streaming into a nightclub. "I didn't ask for specifics, if that's what you're worried about."

I caught the echo in his mind. "You didn't

have to, did you? He told you everything. *Everything!* Oh, my God, he told you about me insisting on the light being off?"

"He said you were very modest."

I could feel Kristoff desperately trying to shove thoughts back out of the way so I couldn't pick through them, but I pounced on a mental image that made my skin burn. "Oh, my God! He told you he didn't . . . that we didn't . . . Oh, my God!"

"You're making too much of this. Alec and I have always discussed women, although I do not go into specifics as he does."

"Oh, really? And did you tell him all about you and Angelica?" The words were off my tongue before I could stop myself, but I regretted them the instant I heard them.

Kristoff's jaw tightened. He kept his gaze grimly on the people milling around as he inched through them. "No."

The familiar stab of anguish I was coming to think of as Angelica pain lanced my chest. Of course he didn't talk to Alec about her. She was special. She was the woman he'd chosen to spend his life with, not one who had been thrust on him by circumstances and fate.

Unreasonable and unwanted tears pricked the back of my eyes. "Did you tell him about us?"

"No." He shot me another swift glance. "Would it make you feel any better to know I was pleased when he told me that he had not engaged in anything other than oral sex with you?"

"You were?" I asked, looking at him despite my embarrassment. "Really? Why?"

He nodded, a slightly chagrined expression on his face. "I've been told in the past that I can be overly possessive where women are concerned. You had expressed your preference for Alec, and I accepted that, but I could not help but be pleased that he did not possess you completely."

I didn't quite know what to say to that, other than to acknowledge my own little kernel of happiness that he, too, could be jealous. "Possessive, hmm?"

His lips turned downward, his eyes steadfastly on the street before us. "It is not unknown for Dark Ones."

"Given what I've seen," I said, thinking of the vampires I'd met, "I'd say that is a fair statement. I have to admit that I kind of like it."

One of his lovely sable eyebrows rose. "I thought women did not like possessiveness."

"A little of it can be nice," I said with a little smile to myself. "Too much is obnoxious, but a little . . . It makes us feel wanted."

He said nothing as he pulled into a parking lot next to what looked like a government building, but allowed me to feel the need that always seemed to be simmering within him.

I was a bit surprised to find my body answering his with a little hum of excitement. "Do you need, for lack of a better phrase, topping off?" I asked as we sat together in the warm, intimate darkness of the car.

"Do you really want to have sex here in the parking lot, where anyone could see us?" he asked in return, his eyes glittering like a cat's in the night.

I considered, for a few seconds, that very thing. "I don't suppose you could eat without us going at it like bunnies?"

He pursed his lips at me, and before I could stop myself, I leaned into him and licked them. With a low growl he wrapped both arms around me and pulled me onto his lap, claiming my mouth in a way that left me breathless and mindless of everything but him.

Does that answer your question? Reluctantly, he released my lower lip and looked down into my eyes, the teal fire in his bathing me in the warmth of his desire.

I suppose it does. My skin tingled where I was pressed against him. We sat like that for a moment, unwilling to part, but a slight snore from the backseat had me pushing myself off him. "Later?"

"You can count on that," he said with a look that almost seared my clothes. "I know of a place here you will like. I will feed there."

"Deal."

"You think it's OK to leave him here?" I asked as we got out of the car. Mattias was snoring away happily, hugging my sweater to his chest.

"Unfortunately, yes," Kristoff said with a sigh.

I poked him in the side, and then took his hand when he offered it. Despite the chilly air of the evening, I fanned myself as we walked toward the building on the other side of the government offices, secretly delighted. It was shameless of me, I knew, but dammit, if I had to spend the rest of my life bound to this man, I was going to enjoy every minute.

My libido had calmed down enough that I could think coherently by the time we stood at the back of the old stone building. "You're sure that no one will have contacted the vampires here to warn them we'll be coming for Kristjana?"

"It's not likely." Kristoff examined the back of the building, his gaze going from window to window, upward along a permanent fire escape, and he stepped back so he could look at the top of the four-story building. "Andreas will expect that we'll be taking the sacristan to the nearest group of reapers, and that is in Rome."

"Why would he think we wanted to get rid of Mattias?" I asked softly, scooting a little closer to him. The alley we were in wasn't even remotely dirty, but the large trash bin next to me loomed up with a menacing shadow. "He's docile as a lamb so long as I keep him light-bound."

"He knows I will have to feed more frequently than normal for the next few days," he answered, slipping off his long duster and tucking it behind the garbage bin. "Stay here. I'm going to climb up and see if anyone has alerted them that we've escaped with the sacristan."

"Oh, no," I said, glancing around at the shadows. "If you're going, I'm going, too."

"No, you're not. I just want to reconnoiter. Until I know if they're watching for us, you stay here."

"I could go around front and be a distraction while you snatch Kristjana," I suggested generously.

"Do you seriously believe she will come with me without screaming down the entire town?" he asked.

"I suppose not. I'll have to do the light thingie with her, too, I guess."

"Exactly. Stay here while I see what sort of security the Dark Ones have in place."

I glanced around at the shadows in the alley. "All right, but don't take too long. I have the feeling we're not alone here."

"Stay hidden," he ordered before he jumped and caught hold of the bottom of the metal ladder, hauling himself upward.

I have a better idea. I'm going to take a look around this area and see if I can find signs of Ulfur.

He didn't like that idea much, I could tell. *Stay in the shadows as much as you can. I don't know who here will recognize you.*

I didn't let him feel me rolling my eyes at such a silly statement, but I did stick to the shadows as much as possible as I made a quick tour of the blocks surrounding the building.

Everything OK? I asked after about five minutes of silence from him.

Yes. There is an elaborate security system in place. It's taking time for me to avoid setting it off.

No problem. I'll just keep looking around. So far I haven't found any spirit to ask about Ul-fur. I thought he said Reykjavik was crawling with ghosties.

I rounded a corner about two blocks away from Kristoff, pausing as I examined a pedestrian zone. Despite the late hour, a brightly lit neon sign and the faint sounds of jazz were proof that the Icelandic night-life was alive and kicking. A couple passed me on their way into the club. I gave the small clutch of people standing outside a quick once-over, making sure there was no one I recognized. I was just about to move on when a woman across the square on her way into the club glanced my way, did an obvious double take, then waved as she hurried over.

"Oh, hello! You're a Zorya, aren't you?" she said in a breathless voice. "Just who I need!"

I gave the moonstone hanging from my wrist a quick check. She followed my gaze, laughing as she put a hand on my arm, giving me a little squeeze. "Oh, I'm not a ghost! I'm a real person. I'm Siobhan. Siobhan Gullstein."

I must have looked surprised at her name, because she grinned. "Mummy is an Irish pagan, and Dad is a rabbi from the Bronx.

They're not quite your typical love match, but they're happy, so who am I to quibble?"

"Er . . . hi. Pia Thomason," I said, holding out my hand and trying to remember if I'd met her before. She didn't look familiar, her dark hair and eyes and rather elfin manner reminding me of Demi Moore at her most dewy-eyed. "How did you know I was a Zorya?"

"I'm a vespillo," Siobhan said matter-of-factly, as if that explained everything.

"Are you, indeed?" I said politely, trying not to look utterly clueless. *Boo, what's a vespillo?*

A vespillo? Why do you want to know?

Because I just met one.

I felt his sudden alertness. *Who?*

She says her name is Siobhan. Why, what is she? I hate to ask. It seems so rude.

His sudden spurt of concern faded away. *I do not know her. She is probably no danger to us. A vespillo is an assistant to a necromancer.*

Oh, that's a lot of help.

Do not speak to her, regardless. I am almost into the building.

Siobhan had been eyeing me with amusement while Kristoff and I had the quick conversation. "I hope you don't take this the wrong way, but are you new to all this?"

222

I relaxed a smidgen, giving a wry smile. "I'm afraid so. I know that vespillos are assistants to necromancers, but beyond that I'm a bit fuzzy."

"Don't worry. It took me forever to get the terminology down," she said with another friendly grin, then waved toward the nightclub. "Why don't we go have a drink, and I'll tell you all about life as a vespillo."

"I'm afraid I'm waiting for someone," I said, hesitating.

"Ah. Gotcha. I've got some friends waiting for me inside, but I thought I'd say hi and see if you're doing anything tomorrow."

"Tomorrow? I'm not sure what we're doing. We're probably leaving soon."

"Really?" Her brow wrinkled. "I thought you were here because of the Ilargi, but I guess I'm wrong. Well, nice meeting you. If you're still here tomorrow, I'm at the Hotel Reykjavik. Give me a jingle if you're available to help a poor, overwhelmed vespillo."

She started to turn away, but I caught her sleeve, stopping her. "Wait a second — you said Ilargi. You don't mean reapers, do you? The Brotherhood of the Blessed Light?" I wondered if she'd seen Kristjana, although I doubted if the vampires had let her escape their clutches.

"No, Ilargi. You know, the soul suckers?"

She squinted a little at me. "You really are new, aren't you?"

"I think we'd better have that drink," I said, considering telling Kristoff, but deciding he had enough on his mind trying to determine what was going on with the vampires holding Kristjana.

She grinned. "My kind of girl. We'll have a quick one at the bar before I join my friends, OK? They're a good lot, but kind of noisy."

I followed her into the club and was immediately enveloped in a dark, womblike warmth. Siobhan steered me toward the bar farthest away from the musicians. I ordered a glass of wine, waiting until she returned from checking in with her friends before settling down on a barstool.

"Let's start at the beginning," I said, accepting my glass of wine. "What exactly do you do?"

"Well, originally, 'vespillo' was the name they gave people who carried out the dead for burying," she said, sipping a giant stein of beer. "But something like a millennium ago, the name was used by a necromancer's assistant, and it kind of stuck. Not that we're mere assistants anymore — we unionized, you see. So now we're considered sort of a cross between a necromancer and a metal detector."

"All right," I said slowly, wondering how I could admit that I was just as much in the dark as ever.

"We find essences of unbound bodies," she said, evidently noting my lack of understanding. "Hence the metal detector reference."

"Unbound bodies. Like . . . ghosts?"

"No, not spirits. Everyone has an essence, right?"

"Your soul, do you mean?" I asked.

She made a so-so gesture. "Kind of, but not exactly, if you know what I mean. An essence is something unique to each person. When they die, their soul and spirit are bound together and take off for wherever. Well, that's where you come in, right?"

I nodded.

"But their essence remains with their body. Think of it as kind of a marker that stays with their bones, and even after, when those turn to dust."

"And you find that essence?"

She took a sip of her beer and nodded. "That's what a vespillo does. We can see them. They look like swirly blue glowing things, generally, although sometimes their pattern is weak and hard to see."

"Why would you want to find the essence

of anyone?" I couldn't help but ask.

"Ooh, peanuts. Yum." She pushed the bowl toward me after scooping out a handful. "Necromancers use us, mostly, since they're the ones who can really do anything with the essence, but sometimes I get the odd legal request to locate the remains of someone who's gone missing and presumed banished to the Akasha."

I searched my mind for any clues as to the purpose of a necromancer. "I realize I'm sounding horribly ignorant, but what does a necromancer *do* with the essence?"

"Raises them as a lich, of course," she said, popping another handful of nuts into her mouth. She added around the mouthful, "That's how you make liches. You raise the remains of a person or, if the body is not present, raise the lich from the essence. It's easier with a corpse, of course, but a good necromancer thinks nothing of raising from an essence."

"Ah, liches." I frowned, trying to remember who'd mentioned them recently. "The . . . er . . . zombie guys, right?"

She took another swallow of beer. "Eve would yell at you for that. Eve's my girlfriend, and a fourth-class necromancer. We normally work together, although sometimes I get gigs without her. The difference

226

is that revenants aren't bound to the person who raised them, and liches are. And then there's that whole magic thing, but that's really neither here nor there."

I thought of asking her for more information, but a glance at the clock behind the bartender reminded me that Kristoff was probably going to need my services in a few minutes

Everything A-OK?

I am in the building, but there are several Dark Ones here.

Be careful, I told him before returning my attention to the peanut-munching woman in front of me. "You mentioned an Ilargi in the area. There was one here a few months ago, but I never found him. Have you seen him?"

"Nope, but I gather from the lack of spirits in this area that he's been really active, sucking back the souls of all the ghosties he could find. I've only found one he missed, in fact."

My skin crawled with horror. "Dear God. The ghost you talked to — was his name Ulfur, by any chance?"

"No, this was an old woman who is parked out in the harbor. She's afraid to come ashore. Ulfur, you say? Just a second." She dug through the messenger bag that was

227

slung across her chest and pulled out a battered notebook, paging through it. "Let's see, new curse I saw in Barcelona, list of wards useful against phantasms, recipe for a whole-wheat challah —" She flashed me a grin. "Dad loves to cook. Oh, here it is."

She pulled out a piece of paper from the notebook, running her finger down it until she nodded. "Got it. Ulfur Hallursson. He's on the list."

"What list?" I asked, panicking slightly. I'd left Ulfur here because he'd assured me he'd be fine wandering around and watching the tourists until I could find a way to send him to Ostri so he could be with the rest of his village.

"The list of people whom Eve is supposed to raise. See?" She held out the paper for me. "It's a group of about twenty folks. Ulfur got washed into the ocean a hundred and fifty years ago, evidently. That's what I was asking if you could help me with — the Ilargi evidently had no idea exactly where on the coast the village used to be. I wondered if you'd go out with me to grill any spirits who remained."

I stared at her in growing horror. "The *Ilargi* hired you?"

"No, not me. Eve. Technically, Eve should have hired me to find the essences, but I give her a break on large jobs, and she gives me a cut of her fees. It works out well," she said, sipping her beer and reaching for more peanuts.

"But . . . Ilargis suck souls."

"I know, and I don't really like working for them because of that," she said, giving me a sympathetic look. "But a girl has to live, and really, if the Ilargi has already sucked their souls — and Eve says he has — then the harm is already done. Raising them isn't really going to make things worse for them, is it? In fact, it'll be better, because they won't be phantasms anymore."

My mind whirled in a miasma of horror and disbelief. Spirits feared losing their souls — which turned them into hopelessly forsaken phantasms — more than anything. My heart wept at the thought of sweet, self-sacrificing Ulfur ending up as one. But if Siobhan was right, then perhaps there was still hope. "I had no idea there was a way out of being a phantasm," I said slowly. "You're sure that the Ilargi told you he'd taken the souls of the people on that list?"

She nodded, chewing for a moment before she answered. "I told you he'd been busy on the island. But he didn't tell Eve where the village was."

"The village . . . it's south along the

coast," I answered absently, still trying to sort through the confusion in my brain. "But I sent the villagers on to Ostri. All but Ulfur."

"That's part of the problem. He's the only one from that village on my list, so it's almost impossible to find it. Will you help me?"

I was silent for a moment, my fingers rubbing the stem of the wineglass. "No."

"Oh." Her face fell.

"But I will hire you," I said, making a decision.

"For what?" She set down her beer, clearly interested.

Dio!

"I want Ulfur. That is, I want his spirit or whatever is left of him returned the way it was." *What's wrong?*

"Mmm." She frowned for a moment. "Can't do it. The Ilargi has his soul now."

This woman is a she-devil! She's alerted the Dark Ones to me.

Wait a second. You're tackling Kristjana without me?

"Leave the Ilargi to me," I said with far more confidence than I felt. "You said your girlfriend can raise Ulfur, right?"

She was alone. I thought I could knock her out and take her out through the window. But she screamed before I could silence her.

"Yes, but the lich is bound to either the person who raised him or the person who holds his soul. So I'm afraid that means he'd be bound to the Ilargi."

You're supposed to wait for me so I can brain-zap her! I said, digging through my purse for a few coins. Hastily, I pulled out a pen and a receipt, scribbling our hotel name and room number on it before shoving it at Siobhan. "I'll worry about that later. I just don't want poor Ulfur in the hands of some clearly deranged madman. I'm sorry, but I have to go. My husband needs me. Here's where we are, under the name Vincenzi. Call me in the morning and we'll work out all the details."

She took the paper, watching with raised eyebrows as I gathered up my things. "All righty, although Eve is going to be a bit touchy about two-timing her employer."

"Her employer is an evil soul-sucking bastard who gets what he has coming to him," I answered, pulling on my coat and waving as I dashed out of the club. *On my way!*

231

CHAPTER 9

"Boy, am I glad you're . . . here. . . ." The sentence trailed off as I saw who it was knocking at my door. "Oh, hello. When I called the dial-a-reaper number, I hadn't expected you two would be the ones to make the pickup."

"The director thought it would be best if we limited exposure of Brotherhood members to one who so clearly does not embrace the true glory of the light," Janice Mycowski said primly as she pushed past me into the hotel room. "You have Kristjana and Mattias here?"

"Yes." I closed the door behind Rick, trying to summon up a welcoming smile.

"You look well," Rick said politely. "Iceland must agree with you."

"Thank you. No!"

Rick looked startled for a moment until he realized I wasn't shouting at him.

Mattias, who had been forbidden to leave

his chair, grabbed the seat and chair-hopped his way toward me. "Pia!" he called as I reentered the living room of our hotel suite.

"I told you to stay!" I said, pointing back at the corner where he'd been.

His face shifted into a pout. "But Kristoff is not here. You said I had to stay out of his way, but he is gone. Smooches!"

Rick and Janice looked at Mattias with obvious surprise, the former turning a bemused glance upon me.

"Er . . . he's a bit . . . affectionate," I said, blushing a little as I hissed to Mattias, "I told you there will be no kissing!"

"Piiiia," he said, drawing out my name in a depressed sigh.

"You've light-bound him!" Janice declared after giving him a good long look. She turned her fierce gaze upon me. "You dare!"

"You bet your butt I dare," I said, squaring my shoulders and looking like I would be prone to light-binding anyone who annoyed me.

She took a step back.

"It's keeping him happy and me sane, so I don't want to hear one word about that. Kristjana is through the bedroom to your left." I gestured toward the appropriate door.

She marched to it with a glare that probably could have cracked cement. "I shall be sure to tell the director just how you treated our members!"

"Oh, I'm sure Frederic has a much worse image of me than as someone who dazzles a couple of troublesome reapers," I said, following her into the room. I was braced for a scream of outrage, which was forthcoming immediately.

"What have you done to her?" Janice yelled. I stood in the doorway and smiled somewhat weakly as Janice fussed around the prone woman lying on the bed. "Goddess above! You've killed her!"

"No, no, she's not dead. She's just sedated. She was a wee bit upset when we got her out of the room she was being kept in, and the doctor thought it would be best if she had a little downtime to recover. I'm not quite sure why, but she was resistant to the light-binding, so we gave up trying to make her happy and just let her go to sleep instead."

"Downtime!" Janice shot me a look of purest venom before she began patting Kristjana's cheeks in an attempt, I assumed, to bring her around. "You have become one of the monsters you should be destroying."

"She appears to be injured," Rick said, peering over his wife's shoulder.

"Not really," I said quickly. "Not seriously, anyway. There was a little incident on the fire escape when she tried to break free, and Kristoff was slow in grabbing her, so she went over the edge, but we were at the bottom of the fire escape, so she didn't fall very far. The doctor said it looks far worse than it really is. The black eye should fade in no time."

Both of them gave me identical looks of horror.

"We had her X-rayed and everything," I reassured them. "I managed to get her light-bound for the duration of the hospital visit, and she checked out fine, so really, there's nothing to worry about."

"Do you need me? I'm here if you need licking anywhere," Mattias called from the doorway, blowing me a kiss as he beamed at Rick and Janice.

"His things are all packed and ready," I told Rick with an urgency that I feared was unmistakable. "I'm afraid we didn't have time to get Kristjana's things, but with the town crawling with vampires, we thought it best to sit tight and not worry about her clothes and such."

"Kristoff!" Mattias called happily from where he still sat in the doorway, his head turned to the door of the suite. "Pia said I must sit in the chair until you returned. Now I can go to her. She needs me."

Kristoff! I told you the Brotherhood people would be here to pick up Mattias and Kristjana! Go away before they see you!

Dio, he swore. *I thought they would be gone by now. Did you find out where Alec is?*

No, I haven't even brought that up.

"Kristoff?" Janice said, suspicion tainting the word.

"Yes, he's my . . . er . . ."

"Husband," Kristoff said, appearing in the doorway. He eyed the two Brotherhood folk for a moment. *I do not know them. Where are they from?*

Seattle.

Then they will not know me, either. I have not worked in the United States. "Kristoff von Hannelore," he added, making a little bow.

Von Hannelore? I asked, somewhat surprised by his surname. I had been too flustered at our rushed wedding to notice what name was listed for him on the papers, and hadn't thought to ask him about it since. *Isn't that German? I thought you were Italian.*

My parents were from a small principality in what is now Germany. I lived there in my youth.

"But . . . you're married to the sacristan,"

Janice said, frowning.

Mattias took my hand and kissed my fingers. "Yes, she is. My Pia. My wife. She needs me. Licks?"

Kristoff pried Mattias's fingers off my hand, taking it himself. "She was married to me first."

"It's a bit complicated," I said, wondering how on earth I could explain Kristoff.

"Kristoff is my friend, too," Mattias added, beaming at him and trying to take his hand.

Kristoff growled, *I am not used to having to be explained.*

Yeah, well, people who charge in on meetings with their mortal enemies just have to tough out what they find.

"You have two husbands?" Rick asked a bit hesitantly. "Is that legal?"

"Well . . . technically —"

"Yes," Kristoff said quickly.

They don't seem to realize you're a vampire. I'm glad, but I have to say that it surprises me a bit.

It's not like we walk around with a big sign pointing to us proclaiming, "Dark One," you know.

Yes, but you're their area of specialty. Shouldn't they at least sense something different about you?

Experienced reapers might. These two ap-
pear innocuous.

"I like licking," Mattias said, apropos of nothing.

"You try and you'll find yourself without a tongue," Kristoff threatened as Mattias grinned at him.

"Mattias! Sit!" I ordered, pointing to the chair. "No licking! No kissing! And stop trying to hold Kristoff's hand."

"Pia, Pia, Pia," was his sad little refrain as he obeyed my command and sat in a chair next to me, pouting slightly as he clutched the hem of my gauze skirt.

"What you have done to that poor man — to both of them . . ." Janice said, her face dark with malevolence. "You will answer to the governors for these crimes; oh, yes, you will!"

Rick had been giving Kristoff a thorough visual examination, and said finally, a puzzled frown between his brows, "You are not a member of the Brotherhood?"

"No," he said, tensing.

"Kristoff is helping me with . . . er . . . finding Ulfur," I improvised, hoping the mostly true statement would pass muster. "Which isn't going to be easy at all. An Ilargi has taken his soul."

"Ilargi!" Janice gasped. "Here? You must

stop him!"

"Easier said than done. Kristoff is here to help me find Ulfur's remains, his essence, so we can raise him as a lich and get him away from the Ilargi."

"You are a vespillo," Rick said to Kristoff, nodding at my deception. "You have a necromancer already?"

I am not a vespillo!

No, but it won't hurt if they think you are. I'd rather not have them poking around and figuring out you're a vampire.

Bah!

"Yes, her name is Eve." I glanced at my watch. "In fact, we have an appointment to meet with her and her . . . er . . . assistant in half an hour, so we really should get down to business."

"What business would that be?" Rick asked politely as Janice gently shook Kristjana.

"She's asleep," Mattias said helpfully. "She was not nice to Pia, so we put her to sleep. She threatened to rip my lips off, too."

"You have fulfilled only part of your bargain," Janice said, giving up on Kristjana. "You must also retrieve the spirit left behind and escort him to Ostri. Which" — a slow, evil smile crept over her face — "considering he is now a phantasm, is going to be very difficult."

"But not impossible once he's a lich," I said, hoping that was true.

Evidently it was, because her face darkened again, and she turned away with a muttered word.

"I'm afraid we cannot help with your spirit, if that's what you are asking," Rick said. "It would violate the terms of the agreement, you see. I wish we could help, but our hands are tied."

"My hands were tied earlier," Mattias piped up. He sent me a loving look. "Pia tied my hands to my feet and made me lie on the floor while she took a bath. I pretended I was her bath mat."

"We weren't going to tell people about that," I reminded Mattias with a weak smile at the others. "It wasn't like it sounds. . . ." Kristoff's look had me stammering to a halt. "But enough about that. The business I referred to actually concerns the board of governors. You see, there's a vampire I want to find, and I think they can help me."

Janice bristled. "You dare to use us in that way?"

"You know, you keep asking me if I dare to do things, and I think by now we can take it as read that yes, I dare. I dare a lot, actually. Why? Because I have to. So if we could move past the dramatic gasps of horror and bugging-out eyes and pointing fingers and whatnot, and stick to the facts, I'd be really grateful."

"I love you," Mattias told me, and proceeded to suck on the bit of my skirt hem that he held.

Janice's face turned beet red. "You dare —" She caught herself in time. "You can't seriously believe that the governors would in any way aid someone who so clearly does not follow the precepts of the Brotherhood. You think we would turn over to you our database of vampire locations?"

"No, but that's interesting that you have one." *Did you know that they have a database?*

Yes. It is sorely out-of-date.

Good.

"That's good, because I can assure you that the governors will do nothing — nothing — to aid one of the evil undead. Unless, of course, you're referring to cleansing them of their darkness and bringing them into the light, as they all should be."

Kristoff stiffened beside me.

Relax. That's how they all talk. That is not a thought prone to inducing relaxation, he answered with a mental grimace.

I fought the urge to touch him, knowing

241

full well that I couldn't do so without wanting to jump him.

Kristoff's lips curled slightly.

You could at least pretend you don't hear my smutty thoughts about you.

Why not? I enjoy them. I particularly liked the one you had about massage oil, although I prefer cherry flavor to orange.

"What exactly did you want to know?" Rick asked.

"I have reason to believe that one of the vampires has been held by the Brotherhood," I said, picking my words carefully. I didn't want to outright accuse them of nabbing Alec if he had gone along willingly. Then again, I didn't know if he had done that. "I'd like to know where he is, and if he's OK."

"No," Janice said abruptly.

"You don't seem to understand," Kristoff said, wrapping his arm around my waist. "Pia is not asking. She is telling you what it will take in order for her to turn over these two reapers."

Mattias rubbed his head on my hip.

"You will turn them over because that is part of the agreement," Janice said slowly.

"I'm changing that," I said simply. "Now in order to get them, I want to know where Alec is."

"Alec?" She frowned and glanced at her husband.

He shook his head, shrugging.

"Alec Darwin. He's a vampire who was in Iceland two months ago. He disappeared not long after I went home."

"Why do you care?" Janice asked.

I thought for a few seconds of lying, but I'd done enough indulging in half-truths for the day. "I had a relationship with him at one time, and although it's over, I am concerned for his well-being."

"Relationship?" Janice asked, horrified. "You gave yourself to a vampire?"

"Pia was not a Zorya at the time," Kristoff said, taking us all a bit by surprise.

"That's right," I agreed. "And we weren't together for very long, but I still would like to know what's happened to him."

"I'm sure he's dead by now," Janice said with malicious enjoyment. She bared her teeth. "If he is in the power of the governors, then he has been cleansed."

"So they'd take him to the Brotherhood headquarters?" I asked.

Janice looked sullenly at her husband when he answered, "Most likely. That's where the big storage facility is, you see. Where they keep the vampires before they are cleansed."

I felt a bit sick to my stomach at the thought of such a thing.

Beside me, pain spiked through Kristoff. I leaned into him, offering him wordless comfort.

"Do not tell her any more," Janice ground out through her teeth. "You have said enough."

"Alec may well be dead," I said calmly as he tensed up again. "But I'd like to hear that from Frederic himself."

"Monsieur Robert does not wish to speak to you," Janice said, whipping out her cell phone before she remembered that it wouldn't work in Europe. She jammed it back into her bag. "But if you demand proof of that yourself, I will call the Brotherhood headquarters. I will use this phone." She gestured to the phone next to Kristjana.

"Be my guest. Mattias, come along. Rick, can I offer you some coffee while we wait for Janice?"

Beloved, these are reapers, Kristoff protested as he followed Mattias and me out of the room and into the living area. *You do not offer them beverages.*

You may not, but I do. I like Rick. He's not at all snarky like his wife. Besides, he said he was a historian, and I'd like to know more about the Brotherhood.

Why? he asked quickly.

Just curious about how they got started going after you guys. "So, Rick, you're a historian, right? You must know a lot about the origins of the Brotherhood. How do you like your coffee?"

"Black is fine," he said, sitting down on the couch next to where I parked Mattias, giving me a bit of a bemused look. Kristoff sat gingerly on the chair next to him, eyeing long fingers of sunlight as they spilled onto the highly polished oak floor. "And I know something about it, but unfortunately not a lot. The archives dealing with the history of the Brotherhood really only included resources that cover the time after the Lodi Congress."

The what?

It is the name given to the body that organized the first hunt of Dark Ones.

"Huh. I know they used to just deal with helping dead folk, but then something happened to switch their attention to vampires. What exactly was that?" I asked, giving Mattias a cup before taking one for myself and plopping down on the arm of Kristoff's chair.

Kristoff shifted uncomfortably. The finger of sunlight was creeping ever closer to our feet.

"It's a little hard to piece together precisely, but I gather that there was a Bavarian Zorya who killed a vampire's mate in a jealous fit. The vampire, in revenge, slaughtered both the Zorya and her husband, the sacristan for that area. The Brotherhood was so outraged at their deaths, it started a movement to cleanse the darkness that threatened to consume not just Brotherhood members, but all who stood in the way of the vampires."

"A vampire started it?" I asked, finding it hard to believe.

Kristoff swore in Italian, fortunately only in my head. I had to admit I agreed with his sentiment. *What do you bet there's more to the story than that?* I asked him.

There is.

I peeked at him out of the corner of my eye. *That sounded like more than just a general condemnation of the reapers. Do you know how the Brotherhood got started on their vendetta against you guys?*

All who hunt the reapers are familiar with their history.

Good, then you can tell me what happened. "Are you absolutely sure that a vampire started it?" I asked.

"Without a doubt, yes. I've seen the primary sources."

"I'm surprised primary sources survived so long." *Kristoff?*

Why do you care how the war started? It's ending it that I care about.

Rick said as he set down his coffee, "There is only one that I've seen. Or, rather, seen photocopies of. It is a diary that mentions the origin of the Lodi Congress."

I was a bit surprised at Kristoff's snappish tone but kept my smile serene. "Fascinating stuff. I wonder —"

"I have spoken to the director," Janice announced with a dramatic wave of her hand as she entered the room. Judging by the gloating smile on her face, she was enjoying every moment of this. "The director, as I told you, has no desire to speak with you personally, and asked me to inform you that your agreement to the original terms is binding, and is not open to amendment. Further, he was appalled and shocked to hear how you've been abusing the priestess and sacristan, and asked me to tell you that separate charges may be made on those accounts."

No surprise there, I said. *But we got what we wanted.*

They didn't confirm that they have Alec, Beloved.

They didn't deny it, either, and thanks to

247

Rick, we now know where he would be likely to be held.

"We will take them now," Janice said, gesturing to her husband. "I just pray to the goddess that they will survive your abuses without permanent damage."

"Mattias, how would you like to go to Los Angeles?" I asked as she and Rick went into Kristjana's room.

He thought for a moment. "Would I?"

"Yes, you would. You'd have fun there, and meet new people, and see new things."

"New things are good. Are you going?"

I leaned forward to whisper in his ear, "Not right now. Don't tell anyone, but I will be there soon, and I'll see you then."

"Piaaaa," he said, his eyes filled with adoration. He turned his head to kiss me, but I jumped back. He smacked his lips a couple of times at me. "Good-bye kiss?"

"No," Kristoff said, slamming Mattias's bag into his arms, sending him staggering back a couple of steps. "Don't let the door hit you on the —"

"Kristoff!" I glared at him. *You don't have to be rude to him! He can't help being like a gigantic human puppy when he's under the influence of my womanly wiles.*

He might not be able to help it, but I'm tired of him always trying to fondle you.

Jealousy ill becomes you when it concerns someone light-bound. "The doctor says she should be out for another hour or so," I told Rick as he emerged from the room with a limp Kristjana in his arms. "But she should be fine. Go with Janice and Rick, Mattias. They will take you to LA."

"I am going with Janice and Rick," he repeated, following them to the door. "I will be good."

"I'm sure you will," I said, standing at the door to the suite and waving at Mattias until the door of the elevator closed on them. I slumped against the wall, relieved to be rid of the stress of keeping Mattias under control. "Whew. That's done. I can feed you now. I know you're hungry, and we should have a few minutes before we have to go spirit hunting —"

"Pia!" I de-slumped when a familiar dark-haired woman emerged from the other elevator, tugging a tall, thin woman after her. "Hi! We're a bit early. You don't mind, do you?"

CHAPTER 10

"I thought we'd get a good jump on searching for your spirit. This is Eve. Wow, nice room! Oh . . . er . . . hi."

So much for feeding you. I'm sorry.

There wouldn't have been time for the food I was interested in, he answered with a mental image that threatened to buckle my legs.

Oh, that is not playing fair. "That's my husband, Kristoff."

"Siobhan Gullstein. This is Eve Voorhees, who is the necromancer I told you about, Pia."

"Hi," Eve said, holding out a hand. She was as tall as Kristoff, freckled, with short sandy blond hair and wire-framed glasses. Her gaze was straightforward and earnest. She looked absolutely normal, not in the least as if she were the sort of person who raised the dead for a living. "Siobhan says you know where the essence is?"

"Not exactly, but I know where the village was before it washed into the ocean."

"I see." Eve had a slight accent — Dutch, I assumed by her name — and although her manner wasn't as friendly and open as Siobhan's, I liked her. She hesitated a moment, biting her lip before she continued. "I don't normally do this. I may be old-fashioned, but I like to honor my commitments, and I don't usually betray a client in this manner."

"I absolutely understand, and I would never ask you to do so except this is really an emergency."

She nodded. "Siobhan told me that the spirit in question belonged to you, but his soul was taken by the Ilargi who hired me. I do not judge those for whom I work, but I do not agree that it is right to take the soul of another."

"I'm glad you feel that way," I said, relieved. "Naturally, we will pay you the going rate for lich raising. Er . . . what is that?"

She named a figure that had me reeling for a moment.

Kristoff made a face and pulled out his checkbook.

Thanks, Boo.

"Excellent," Eve said, folding the check and tucking it away. "Shall we go?"

"Sure," Siobhan answered.

"I will meet you downstairs," Eve said, heading for the door.

"She left the car parked illegally, and is worried about it getting towed. You have no idea how on top of those sorts of things the Icelanders are," Siobhan told me.

Kristoff murmured something about getting our coats as he disappeared into our room.

"Wow, he is . . . Hoo, mama! Some kind of gorgeous," Siobhan said in a whisper, taking a few steps to the side so she could watch Kristoff gather up his coat and hat. "I love men with cleft chins! It's so sexy! I bet you suck it, huh?"

I blinked at her in surprise.

"Sorry," she said with a little giggle. "Didn't mean to shock you or anything. It's just that you didn't tell me you were married to a fashion model. My God, those eyes! Mmrowr!"

"I thought . . . Aren't you . . ." I gestured vaguely toward the door through which Eve had just left.

"Oh, I am. That is, I like both sides of my bread buttered," she said, winking as Kristoff came back into the room with my jacket.

Why are you looking so odd? Kristoff asked a few minutes later, as we emerged from the hotel. He held me back for a second, his eyes bright even in the shadow of his hat as they searched the street.

Because Siobhan just asked me if I sucked your chin.

He shot me a startled look before gesturing that it was all right to proceed.

She thinks you're gorgeous.

Ah.

"Which way?" Eve asked as Kristoff held the back door for me to climb into the car. She had a map spread out on the steering wheel, while Siobhan was poking at the GPS unit.

"It's broken," she said, waving toward it. "So we're going to have to do this the old-fashioned way."

"This is the wrong map," Eve said, frowning at it. "Shivvy, get me the other one."

"Sure thing." Siobhan turned and reached back between Kristoff and me, inadvertently knocking his hat off in the process.

Kristoff ducked away from the window, lunging over me to avoid the sunlight coming in on his side.

"Sorry. I . . . er . . ."

Are you OK? Did you get burned?

I grabbed the hat she held out and gave it back to Kristoff, who got it adjusted so he could sit up.

Barely. I'm fine.

Eve watched us with curious eyes via the rearview mirror.

Oh, crap. You think they know? I turned in my seat to grab the couple of maps in the storage area behind us. "I'll get the map."

Siobhan took them from me with a look at her partner. "Er . . . you're a Dark One?" she asked Kristoff.

"Is there a problem with that?" he asked with absolutely no expression on his face.

You're really good at that. I bet you clean up at poker.

"No, I'm just a bit surprised. Eve . . ." She waved toward the other woman. "Eve has always wanted to meet one."

Eve nodded quickly, an excited light in her eyes. "I'm doing a thesis on the relationship between the otherworld and mortal literary conventions. I'd love to talk to you about Dark Ones versus vampires in the popular culture."

"Everyone loves a hunky vampire," I said, smiling.

Eve grinned for a moment, then sat back, but she positively hummed with excitement.

"I've only seen one Dark One before, and never up close. Oh, my God!" Siobhan's jaw dropped for a moment as her gaze moved over to me. "You said you guys are married. Does that mean you're —"

"A Beloved? Yes." I gave Kristoff's leg a possessive pat. "And yes, I am tempted to suck his chin. That cleft drives me wild, too."

Kristoff went into martyr mode, not actually rolling his eyes, but the urge was apparently almost overwhelming.

Oh, stop looking that way. You love it. What man wouldn't like random female adoration?

I am only interested in adoration from one person.

I withdrew my hand slowly, not sure if he was referring to his girlfriend, Angelica, or to me.

His fingers captured mine and returned them to his leg, where he held them.

Warmth pooled low in my belly.

"Hee, hee, hee," Siobhan said, turning back in her seat, although I noticed she lowered her sun visor so that she could see him in the mirror. "I don't blame you one bit. Man alive, a Dark One and his Beloved. That's so awesome. How did you guys meet?"

A heavily edited version kept Siobhan occupied until we had reached the small village south of the town I had stayed at two months before. It wasn't until we had climbed down a rocky, steep slope from a tiny stone church that sat atop a cliff that

255

she finally turned her attention to the reason we were there.

"There are several essences here," Siobhan said as she wandered up and down the rocky shoreline, dashing first here, then there, like a shorebird on the trail of a tasty morsel. "There're a number clustered right here," she added, having taken off her shoes and socks and rolled up the legs of her pants to wade into the water.

"Do you see a horse?" I asked, eyeing the water. I knew it must be very cold, and I didn't particularly want to have to swim. "Ulfur had a horse named Ragnar who died with him. They were very close."

"Horse . . . horse . . . no, no horse. Let me try farther out. Good thing I put on the suit under this, eh?"

She returned to shore just long enough to strip down to a long swimmer's bodysuit, Eve doing the same. "No spirits around here, are there?"

I looked at the stone dangling from my wrist. "None that I see."

"Hell. So much for the easy way. I guess there's nothing for it but a little swim in the icy drink. Brrr. Here goes nothing."

It took them two hours and several trips back to shore, where they stood huddled in blankets guzzling coffee from a large ther-

256

mos Eve produced, before Siobhan called out from about thirty feet off shore, her hand held high in the air as she swam back to shore.

"Got it!" she said rather breathlessly as she stopped in front of us, both she and Eve bright red with cold. I handed them towels, holding blankets at the ready as Siobhan explained, through chattering teeth, how she was just about to give up when she spotted the essence of a horse, and followed that to Ulfur's final resting place. "We may get pneumonia from this, but by God, it was worth it. Behold, the essence of one human named Ulfur Hallursson."

I looked at the empty palm she held out for inspection.

Do you see anything? I asked Kristoff.

He frowned. *No.*

"Um. Are you sure it's there?" I asked her.

"Oh, yes, it's there. Only vespillos can see the essences — otherwise, we'd be out of a job. He's right here, swirling around like a piece of blue dry ice."

Eve had been peeling off her wet suit under the cover of a blanket. She emerged now fully clothed, with her head wrapped in a towel, rubbing her hands to get the warmth back. "Do we want to do this here?"

"Sure," I answered, glancing around. "No

one else is here, and I know you guys want nothing more than a hot bath."

Have you ever seen a lich raised before?

Not raised, no, Kristoff answered, his gaze interested as he watched Siobhan gently set her handful of nothing on a flat rock. *I've seen liches, of course.*

What do they look like? Is Ulfur going to be all green slime running off his oozing flesh, and empty eye sockets? I asked nervously, trying to brace myself for the sight of Ulfur as an undead, albeit corporeal being. *Or is he going to be nothing but a skeleton, like in those role-playing games?*

Liches don't look any different from a mortal, other than having black eyes.

Soulless, dead eyes that leach the life from people around them, you mean?

Siobhan changed into her clothing as Eve sat cross-legged on her blanket, her eyes closed, her hands held out as she swayed and chanted softly. "It shouldn't be long now. Eve is pretty quick. She doesn't do all the fancy ceremonies unless someone really wants them."

Kristoff gave me a long-suffering look. *I will be glad when you move past the point of believing everything you've read or seen in the movies.*

Don't get snarky with me, Boo. As of a

couple of days ago, I had no idea liches even existed, let alone what they were.

Eve got slowly to her feet, her eyes still closed, her hands held out palms down over the rock. Suddenly she froze for a moment; then her eyes shot open and she brought her hands together with a loud clap that sounded like a shot, causing me to take a step back.

"Holy . . . Ulfur!" I jumped forward in joy at the sight of the familiar face, even if it was a bit wavery and wispy, as if it had been projected on a curtain of smoke. "Thank God! I thought I'd lost you!"

"Pia?" The smoky figure solidified before our eyes, Ulfur looking down at his hands for a moment.

"Yes! It's me! I can't tell you how glad I am to see you. Oh, well-done, ladies, well-done. Ulfur, I wouldn't blame you in the least if you were pissed at me for leaving you to be sucked up by an Ilargi, but I assure you —"

"Dear God, what have you done?" Ulfur asked, his eyes as black as Kristoff had warned they would be, shiny and filled with horror.

Before I could say anything, he dissolved, just dissolved into nothing.

"No!" I wailed, waving my hands around

in the spot where he had been.

"I thought that might happen," Eve said, shaking her head. "Not good."

"Not good? Not good? What happened? Where's Ulfur? Why did he say what he did?" I asked, panicking. "Why did he go away?"

"His soul is held by the Ilargi," Eve answered, her thin face pinched. She glanced at her friend. "I'm sorry; I had hoped that you would have a little time with your spirit before he was summoned from you, but the Ilargi must have been waiting."

"But . . . but . . . I don't understand!" I felt like pulling my hair out, near tears at the thought of being so close to rescuing Ulfur.

"Let us discuss the issue in the car," Kristoff said, glancing over my shoulder. "The sound of the raising has caused some interest in the village."

I turned to see a line of people streaming toward us. We didn't hesitate in packing up our things and returning up the rocky path to where we'd left the car. I crawled into the back next to Kristoff, miserable and sick at heart at the thought of Ulfur suffering any more.

"You're going to have to get the soul away from the Ilargi if you want your friend to be free," Siobhan said a short while later, when we were heading back to Reykjavik. "I'm really sorry, Pia. As I told you, normally liches are bound to the person who raises them, unless, as in this case, their soul is held by someone else. I really thought the Ilargi wouldn't even know that we raised Ulfur, but evidently he's keeping a close watch on the souls in his possession."

Kristoff's hand was warm on mine, providing me comfort just through the touch of his fingers as they stroked the back of my hand. *Do not distress yourself, Beloved. You knew we would have to do something about the Ilargi in order to free him.*

Yes, but I thought that he'd get to be with us while we did it. Poor Ulfur. He looked so horrified, so appalled. And it's all my fault.

Unless you have taken to sucking souls on the side, it is not your fault.

Do you ever sometimes think that life is using you like a toilet? I asked miserably, listening with only half an ear as Siobhan and Eve alternated apologizing.

Not frequently, no.

Lucky you. Honest to God, Kristoff! Like we don't have enough to do trying to find Alec, now I have to take a soul from an evil soul-sucking reaper? How on earth am I supposed to do that? I almost wailed into his head.

261

You will do it just as you do everything else — one step at a time, he answered with infuriating calmness.

By the time Siobhan and Eve dropped us off at the hotel, I was panicking a bit less, and starting to sort through the advice they offered.

"The best I can do is give you this phone number," Eve said as we parted ways in the hotel lobby. She pressed a small piece of paper into my hands. "I wish I'd thought to ask the Ilargi his name, but all transactions are done through the Akashic League. They send me out a list of people I'm to raise, and any pertinent details. They're very big on confidentiality. The only reason I got the phone number for the Ilargi is because there was some confusion about the location of your friend. If it helps, it's a U.S. number."

"Thank you both for all the help," I said, narrowing my eyes at the phone number. "Good luck with your thesis."

They both waved as I headed for the bar. "I need a drink before I call this ass-hat and ream him a new one for doing what he's done to poor Ulfur and all the others."

Kristoff grabbed my arm, stopping me. "You need rest. You're exhausted."

"Drink first, then reaming, then bed." I eyed him for a second, aware of the growing hunger within him. "Or rather, drink, then feed you, followed by reamage of the Ilargi, and after that, bed, so I can molest you as you've never been molested before."

"You need rest above all else. I can feel how tired you are —"

"There you are! We've been waiting for you forever! Where have you been?" Magda bustled out of the bar as I tried to peel Kristoff's fingers off my arm. "Hello again, Kristoff. So, what's been happening? Did you find Ulfur? Did you find Kristjana? Where's your boy puppy? Oh! We saw your brother at the airport in Rome, Kristoff, but we gave him the slip, didn't we, honey? Honey? Where'd Ray go now?"

Magda turned around in a full circle before spotting her boyfriend over at the reception desk, where he was unpacking several cartons of film and placing them into his camera bag.

"I'm so glad to see you," I told Magda, giving her a little hug. "Good job on ditching Andreas. And yes to both questions, although the bit involving Ulfur is kind of long and . . . well . . ."

A lump suddenly clogged my throat as tears threatened to form at the thought of having failed Ulfur.

"I'm sorry," I apologized, making an effort to get a grip on myself. "I don't normally cry."

She eyed me with a critical eyebrow raised. "You look like hell, Pia. I mean that in the nicest way, of course, but you really do look like you've been put through the wringer. Maybe you need a little break."

"That's exactly what she's going to get," Kristoff said, wrapping his arm around me and pulling me to the elevator.

"Oh? Oh!" Magda grinned. "Gotcha. I'll see you tomorrow, then?"

"You'll see us tonight if you come with us," Kristoff said just before the elevator door closed. "Blue Lagoon. We leave in half an hour."

CHAPTER 11

I waited only until I'd changed into dry shoes before dialing the phone number Eve had given me.

Kristoff was on his cell phone to one of his cohorts, who evidently didn't believe him guilty of the crimes so wrongly tossed at his feet, giving a concise rundown of the events of the last few days.

I tapped my fingers in irritation on the table upon which the phone rested, mentally going over the things I wanted to say to the bastard who had ripped Ulfur's soul from him, but a click and the slightly mechanical note to the voice that spoke in my ear heralded voice mail rather than a live person. I listened with growing disbelief until the recording ended, then slowly hung up the phone.

Kristoff broke off in the middle of telling his friend about how we'd been charged with finding Alec, covering the lower half of the cell phone to ask, "What is it?"

"That phone number. It belongs to Alec."

He frowned. "Are you sure?"

I nodded, waving at the phone. "The voice mail is his. His voice and everything. Kristoff, what the hell is going on? Alec isn't the Ilargi. Is he?"

I slid down the wall into the chair that stood next to the phone table, my mind whirling with disbelief.

Kristoff said nothing to me, switched to Italian, and continued speaking to his buddy. By the time he was finished and had come to squat at my feet, his hands on my knees, I was a mess.

Why do you cry?

Because nothing makes sense. Because I was so deceived by Alec. Because nothing is what it seems. You're not the horrible, evil monster I thought you were, and Alec isn't the nice, loving man he appeared. Ulfur wasn't happy we raised him as a lich — he was horrified. Honestly, Boo, at this point, I'm going to expect that Magda turns out to be the new Zenith, and Ray is her hired assassin!

Kristoff smiled into my head as he gently pulled me from the chair and into his arms, cradling me against his chest as I sniffled my tears of self-pity. "I do not believe your friends are anything but what they appear."

266

"Yeah, but you don't know, do you? Look at Alec, Kristoff! Even you were fooled! If he can be your friend for so many centuries, if I can sense nothing bad about him to the point where I slept with him — kind of — and if your whole entire Moravian group didn't know he was an Ilargi on the side, then how on earth are we expected to know anything about anyone?" I wailed.

"You must trust this," he said, sliding his hand into my bra, his hand warm on my breast.

"My boobs might like you a lot, but in general they're not very insightful about people," I said, sniffling.

"I meant you must trust your heart, which you well know. Being a Dark One or his Beloved does not mean we suddenly possess all knowledge there is to know, Pia. We cannot see the future any more than we know the truth that is in others' hearts. Alec has served me as a friend for more than three hundred years, and although his actions confuse me, I am not convinced that he has become a traitor."

I thought about this for a moment, idly kissing his Adam's apple. "Your brother and cousin didn't show any faith in you."

"They must follow their hearts as well," he said simply, hunger rising swiftly in him as I switched to nibbling his earlobe. "Beloved, if you start that now, we will never get to the Blue Lagoon, and I would very much like for you to see it."

I sighed and released the earlobe I was sucking. "What are we going to do about Alec?"

He stood up, letting me slide down his body. "Rest first; then we will discuss plans." He put a finger over my lips as I was about to protest. "Be assured we will take action."

That was all I got out of him. He refused to talk more about Alec, repeating that I was exhausted and needed some rest and relaxation. So it was that a short time later I trotted down the hotel steps and stared with absolute surprise at the sight that met my eyes. "I don't believe it. Have we entered some sort of a warp where time is standing still?"

Magda stood next to me and stared at where I was pointing. "Good Lord. I think we have."

"What's going on?" Raymond asked, coming up behind us, fussing with a camera. He looked up, a delighted smile blossoming on his face. "Is it another holiday?"

"I don't know, but look! Dancing! Ooh, Ray! Let's join!"

Raymond shot me a quasi-apologetic look

as Magda grabbed his hand and hauled him off into the throng before us. The strains of "Unchained Melody" filled the soft summer evening air, reminding me of our first night in the nearby town of Dalkafjordhur. There'd been dancing the last time I was there, too.

"I just had a phone call from a friend," Kristoff said as he emerged from the hotel. "He said that there has been a sudden increase of activity in the reaper headquarters in Los Angeles."

"Sounds like something is definitely up. Extra security around Alec, do you think?"

He shrugged and tucked his cell phone away in the inner pocket of the soft leather jacket that I remembered him wearing the first time I'd seen him. "Possibly, but that assumes Alec is being held captive. At this point, we don't have any solid proof either way."

"But it does give credence to what Rick said about him being there. I guess we'll be California bound, then. Although I wish we could stay here to search for the Ilargi who has Ulfur."

"As the necromancer told you, he didn't have to be physically near in order to summon a lich under his control."

"I know." My shoulders slumped.

"I've told you that we will find him," Kristoff said, his gaze slightly critical as he examined me. "Later, after you've had a rest."

"We all could do with a break," I said, shaking off the glum mood. Kristoff meant what he had said — he would help me find Ulfur and his soul, so there was no use in giving in to self-pity again.

As the music ended and people applauded, a memory flitted across my mind, the memory of him standing in the small square, cloaked in the shadows from a nearby building as he talked with Alec. For a moment, I was intensely glad that fate had thrown him my way.

"You look very pretty," he said out of the blue.

"It's the dress. Magda insisted I buy it before we left for Vienna. She said it was flirty and would make you want to ravish me on the spot. Does it?"

He looked at me again, longer this time, his gaze lingering on the swell of my breasts as they threatened to overflow the fitted bodice of the simple yet elegant white dress. His gaze continued downward, stopping briefly on my hips, before proceeding down to the full skirt that flared out in graceful folds, ending just slightly below my knees.

Kicky summer sandals and delicate shell pink toenail polish completed the ensemble. I held my breath for some reason, wanting him to find me sexy, yet unwilling for him to think I'd dressed with such care just to meet his approval.

No, it doesn't make me want to ravish you.

My heart dropped to the very same shell pink toenails.

It makes me want to worship you passionately, starting at your delectable toes and moving upward along legs that are both feminine and enticing to thighs that leave me feeling weak with need. It makes me want to take your essence into me. It makes the hunger rise in me until I'm nearly mad with desire. "Ravish" implies an impersonal act of sex. So ravish? No. Possess and consume and lose myself in you? Absolutely.

My heart, back in its accustomed place, melted into a great big puddle as I leaned into Kristoff, my lips teasing his. "I'm falling in love with you, you idiot man. You can't say things like that to me and not expect me to swoon entirely."

Passion flared to life in the depths of his lovely eyes. He took my arm, and I thought he was going to kiss me until he pulled me after him, stopping at the edge of the bodies moving in time to the music. I caught a glimpse of a woman with a white veil, and a couple of men in tuxedoes, before Kristoff twirled me around and pulled me up into a close embrace, his hands on my hips.

"I didn't think you noticed the party," I said, giggling a little as the music stopped again, ending our dance before it even got started.

"I may be distracted, but I'm not blind," he answered, looking over the crowd to the band as they started in with a number from *Dirty Dancing.* Kristoff cocked an eyebrow as his gaze returned to me. *Do you dance?*

Not very well. But I love this song, and I've seen the movie about a hundred times.

A rare smile flirted with the corners of his mouth as he took my hand in his, putting the other on my waist.

You don't think you're going to . . . I stopped, suddenly breathless as he spun me away, pulling me back immediately, only to bend me backward. His mouth was hot on my chest for a moment before he pulled me back and started moving with the song, guiding me into dance moves that I never in a million years thought I could do.

Dear God, I'm dancing! I couldn't help but laugh. *I never dance! Not like this!*

You never had me to dance with, he answered, sending me into another twirl. Part of me felt self-conscious and clumsy, well aware that I lacked grace and coordination, but the other part of me, the part that touched Kristoff's mind, rejoiced at the spontaneous gesture on his part.

You're an excellent dancer, I said, giggling again when he pulled me up tight to his hips, grinding them against me in a highly suggestive manner.

You should see me do the cinque passi, he answered.

The what, now?

It was a dance step very popular about five hundred years ago.

I twirled away again, then returned, struggling with the odd sense his words brought. *You really are four hundred years old, aren't you? I know you said you were born in the seventeenth century, but it just didn't really hit me until now. You lived during the Renaissance. You were alive when Galileo was alive! You must have seen popes and kings and even countries rise and fall.*

Galileo was an old man, blind and sick, when I saw him.

I stopped dead in my tracks as I stared up at him. *You actually met Galileo? You saw him in person?*

Yes. For some reason, I felt him emotionally withdraw from me. His body still moved in time to the music, but the joy had gone out of the moment.

But you must have been a very young man, I said cautiously, wondering why suddenly his mental barriers were in place again, excluding me from some of his thoughts.

Yes.

He said nothing else, and I debated pressing him for details, but I hesitated to do that. Neither of us had wanted this relationship, but he was clearly trying to make the best of it. I didn't want to aggravate a situation that was starting to become more and more painful, at least for me, by pressing him when he wished to withhold himself.

The music ended. I stood watching him for a moment, suddenly sad at the situation. How on earth was I going to get through a lifetime of being held emotionally at arm's length when just a couple of days had me wanting to shake him?

Behind me, women squealed and called out excitedly as a bride was helped onto a table in preparation for throwing her bouquet.

"Bah. Competition is nothing," Magda said, fanning her face as she and Raymond returned. "I could blow those skinny Icelandic women down with one breath, but I don't need a bouquet that bad. What's

274

wrong?"

She had addressed the last comment to me.

I shook my head. "Nothing. Let's go before someone of the fanged variety spots us. Our plane leaves in ten and a half hours, so that ought to give us enough time to visit the hot springs."

"Amen," she said, taking Raymond's arm.

Kristoff held out his hand for me, his eyes bright with passion, but it was not his sexual interest I doubted.

That thought remained, even two hours later when I found myself in heaven.

"I don't care how you ended up with this money. I don't care if you get to keep it. I don't care about anything right now, to be honest." I heaved a blissful sigh and sank up to my neck in the warm, milky blue, algae- and mineral-laden water of the famed Blue Lagoon hot springs. "Other than the fact that we have three whole hours of this. Who needs sleep when we can soak here?"

"This is not a replacement for proper rest, but it is the best I can do, since you refuse to sleep. You will do so on the plane, however." Kristoff's voice drifted out of the private lounge he'd reserved for us. Although the Blue Lagoon covered a large area shaped by the surrounding volcanic rocks, the main section did not offer privacy. The spa offered a couple of areas (for a hefty fee) that not only included personal changing rooms and a lounge where one could relax on some very modern-looking furniture, but also a tiny private lagoon.

"You said I was immortal now that I'm officially your Beloved." I wriggled my toes into the soft mud, allowing myself to bob gently in the water. I had read in the spa brochure that the water was famed for its therapeutic qualities, and that the white silica mud was much sought after for its antiaging properties. I reached down and scooped up a handful of the mud, letting it slip through my fingers. It was chalky white, but smooth, like very fine sand.

"That doesn't mean you don't need sleep." Kristoff emerged from the lounge behind us. He was still fully clothed. I frowned.

"Why am I here, naked, in our very own private watery paradise, and you're not molesting me as is my due?" I asked.

"We're here because I thought you would enjoy it. Also because it is likely that the Dark Ones will be canvassing hotels in the area. But mostly because you need somewhere to rest and are too stubborn to do so elsewhere."

"Boo."

"What?"

"You know full well what I mean. Why aren't you here in the water with me, naked, so I can ply my womanly wiles upon your fabulous, if still slightly too skinny, male body?"

"There are things that must be done, Pia. I have a few friends remaining upon whom I can call, and I have done so."

That got my attention. I bobbed my way over to the wooden planking that edged one side of our pool. "Call for what?"

Kristoff squatted and ran his fingers across the top of the water. "Information regarding reaper movements in California. And to track Alec's last known movements."

"Oh, excellent. What did you find out? Where did he go?" I asked.

He was silent for a moment. "Nothing has been discovered yet."

I frowned. "Damn. What about the Brotherhood people? Is anything going on besides the fact that they're hunkering down for a fight?"

"Nothing that I haven't already mentioned."

"Hmm. I was thinking about this on the ride out here."

"You were not," he countered. "You spent

the trip out here fondling my leg and thinking the most erotic thoughts that a man can
bear. And a couple I couldn't."

"I did both. I'm a woman — I can multi-
task. Anyway, I was mulling over the situation with Alec and the reapers, and I think I
see the truth. It all comes back to Frederic."

One eyebrow went up.

"You have the most expressive eyebrows. I
love that about you," I said, smiling before I
continued. "See if you follow my reasoning,
which I admit right now might be the teensiest bit flawed, because I'm a bit rummy
from lack of sleep. One." I held up my
fingers to tick off the items. "Denise was
protecting someone."

"You don't know that for certain."

"I'm pretty sure of it. It's the only thing
that makes sense. Two, Frederic killed her."

He nodded.

"Three, with the Zenith gone, the director
of the board of governors is more or less in
charge of the whole shebang."

His nod was slower in coming this time,
but it came at last. "There is a new Zenith,
though," he pointed out.

"Sooner or later, yes. But what if the later
is much, much later? What if Frederic
wanted to be in charge but, because he's
male, could never be a Zenith? What if he

set up Denise, giving her some convincing line of bull that had her believing he was a good guy, but in reality he was setting her up for the fall? And then when she did fall, he shot her to keep her from talking? Voilà. Instant leader of the reapers, with no witnesses and no questions asked."

He thought about that for a few minutes. "It is possible, I grant you. But where does Alec fall in this theory of double cross and hidden agendas?"

"Oh, Alec." I sank back into the water, enjoying its warm, silky feeling on my naked flesh. "Well, we know vampires can't be reapers, even if they're from the Ilargi side of the family, right?"

Kristoff made a vague gesture.

"Right, so, he can't be an Ilargi, but he can work for one."

"Why would he wish to participate in the stealing of souls?" Kristoff asked.

"He doesn't want to. Or rather, it's a necessary evil in order for him to ingratiate himself with Frederic."

"The director?"

"Yes! Frederic is the Ilargi! Don't you see? He's doing a double-cross thing, just like you said. He got Denise out of the way, and now he's going around eliminating ghosts so Zoryas can't do anything with them. Alec probably contacted him with some weird tale of wanting to help the reapers without letting him know he was a vampire, so Frederic set him up to appear to be the Ilargi, just in case anyone nosed around."

"Less experienced reapers would not recognize a Dark One as being such on sight, but I assume the director would," Kristoff pointed out. "Sooner or later he would come face-to-face with Alec and know that he was not what he appeared."

"Exactly." I back-kicked a couple of feet. "But by then the illusion of Alec being the Ilargi was in place. I don't doubt that he's innocent, as your gut instinct said. They probably have him in maximum security back in Brotherhood Central. The reason he's still alive is because they don't have a Zenith, so therefore, they can't fire up the local Zorya and get her to off him."

"I hesitate to ask this, but my curiosity to hear your explanation outweighs my better judgment: Why would the director wish to effectively destroy the ghosts his organization was created to protect and aid?"

I smiled. "Because he's mad, of course. He doesn't care about ghosts anymore. All he wants is to rid the world of you guys, so he's eliminating any distractions that would keep Zoryas from performing his purposes

— killing vampires."

"But there is no Zenith, and thus the murders can't be performed."

"That had me confused, too, until I realized something really obvious — the original purpose of the Zoryas was the ghost bit, right? And all the ceremonies and such were created around that. The stuff with the vampires came later, much later, so it's quite probable that the rules just got grandfathered in. I'm willing to bet you that if a group of Brotherhood guys got together and started that evil cleansing ceremony, so long as they had a Zorya present, she could smite the hell out of her victims. The Zenith thing is just a holdover from days long past. And before you say we have no proof of that, may I remind you of this?"

I summoned a tiny ball of light and let it dance in front of his feet.

He looked at it without moving.

"If I wanted to, I could probably pull down enough light to seriously harm you, Kristoff. It may take a ceremony with a couple of Brotherhood guys channeling their powers to finish you off, but I'm sure we wouldn't need a Zenith to do so. Frederic must have found this out. Remember that Denise was a Zorya before she was the Zenith. I bet somehow they found it out, and that started his convoluted plan."

"Convoluted, indeed," Kristoff said, still watching the light bobbing at his toes. I waved a hand and dissipated it.

"I just bet you that Frederic is making sure another Zenith isn't named. Which all points to one very clear conclusion."

"Yes, it does. It says that you are more tired than either of us realizes."

I made a face at him. "No, silly. It means we're going to have to deal with Frederic."

"I agree. We will kill the director."

I gawked at him. "How on earth did you jump from 'we need to give Frederic the third degree' to killing him?"

His eyes lightened a few shades. "He is manipulating you, Beloved. Your theory is interesting, but unproven at this time. It is more likely that if the director is not working with Alec, he is probably holding him prisoner. And since he is fortifying his defenses, he must expect an attack by us. You are my Beloved, a fact he knows. Do you honestly believe he will not attempt to destroy us should he be given the opportunity?"

I was silent for a moment, remembering the pain of the knife Frederic had wielded as it sank deep into my flesh. "I don't condone what Frederic has done in the past.

And I don't appreciate him manipulating me, and he's definitely up to no good. God knows I certainly don't support the war between the Brotherhood and you vampires, but someone somewhere has to draw the line and end the war. Someone has to stop the killing. And I choose to be that person."

To my surprise, a faint smile was visible on Kristoff's adorable lips. "My mother would have liked you. She was frequently in the stocks for what the local nobleman who ruled the town called gross impertinence to his position. She always championed the downtrodden, and more than once came close to the gallows for her attempts to right what she saw as wrongs."

"She sounds like she was a marvelous woman," I said, and, tempted as I was to continue that line of conversation, I set it aside for a bit. "You're not going to distract me from the discussion, Boo. Especially since you know I'm against unnecessary violence."

He sighed, a weary expression on his face. "What would you have me do? Promise that no harm will come to any reaper?"

"No. I would like you to think about ways to get what we want without anyone dying."

Water lapping gently at the rocks was the only sound for a few moments.

"I will not risk your life," he said finally.

"Nor would I expect you to. Just don't go into this with a no-quarter stance, OK?"

His expression was sour, as if he'd tasted something bad. "I do this under protest."

"So noted." I swam backward a couple of feet, determined to enjoy the few hours of respite granted to us. I allowed myself a few smutty thoughts about what I'd like to do to him before continuing. "Back to my original question — why aren't you soaking in here with me?"

"My friend is continuing to track Alec's last-known movements." He glanced at his watch. "I expect the answer to come in shortly. Much as I would like to make love to you, Beloved, I must attend to this first."

"You know what I say to that?" I asked, reaching beneath me to scoop up another handful of the white silica mud.

"Something that's intended to irritate me, I'm sure," he said with a mock sigh.

"No. I say: incoming!" I hefted the handful of dripping wet, slippery mud and flung it at his head.

The mud hit him full in the face with a wet splatting noise. He stood stunned for a moment before turning a really top-quality glare on me. "That was uncalled for," he snapped, reaching for a towel.

"Oh, come on, Kristoff! Just come have a little dip with me, and then you can do all the tracking down that you like. I'll help."

He just continued to wipe the mud off his face and upper part of his shirt.

I scooped up another handful, and thought about pelting him until he gave up and came after me. But I didn't want to force him into having a little fun. That would defeat the purpose of him having a few hours of relaxation. No, he just needed a little persuasion, something that would convince him of the benefits of taking a little time away from the burdens we both bore.

I smiled to myself, swimming toward the stone steps that led out of our private lagoon to the lounge. When I was close enough that the water was about waist-deep, I stood up.

Kristoff, dabbing off the last smidgen of mud, froze. I arched my back a little, thrusting my bare breasts forward.

"It's too bad you can't find a little time to relax," I said, caressing my breasts with the chalky white mud, allowing it to slide slowly down my chest, trailing my fingers down after it with long, sweeping strokes.

His eyes glittered with blue fire as he watched me.

"According to the spa brochure, this water

is supposed to do all sorts of good things for you," I cooed, scooping up two handfuls, pouring them over my now white breasts. "They have all sorts of treatment and massages available in the water, for a variety of ailments."

His eyes widened, but he didn't otherwise move.

I bent and got another handful of mud, slowly walking forward toward the stairs until the water was at my pubic bone. I slathered my belly with the mud, making little swirls and circles in it as I spread it lower.

I thought Kristoff's eyes were going to bug right out of his head.

I dipped my fingers even lower. "But if you don't want to experience the benefits and pleasures it is sure to give you, I'll just have to enjoy it all by myself."

A splash momentarily blinded me, water flying everywhere. I laughed when Kristoff, still fully clothed, stood before me with two handfuls of white mud.

"It would be a shame to miss such a natural phenomenon," he agreed, his voice husky as he spread the mud on my breasts.

"You still have your clothes on," I pointed out, then gasped as his head dipped and he took the tip of one breast into his mouth.

"Oh, dear God. Kristoff!"

The last was in response to his hands, which had gone beneath the water and were busy with hidden parts of me. My knees threatened to buckle as his fingers danced along sensitive flesh.

You taste salty, he said, his mouth moving along my breastbone. I could swear his tongue was made of fire as it swirled and lapped.

It's the water. It's two-thirds seawater and one-third fresh. I read that in the brochure. . . . Boo!

He smiled into my neck as two fingers suddenly dipped inside me. Hundreds of normally dormant nerve endings suddenly sat up and took notice of him, tingling with delight at his touch.

You have too many clothes on. I whimpered, trying to get my hands to strip the wet clothes off him, but my body was too involved in the sensations his mouth and hands were generating for me to do much but stand and quiver with rapture.

Yes. I have clothing on, and you do not. It's very wicked, is it not?

Definitely, but it also is keeping me from touching you, I said, groaning as a third finger joined the other two, his thumb making little swirls that almost had me sobbing.

287

My brain didn't know whether it should focus on the wonderful feeling his fingers were generating, the sensation of my breasts rubbing against the slightly abrasive wet cloth of his shirt, or the fire that his mouth was trailing as he kissed a wet path along my shoulder.

Perhaps I do not wish to be touched, he answered, his teeth nipping the flesh of my upper arm.

I let him see a mental picture of what exactly I wanted to do to him. He froze for a moment, then in a move that was literally too fast for me to see, he stripped off all his clothing, the dull thud of his shoes hitting the stone floor of the lounge the last thing I heard before he was back in my arms, his body, wet and warm and hard as the lava rocks around us, holding my entire attention.

Where were we? he said, then smiled into my mind. *Here, I think . . .*

I squealed as his fingers resumed their previous activity. "Two can play at that, mister."

I had a handful of mud ready, and slid it down his chest and stomach, gently biting his shoulder as I let my hands go even lower, down to his erection. "Now, see? I knew this would benefit you. Sparky is all happy."

"Sparky?" he asked, nipping my earlobe. "I can live with a pet name for me, but I draw the line at naming body parts."

"Oh, really?" I asked, taking him in both hands, gently exploring the territory. "So you wouldn't approve of my calling your penis 'Raging Stallion'?"

His eyes crossed for a moment as I discovered a particularly sensitive spot. "Raging Stallion works for me," he said with a gasp.

"I thought so. Now, why don't you go sit over there on that bottom step, and I think we'll be far enough out of the water so I won't drown while I perform a therapeutic genital massage."

The fire in his eyes kicked up a couple of notches. "Did you read about that in the brochure, too?"

"No, that's something I thought of on my own. You look like you need a little personal attention. Sit."

An oddly obstinate look crossed his face. "I prefer to stand. It is you who will receive the personal attention."

His hands slid up my hips to my breasts. I stopped them before they could go any farther. "I want to give you pleasure, Kristoff."

"As I do you." His eyes lightened a smidgen, which I was beginning to realize meant he was annoyed.

We stared at each other for a few seconds.

"I can't believe we're having an argument over who gets to do what first," I said.

"Neither can I."

A few more seconds of staring passed, while we both waited for the other person to give in.

"One of us is going to have to let the other one have her way," I pointed out.

"Yes, you will."

I narrowed my eyes at him. "You get your way an awful lot. I think you've used up all of your bossy points. Therefore, you will sit and I will give you a blow job so incredible, you won't be able to think straight."

He stood up a bit straighter. All of him. "I am a Dark One," he declared, projecting into my mind mental images so carnal, I'm surprised the water around us didn't start to boil. "You are my Beloved. You will bend over that rock and let me make love to you in such a manner that will not only keep you from thinking straight. You will also walk funny for a week."

My jaw dropped at his pseudothreat. "Oh! That is so . . . so . . ."

"Truthful?" he asked smoothly.

"Underhanded! Sending me smutty images like that. Well. Two can play at that game." I crossed my arms and thought of the most erotic acts I could perform upon his body.

His Adam's apple bobbed a couple of times, and when he spoke, his voice was hoarse. "I did not include massage oils in my mental imaging! Or ice cubes. If anyone is being underhanded, it's you."

I smiled. "You want underhanded? Try this." I dwelled in loving detail on a plan to use not only slick, warmed lotion on him, but on my breasts as well, rubbing myself along his body until he exploded with pleasure.

"Exploded?" he said, his eyes as black as midnight.

"You heard me, buster."

He trembled with strain for a moment, just a moment, and then he had himself in control again. "This is a waste of time. Submit to me so that I may make you walk funny, and then you can explode me."

"Boo!" I said, slapping my hands down on the water. "I want to do this for you!"

"No more so than I want to provide pleasure for you," he said, still obstinate.

"Argh!" I yelled, thinking furiously, but the images he kept sending me about just what he wanted to do were weakening my resolve. "Oh, this is stupid," I said, wading over to him, wiggling against his body so that my breasts rubbed against his wet, slick chest.

"Exceedingly so," he answered, his head dipping to my neck. He breathed on the spot that never failed to send all my nerves into tingly overtime.

"We'll both do it, all right?"

"That would seem fair. I get to go first, though."

"You, sir, are a bully, and nothing but a bully," I said, poking my finger into his chest. I stopped, eyed the chest, then spread my fingers along the wet skin, stroking the lovely muscled curves. He sucked in a lungful of breath. "What the hell. You go first; then it'll be my turn."

"Agreed." He spun me around so that my back was to him, pushing me slightly forward so I had to catch myself on the rough lava rocks that lined our little lagoon. *If you have the strength after I'm through with you,* came an echoed thought.

"I heard that!" I said, but before I could protest any dirty tricks, all sane thought left my head as his teeth pierced the flesh of my shoulder at the same time he thrust hard into my body.

The warm water swirling around us, the sensation of bone-deep satisfaction that filled Kristoff and spilled out into me as he drank, the ever-increasing tension that wound inside me combining with his, pushing us both higher, joining with a million other sensations, threatened to overload my senses as I clutched the sharp lava rocks. But it was the more profound merging, the blending of souls as he both took life from me and returned it, that sent my spirit soaring. All the dark places inside him, all the inky despair, and pain, and shadows of loneliness that still remained were obliterated at that moment. I fed him not just my blood, but my very sense of being, filling him with light and hope and happiness. And as his tongue swirled a path of flame over my shoulder, as his body tensed in mine, I gave him the last thing I had.

"I love you," I cried as he spun me around, his mouth muffling the words. I wrapped my legs around him when he hoisted me up, clutching his shoulders as his hips flexed with short, forceful thrusts, the muscles in his neck and shoulders as tight as steel. He growled deep in his chest, a primitive, earthy noise that pushed me over the edge. My muscles rippled around him as he gave in to his own climax, an echoed sense of wonderment filling my mind as he stood, legs braced apart, the water lapping at his hips, both our bodies trembling with delightful little aftershocks.

I gave his lower lip one last fond little nibble, then released it and looked down at him, my mind still swimming with our combined emotions.

He was flushed, his eyes glittering with heat hotter than any fire, and on the edges of his adorable lips was the beginning of a smile. No, not a smile, a smirk. Wholly male, utterly arrogant, and completely knowing.

"All right," I admitted as I let my legs drop, aware that he could feel how the muscles in them trembled. "You win. I'm going to walk funny. But I'd like to point out that you did a fair bit of exploding, too."

"Agreed. Where did you learn to do that?"

"Do what?" I asked, wondering if he thought Americans went to school to learn lovemaking techniques.

"When you gripped me like a vise."

I took one step, stumbled, and glared when he snickered. The only thing that saved him from another faceful of mud was the fact that he scooped me up and carried me to the lounge.

"That, Boo, is the result of years of Kegeling. My mother told me to start young so that when I was an old lady I wouldn't have to wear bladder pants like my granny."

"That may be the result of years of intimate exercise, but you haven't been quite so vigorous in the past."

I grinned over the towel I was using to dry myself off. "Just so I know — are we thumbs-up or thumbs-down on the Kegel vigor?"

"Thumbs-up. Definitely thumbs-up," he said, looking down at himself ruefully. Even quiescent, he was still impressive. "Although if you keep it up, you won't be the only one walking funny."

An unexpected sense of peace and happiness filled our remaining hours at the spa.

"How did your parents meet?" I asked after I had recovered enough wits to kick-start my brain into functioning again. I lay draped across Kristoff as he lounged on a plush red curved sofa, clad in one of the spa's thick bathrobes. Kristoff was clad only in me, a fact I much appreciated as I traced the lines of muscles in his chest and upper arm. He was still too skinny for my taste, but I was happy to notice he was filling out nicely with regular meals.

He opened one eye. His hands were lazily tracing shapes on the outside of one of my thighs, the touch casual, but so sweetly intimate it made my eyes burn for a moment. "My parents?"

"Yes. You know, the people who gave birth to you and raised you?"

An odd sense of withdrawal touched my mind. I stopped stroking the muscle of his biceps and looked up at him. Both his eyes were open now, looking at me with suspicion.

"Why do you want to know about my parents?"

"Why shouldn't I want to know about them? We're bound together for the rest of time, Kristoff. I'd like to know more about you, that's all. Is there something about your parents you don't want to talk about?"

He sensed me sensing his emotional withdrawal, and stopped, but there was a wary edge to him, as if he were walking on the blade of a razor. "I've told you about my mother. My father was a tanner. He died when I was very young."

"I'm sorry. That must have been hard for your mom. Were there any kids other than you and Andreas?"

He shook his head, and once again I felt a spike of awareness inside him. He was watching me closely as he spoke. "No. He was born later than me."

"I gathered you were older than him," I

said lightly, continuing to stroke his arm with long, soothing touches, but wondering all the while what it was about his parents that had him so keyed up. "How much older are you?"

"Twenty-two years."

"Really? Wow. That's quite a difference." I was silent for a moment, very aware of his now still fingers on my leg. "You said you were born human. How did you come to be a vampire?"

"I was cursed to it."

"Cursed? Someone can do that?"

"It takes a demon lord, but yes, you can make a Dark One." His voice was suddenly flinty hard. "Why are you questioning me about this?"

"All right," I said, pushing myself up. I swung my leg over until I was straddling his thighs. "What is it that bothers you so much about me asking about your past?"

"Why do you care how I became a Dark One?" he countered, his eyes lightening a smidgen.

I pointed a finger at him. "Don't you dare lighten your eyes at me, Boo! I have no ulterior motive in asking you about your origins other than curiosity about you. It may have escaped your notice, but I just announced to you that I'm in love with you."

"It didn't escape my notice," he said quickly.

Pain stung me. Of course he hadn't missed what I said, but being an honest man, he hadn't lied to me and told me the feeling was mutual. "I'm interested in people I love. I want to know things about them, what they like and what they don't like, and how their childhood was, that sort of thing. And you're just going to have to deal with a whole lot of curiosity about Dark Ones, because up until two months ago, I didn't believe vampires really existed."

Mollified, he released the grip he had on my legs. "I am interested in you, too."

"Good. I'll tell you all about my boring life and family another time. Right now I want to know what happened that had you ending up a vampire."

He was silent for a moment, reluctance thick inside him. "It was an act of revenge. Someone I knew injured another person."

"Someone you knew?" I asked, puzzled why he would be the victim of revenge.

"My wife."

I sat up straighter at that, my mouth hanging open in astonishment for a moment. "Your wife? You were married before me? That is . . . we're not really married, but you thought we were getting married, so it counts."

"We are really married, and yes, I was married before. In 1640, so you can stop pretending you're jealous. My first wife is long dead."

There was no pretense about the quick spurt of jealousy that riddled me, but I ignored that comment just as I ignored the emotion, instead doing a quick calculation in my head. "You were married when you were seventeen?"

"Yes. It was a reasonable age for marriage then. I was apprenticed to a cobbler, and wed his daughter."

A question rose up on my tongue. I tried to fight it, tried to keep my lips from forming the words, but my brain gave the go-ahead without my permission. "Did you love her?"

He looked somewhat startled by the question. "I wanted to bed her."

"Lust and love aren't the same thing," I pointed out.

"No, they aren't." He was silent for a moment. "I suppose I loved her. She was pretty and we enjoyed each other in bed."

"Oh, that really does my self-confidence a lot of good," I said somewhat acidly.

The corner of his lip twitched. "I enjoy you in bed, too."

"Not even remotely near as much re-assurance as you're going to have to provide in order to erase the memory of you hitting it off with another woman," I told him. "But I am nothing if not magnanimous, and am willing to move past your lustful ways, so long as you provide the reassurances later, preferably in tangible form. So your wife hurt someone?"

The closed feeling was back in his mind. "Yes. A woman. Ruth said it was an accident, that an ox she was driving in a cart went mad and ran the woman down, but her companion would not listen. He killed Ruth, and because I was her husband, and thus must suffer as he suffered, invoked a demon lord to curse me forever."

"I'm so sorry," I said, putting my hand over his heart at the sensation of pain deep inside him. "That was truly horrible. I can only imagine what you experienced trying to cope with your own tragedy as well as suddenly finding yourself soulless and a vampire."

His lips tightened. "It was not pleasant. My mother was furious when she found out, and traveled all over the country looking for help, but she was shunned by the Dark Ones she met. After years of searching, she finally found one who would talk to her. He told her there was no hope for me other than a Beloved, but neither of us really believed I'd find one." A wistful note entered his voice. "I would have liked my mother to know that I did, in fact, find you."

"She knows," I said, leaning forward to kiss him. "Just because she's dead doesn't mean she's not still with you."

He said nothing, but his fingers were back to stroking patterns on my thighs.

"How did Andreas come about?"

"The Dark One who consented to speak with my mother is his father." His lips twisted with a wry smile. "My mother was quite attractive, and he always had an eye for women. Something he shares with his son."

"Andreas is a ladies' man, eh?" I said, musing on the irony to be found in life. "I'll remember that. Maybe he would stop being a bastard to you if we found his Beloved."

"I doubt it." Kristoff lifted me off him and set me on the couch, rising to pull on a pair of pants. "Most Dark Ones don't find their Beloveds. It's not as if you can order one up."

I puzzled over Kristoff's unease and reluctance to speak of his past during the subsequent hours, even onto the plane that sent us winging back to the United States.

Part of it could be attributed to the mention of his previous wife; he was obviously astute enough to recognize that I was not yet comfortable enough with our relationship to discuss his past loves, which was one reason why he shunned the mention of his late girlfriend. But even given that, there was something else that he was keeping from me, something that mattered so much, he kept it locked up tight inside him.

Something that I was pretty sure I wasn't going to like.

Chapter 12

"Home at last," Raymond said, stopping next to a small white rental car and taking a deep breath of dirt, diesel, and smog-scented Los Angeles air. "The sights, the sounds, the scents of the city — ah, how I've missed it."

"I haven't," Magda said with a sigh, dropping her suitcase next to the trunk of the car. "I could have happily spent the rest of my life in the Blue Lagoon."

"Oh, don't get me wrong. I liked Iceland a lot, especially the second time around," Raymond said hurriedly. "Without the . . . you know . . . murder and business with the police and everything. But I have to say that it's good to be home. Or near home, in my case."

"I really feel bad about using up all your vacation time running around chasing vamps and whatnot," I said as I leaned against the car, quickly leaping away when the hot metal scorched through the thin material of my blouse. "The offer still stands, you know. You guys can stay in my house while Kristoff and I deal with all this. It's not fair to ask you to help with a problem that isn't of your making, and that way you'd have at least a little fun time before you had to go back to work."

"And miss all the good stuff?" Magda snorted. "Not on your life. We're in it for the long haul, aren't we, pookie?"

"Absolutely," Raymond said, nodding eagerly. "We're one hundred percent behind you, Pia. This is the most exciting time I've ever had, even including the tour to Europe. I never thought I'd become a vampire hunter! I can't wait to blog about this!"

"Er . . . yeah," I said noncommittally.

"Welcome to the City of Angels," Magda said, blowing out a long breath. "And to think I could be soaking in a hot spring at this moment."

"There's Kristoff," I said, sighing with relief as a familiar figure emerged from the elevator. He wore his jacket and hat against the sun, but didn't stick to the shadows, as he had in the past. "Everything OK?" I asked as he hit a button to unlock the car doors.

"I'm not sure," he said, looking thoughtful.

I watched him closely as Raymond loaded the suitcases in the car's trunk. Magda took the keys from Kristoff, murmuring something about knowing her way around LA better than he did.

What's wrong? I asked. *Was it the phone call you had at the rental car place?*

"The phone call was from one of my associates in Paris."

"Uh-oh. That look doesn't bode well. Did your buddy find out something?" I asked, a bad feeling beginning to form in my stomach.

"No. That's the problem. When we left Iceland two months ago, Alec told me he was going to follow up on the rumor of a new group of reapers around Marseilles, and then he'd return to his home. And yet my friend confirmed that Alec never arrived in Paris."

"So where did he go?" Magda asked as Raymond slammed shut the trunk and took the front passenger seat.

Kristoff opened the back door for me. "That's a good question. I'm working on the assumption that he would have gone home if he decided suddenly not to track down the French reapers, but thus far, my contacts haven't found proof he's been here, either."

"Hotel first, then reaper headquarters?" Magda asked.

Kristoff got in after me, immediately pulling me up next to him. I gave myself a moment to enjoy the subconscious move on his part, my heart simultaneously mourning what it couldn't have and enjoying what he could give me. "Neither. We will need to be prepared when we visit the reapers. Alec's house is within an hour from here. We will go there first, and then gather our forces and prepare for the onslaught."

Oh, Boo, I said, filled with gratitude. *You're doing that for me, aren't you?*

"Aye-aye, Captain," Magda said, saluting.

I know how worried you are about your spirit.

You are the sweetest man I know, I said, leaning over to kiss him. *Thank you.*

"Onslaught," Ray whispered to her, patting his jacket for the bulge that was his camera. "Exciting stuff! I've never been part of an onslaught before. I wonder if I have enough film for it."

I agree that Alec is being made to look like he is the Ilargi. I believe we can kill two birds with one stone by searching his house for information on both fronts.

Magda punched the address Kristoff gave

her into the car's GPS, making a little face at the results. "With the traffic, it's going to take us a while to get there. Maybe we should go to the hotel first, then visit the house, then prepare for the onslaught?"

"Alec's house first," Kristoff said stubbornly.

"House it is."

It took exactly two hours and twenty minutes to get there, but as I gazed in awe at the building, I decided it was worth it.

"*Et voilà.* Casa Alec. Ooh. And it is a *very* nice casa." Magda pulled up outside of an arched gate that spanned a drive that curled around to the back of a pale yellow chiffon–colored house.

"That's one heck of a house," Raymond said as we all got out of the car. He took a few quick photos. "Not at all what I expected a vampire to live in."

"Gothic castle with bats circling a bell tower?" I asked, smiling.

He flashed a grin. "Well, maybe. But this one . . . hoo. Must have set him back at least a mill. Maybe two. Do you think it has a view of the valley below?"

"Shall I ring?" Magda asked, poised to ring the visitor's bell.

"Won't do any good. There's clearly no one home," Raymond answered from where he was peering through the brown metal fence to the house. "Looks deserted. Maybe we should come back."

"Not after all we've been through," Magda answered, pressing the bell. "Let's see if anyone answers."

We waited a few minutes, but when it became clear that no one was either home to answer the ring or willing to do so, we decided we would have to rely on our own resources.

"Boost me over the fence, and I'll see if there's a way to open it from the other side," I told Kristoff.

"No," he answered, just as I figured he would.

"You know, I'm not sure that that's not technically breaking and entering," Raymond answered, his voice filled with reluctance. "It might be better if we waited until we can get hold of someone who can legally give us permission to go in the house."

"Don't be so straitlaced," Magda told him with a grin. "A little light breaking and entering is good for you. Besides, I want to see inside. I'm dying to see how a vampire really lives."

"I assure you, we live just as a mortal does," Kristoff said dryly.

"No coffins?" Raymond asked, his curiosity clearly getting the better of him. "No odd servants undertaking mysterious tasks late at night? No mirrors draped in black to hide the fact that you don't have a reflection?"

"He has a reflection," I said, coming to Kristoff's defense. "How do you think he shaves without being able to see himself?"

Raymond's mouth opened and closed a couple of times, like a confused fish. "Well, I . . . I . . . I guess I never thought about it. I just assumed that vampires didn't need to shave. No one on *Angel* ever shaved."

"You mortals watch entirely too much television," Kristoff said as he approached the gate.

Raymond murmured a vague excuse while Magda giggled.

"I just hope the fence isn't electrified or anything like that," I said, standing next to him, eyeing the large brown metal gate. "I assume you want to go first. Just be careful in case Alec has booby-trapped it somehow."

"I don't need to climb the fence; I know the code," Kristoff answered with a long-suffering look at me.

Don't even think of lightening your eyes, Boo.

I don't have the slightest idea what you're talking about, he answered.

Oh, don't you try to tell me you aren't aware vampires can change their eye color.

Some can, perhaps. I wasn't aware I shared that trait.

You do. It's like a barometer for your temper. Light is pissy, and dark is . . .

I stopped and waited.

Dark is what? Happy? he asked.

Aroused. Allow me to demonstrate. I sent him a few memories of our time spent in the Blue Lagoon. His eyes darkened from their normally flawless teal to a deep navy. *See? Your eyes are dark now. You're aroused.*

A fact that will become evident to others if you continue along that particular memory. And that one.

I smiled.

That one, my little temptress, is likely to get you bent over my lap.

Promises, promises, I purred, suddenly standing up straight when Kristoff spent a few moments indulging in just how I was going to be punished.

Luckily, Magda's impatience distracted us before Kristoff's pants grew too tight and I started squirming in earnest.

"Let's go. What are we waiting for? It will be getting dark in another hour." She poked Kristoff in the arm.

Kristoff punched in some numbers on the

recessed panel, and the gate slid open with a nearly silent hiss.

"Take the car or leave it?" Magda asked, poised to do either.

"Leave it," Kristoff said.

"It would be safer inside the gate," Raymond said, looking pointedly up and down the street. "This might be an affluent neighborhood, but you never know. Someone might try to steal it, and I'd hate to have to explain that to the rental company. You'd lose your insurance deposit."

"Stop being such an accountant," Magda said with a fond squeeze of his arm.

"Not that I suspect it's likely to be stolen here, but if we leave it where it is, anyone who comes by will see that someone is here," I pointed out.

"It's easier to get away with the car on the road," Kristoff said with a grim note to his voice.

"Fast getaway," Magda said, nodding her head sagely. "Makes sense. I could always move it down the road a smidgen. There was a spot I could pull off the street, where it wouldn't be quite so obvious it was this house we were at."

Kristoff agreed that would be smart, and accordingly, Magda and Ray moved the car down the road half a block or so.

"I can't believe we're doing this. I can't believe I'm here with a vampire and a sparkling-light lady, and we're breaking and entering a house so expensive, we could go to jail for at least fourteen years," Raymond said as we all trooped up the drive to the house. "This is something straight out of *The A-Team*."

"Sweetie, your middle age is showing," Magda said.

Alec's house, I had to admit, was impressive. It was of modern design, shaped like several square blocks had been stacked one upon another, with bits of it jutting out in an odd but pleasing formation.

"What are we going to do about the lo
—"

Before I could finish asking, Kristoff opened the door and gestured for us to go in.

I frowned at him. "How did you know it would be unlocked?"

"I made sure it was."

"Huh?" For one moment I had a vision of some strange, magical long-distance locksmith abilities known only to vampires.

Now that is so far-fetched, it isn't even in the realm of television.

Then how . . . ?

"The associate who was in California

checking on Alec's movements opened the house up for me. And no, I don't know how — I didn't ask him. Does it matter?" he asked.

"Why are we here if you've already had someone search the house?" Magda asked as she and Raymond walked slowly down a couple of slate steps into a vast living room.

Kristoff evidently knew Alec's house security code as well, since the alarm never sounded after he tapped in a few numbers. "He didn't search the house for anything but Alec. It's our job to see if there is anything here that can tell us whether or not Alec is involved with the reapers."

"Well. All I can say is, viva las vampires," Magda said as she turned slowly in a circle to take in the sights.

I had to agree with her assessment. The house had an open, breezy layout, and I found myself just as curious as Magda and Raymond as to how a vampire lived.

OK, I admit it. I'm surprised, I told Kristoff as I wandered around the large open room, stopping to admire a huge stone fireplace. *Beige suede furnishings and cream-colored accents just weren't what I pictured his house looking like.*

"Green marble in the kitchen," Magda said, emerging from that room. "Ooh,

Jacuzzi on the deck."

"OK, MacGyver, now what?" I asked Kristoff.

He frowned. "My surname is von Hannelore, not MacGyver."

"It was a TV reference, and yes, I'm aware we watch too much of it. Moving on, what now?"

"Now we search."

"Search for what?" Magda asked, coming in from the deck with Raymond. "I'm ready and willing to be put to work."

"Look for anything that has to do with reapers," Kristoff told her as he picked up the phone, punching in two numbers. "Or any travel documents. Anything that could give a hint as to where Alec was last. You two do the ground floor. Pia and I will do upstairs. We'll meet back here to search this floor together."

Magda saluted. She and Raymond headed to the lower floor while I watched Kristoff.

"Anything?"

He listened for a moment, then hung up the phone, shaking his head. "Nothing useful. The last call he made from here was to the Moravian Council, assumedly before we went to Iceland."

"He still has his cell phone, yes?"

"Yes." He held out his hand for me.

I took it, allowing the little skitter of happiness that never failed to follow such a gesture to fill me with warmth. "Now that Raymond and Magda are out of the way, what is it you really hope to find here?"

He shot me a faux-irritated glance. "I should have known better than to try to deceive you."

"Amen. What do you think we'll find?"

"I am hoping that he left behind his reaper journal. Normally, he did not take it with him when he traveled."

"What's in it?" We paused outside of a room. Night was starting to settle in, so Kristoff switched on a penlight and flicked it around the room. It was an unused bedroom. He moved on to the next.

"His notes on reapers. If he has betrayed us to them, there might be some evidence in the journal. Likewise, if not, there may be evidence to that effect, as well. This is his study."

The light was so dim that I couldn't see much of the room.

"And if he's acting as a double agent, pretending to work with Frederic in order to ingratiate himself?"

Kristoff crossed the room to close the blinds on three windows, followed by some heavy gold-and-cream drapes. "There may be some indication of that, too, although he has never mentioned anything like that to me. We should be safe to turn on the light now."

I flipped on the light and breathed in the air rich with masculinity, an intriguing blend of leather, furniture polish, and a faint, lingering citrusy note that I remembered as something inherently Alec.

"You take the desk," Kristoff said, gesturing toward it. "I'll see if there is anything helpful on his computer."

He moved over to sit at a small computer table that butted up against one window.

I touched the corner of the large mahogany desk that dominated the room, running my fingers along its satiny top. It was an antique desk, not terribly old, probably made around the turn of the twentieth century, but meant to impress with its size and ornate decorations. I could easily see some railroad magnate or lumber baron seated behind it, barking out orders with a cigar clenched between his teeth.

"My grandfather used to have a desk like this. I loved curling up underneath it, pretending it was a castle. When he was in a good mood, he'd let me sit at it and cut up papers. I'd arrange books along one side, and have my brother check out books. I loved that desk," I said meditatively, memories swamping me.

"I will buy you one like it later, but you must search now," Kristoff answered, his attention wholly on the computer screen in front of him as his hands flew over the keyboard.

I sat slowly in the chair behind the desk, my fingers caressing the rolled wood that edged the desk, wondering why I felt so oddly reluctant to open the drawers.

"I do not like prying any more than you do," Kristoff said, addressing my unspoken thoughts. "But if he is in danger, there might be something here that will permit us to rescue him. And if not . . ."

He stopped speaking, but his thoughts were readily apparent.

"If not, we'll find that, too. I know." I tried my best to release my feeling of guilt at invading Alec's privacy as I opened the first drawer.

Kristoff swore. "He's password-protected most of the documents. I can't get into them."

"Rats. You don't know his password?"

He shook his head, turning off the computer. "No, and it's useless to try to break the encryption. It would take far too long." He thought for a moment or two. "You keep searching the desk. I will go through his bedroom and the other rooms."

"There're only the three floors?" I asked, a handful of bank and credit card statements in my hands. I glanced through them quickly, but didn't see anything that was out of the ordinary.

"There's an attic, but it's not used. There is a small guesthouse, however. I'll check that when I'm through with his bedroom. It, too, should be empty, but it is better to check. Go through his papers carefully, Pia. There could be something in there that will give us a hint as to his state of mind or plans."

The ticking of the thin marble clock hanging on the wall opposite kept me company for the next forty minutes. Kristoff popped in briefly to say he'd searched all the rooms on this floor, and was going to check the guesthouse before starting on the main floor.

Magda arrived not long after that.

"I'll say this for Alec," she said from where she stood in the doorway, watching me sort through several file folders. "The man has a damned fine wine cellar. I'm afraid we gave in to temptation and opened a bottle of Gaja Costa Russi that's absolute heaven. We saved you guys some."

I looked up from a stock portfolio statement, somewhat surprised by the figures it detailed. Kristoff might disclaim having any wealth, but Alec certainly couldn't deny that he had holdings worth a significant amount of money, even by today's standards. "Thanks, but I don't think Kristoff drinks, and I'm not a big fan of red wines. Did you find anything else?"

She hiccuped and came into the room to plop down in the chair next to the computer. "Nothing that said what happened to him. Everything is shipshape, as far as we could tell. Nothing out of place, no giant map of the world with a big arrow pointing to his destination, nothing but a home theater, pool table, video arcade machines, and the wine cellar. Whatcha got there?"

I tidied the papers and put them back in their file folder, tucking it back in the appropriate drawer. "Just financial stuff. Nothing interesting, unless you want to be amazed at Alec's financial genius, which I have to admit is pretty darned awesome."

"Loaded, is he?" she asked, looking around the room.

"Very. That's the last drawer." I closed it and sat looking at the desk, my hands stroking the polished, cool surface.

"So the trip here has been for nothing."

Her voice reflected her unhappy expression.

"Probably." I was oddly reluctant to leave the dusty hallways of my memory. "I was telling Kristoff earlier about how I used to play at a similar desk my grandfather had."

"Oh, really?" She sat up. "Ooh! Don't tell me your grandpa's desk had a hidden drawer!"

"No," I said, frowning down at my hands on the desk. "I used to beg him to show me the hidden drawer, but he said it didn't have one."

"Damn." She thought for a moment, brightening up to add, "That doesn't mean this one can't have one."

"You're welcome to look. I already did, but two pairs of eyes are better than one, and all that."

Magda hurried over to the desk and, one by one, pulled out the drawers. We checked them for false bottoms and false backs, looked underneath for anything taped to the underside, and more or less gutted the desk. By the time the marble clock chimed the hour, I realized we'd been searching for more than twenty minutes.

"I think we're going to have to face the fact that there's no hidden anything in the desk," I said, rubbing my fingers absently along its rolled edge.

"I'm afraid you're right," Magda said, crawling out from where she'd been on her back underneath the desk, examining the underside. She sat on her heels, her eyes narrowed on my hand. "Why do you keep doing that?"

"Keep doing what?" I looked down at the desk. "Rubbing the edge? I don't know. The carving on it is pretty, don't you think?"

She leaned to the side, peering over the desk. "Yeah, but the desk has that edge all the way around it, and you keep touching just that one spot."

I shrugged. "Coincidence. I suppose we should go report in to Kristoff that we haven't found anything."

I started to get up, but Magda held up a hand. "Hang on a sec. I think there's more to it than coincidence. You had to scoot your chair over a foot so you could touch that spot. It's not something you can reach when you sit square at the desk."

"So? It's just a weird quirk. I like wood. I like to touch it."

"Only that one spot?" she asked.

I frowned at the desk. "Now, that is odd. I guess I have been drawn to this one edge. . . . Oh, Magda, you don't mean to say —"

"Stranger things, my dear, stranger things."

I rolled my eyes.

"Look at it this way." She crawled over to where my hand had been resting, examining that edge of the desk closely. "You're a Zorya. You're not normal anymore."

"Thanks."

She brushed away my grimace. "You know what I mean. You're Pia-plus, and no, I'm not talking about your size. Maybe there's something here that you're subconsciously picking up on. Hand me that letter opener, will you?"

I shook my head but did as she asked, giving her the thin knife that Alec obviously used as a letter opener. She poked at the edge for a few minutes, making me flinch a couple of times as the blade marred the wood.

"Oh, let me do it," I said, nudging her aside. "You're just going to scratch up the lovely finish. Not that I think there's anything to what you're . . . Well, I'll be damned."

I don't know if it was Magda's prodding with the knife that did it, or if I triggered some sensitive spot, but a piece of the molding about seven inches long came off in my hand. I thought for a moment that I'd broken it, but a glance at the minute dovetail work of the desk and molding told me it was intended to come off.

"Look. Is that an opening?" Magda asked, peering closely at the desk. "It is. I think there's something in there. You got a pair of tweezers on you?"

"Do my eyebrows look like I'm the sort of person who has tweezers?" I asked, getting on my knees so I, too, could peer into a thin, narrow slit that had evidently been carved into the thick top of the desk. Like Magda, I could see the faint outline of an object deep in the recess. I used the paper knife, gently guiding the object out. "I think . . . Ah, there it is. Yes, I have it."

"What is it?" she asked, peering over my shoulders at the slim book I held. "Something important?"

"I can't imagine stuffing something trivial in there," I answered, carefully unwrapping a saffron yellow animal skin that had been carefully folded into a bundle. Inside it was what appeared to be a hand-stitched goat-skin journal. It was small, about the size of a PDA, the outer cover brown and stained with age. The pages inside, about ten total, appeared to be made of vellum, also mottled and stained with the effects of time. I rubbed my fingers along the pages, not seeing, for a moment, the thick black handwriting, but admiring the profound sense of age that wrapped around the book.

"Can you read it?" Magda asked, her lips moving as she tried to decipher the handwriting.

"Let's take it to the light." We scooted two chairs over to the table lamp, angling it so the light shone down on the mottled pages.

"It's definitely old," Magda said, hunching over it next to me.

"I think it's a diary of some sort. That's a date, isn't it?" I asked, pointing to the upper corner.

"Looks like it. April? August? Something with an A. From 1642. Wow. Seriously old. I can't make out what the writing says, though. Can you?"

I concentrated on the thick black writing. It appeared to be in a language that I didn't recognize. I ran my finger along the lines of handwriting, trying to pick out words that made some sense.

My finger stopped; my heart contracted. "That . . . that's Kristoff's name."

"What? Where?" She craned to see.

I tapped the word. "Right there. That says, 'Hannelor Kristof,' which has to be a reference to my Kristoff."

"Hmm. Maybe it's when he first met Kristoff."

"Could be. I wonder if this is the reaper journal Kristoff mentioned." I continued searching the diary. There were several more instances of his name, but nothing struck me as recognizable.

"Maybe Kristoff can read it," Magda suggested as I finished running my finger along the lines of text on the last page. Something niggled at the back of my mind, something that I had just seen that was important.

Magda sat back, a look of disappointment on her face.

"Maybe." I looked at the book again, going back to the beginning, where Kristoff's name was first mentioned. My finger traced the centuries-old text, following along until I came to a spot near the bottom of the first page. "Magda."

"Hmm?"

"This, right here. Does that look like *'in tua luce videmus lucem'*?"

"What is that, Latin?"

"Yes."

Her dark head leaned over the book. "Yeah, it does. Why, what does it mean?"

" 'In thy light we see light.' "

"Sounds like a university motto."

I stared down at the page. "It well could

be. It also happens to be something that the Brotherhood people say as part of their rituals."

Her eyes widened. "What do you think it means?"

"I'm not sure. Look, does this say 'Lodi'?" I tapped a word on the following page.

"Um . . . maybe. It could be. Then again, it might be 'loom.' Or even 'look.' The writing is too hard to decipher for sure."

"I think it's Lodi," I said slowly, trying to remember what Rick Mycowski had told us about the origins of the war against the vampires. My fingers slid across the thin vellum until they rested beneath the date noted alongside the entry in question. "It says 1643. That sounds about right for the Lodi Congress."

"The what?"

I explained what I knew of the history of the Brotherhood.

"Gotcha. So this is, like, a mention of the war starting. If so, it's seriously old, and has to be valuable. I wonder why Alec doesn't have this in some sort of archival protective storage rather than shoved into the hidey-hole of a desk?"

I flipped back a page, looking at the dated entry containing Kristoff's name. Why, if the Lodi Congress started the year following that, was the Brotherhood mentioned in the earlier entry? Had Kristoff been one of the first vamps to go after the reapers? I made a mental note to ask him when things were less hectic and he'd be more inclined to chat.

"Regardless, it's valuable enough to warrant having Kristoff translate it," I said, gently rubbing my thumb across the goatskin covering. "If it turns out to be nothing, we'll return it to Alec. Assuming he comes home, that is."

"I guess we're finished here, then," Magda said, glancing around the room.

"We've looked everywhere. We can move on to the floor below us." A thought occurred to me: Kristoff hadn't been in contact with me for over half an hour. While that wasn't in any way remarkable, I would have thought he'd be interested to know of our progress, or lack thereof. *Boo, I'm ready to go on to the main floor. You about finished in the guesthouse?*

Silence was my only answer.

Kristoff? Everything OK?

I stood up as the profound silence filled my head. "Something's wrong," I said, trying to open up my senses to locate Kristoff.

She paused at the door. "What?"

"Kristoff isn't answering me."

She glanced at the phone for a moment before her eyebrows arched. "Oh, the mind thing? Maybe he's busy. Or out of range."

I shook my head, suddenly filled with the strongest portent of danger. "I don't think so. Something has happened to cause him to close his mind to mine, and that can only be one thing."

"Reapers?" she asked, her face losing some of its animation.

I nodded. "Or worse."

She froze for a moment. "Come to think of it, Ray should have been upstairs by now. Even if he had been drinking that lovely Costa Russi, he should have. . . . I'm going to go check on him."

She dashed out of the room without waiting for a response.

Possessed by a sudden sense of urgency, I hurriedly wrapped up the journal, shoved the bit of trim back onto the desk, and without an alternate choice, stuffed the journal under my dress, into the band of my underwear.

I snatched up the penlight that Kristoff had left me, flipping off the room's light before carefully closing the door. The house was dark now that the sun was setting, but the penlight allowed me to pick out the way to the stairs that led down to the main floor.

It, too, was in the dark, and for a moment I hesitated, the primitive part of my mind refusing to march blindly into what felt like certain danger.

My foot had just hit the first stair when a noise behind me startled me, causing me to simultaneously gasp and spin around, one hand clutching the penlight, the other groping the journal as it pressed against my skin.

A face loomed suddenly out of the darkness. My skin crawled in horror for a moment, my body giving in to the flight instinct. I stepped backward and plummeted down the staircase into the inky blackness below.

CHAPTER 13

The pain caught my attention first. It was sharp and hot, radiating out from a spot on the side of my head, dull waves of agony that brought the rest of my awareness to me.

"Unh?" I said, my tongue seemingly made of lead as I blinked my eyes, trying to shake off the last shreds of oblivion that clung to the edges of my mind. "Hrng?"

"Are you awake? How do you feel?"

I blinked a couple more times. Light and shadows flashed on my face, blurred into fleeting shapes that seemed to rush past me.

"Boo?" I asked, trying to adjust my position, and wincing at the pain in my head that followed the movement. "Ow. What the hell?"

The man's voice was a pleasant baritone with a slight German accent, sophisticated and sexy. "You hit your head on the banister when you fell. I caught you before you tumbled down the stairs, so you should be fine. Immortality is just one of the perks of being a Beloved."

Carefully I turned my head to look in the direction of the voice, my eyes still not focusing too well. Slowly, a face resolved itself, dimly lit, but recognizable. "Alec?" I asked, the memory of him emerging from the darkness of his house returning with an impact that had me struggling upright.

Something bound me, holding me back. I struggled with the thing, realizing as a metallic click sounded that it was a seat belt. I was in a car.

"What are you doing here?" I asked, pushing myself up from where I'd been slumped in the passenger seat. Pain bit hard and deep in my head for a few seconds, slowly ebbing away to a dull throb. "Oh, God. I remember now. You loomed up out of the darkness and scared the crap out of me."

"I'm sorry for that, love." Alec caught himself, making a little face. "I suppose I shouldn't call you that anymore. Not since . . . Well. What's done can't be undone."

"If you're talking about Kristoff . . . ," I began slowly, rebuckling my seat belt. With extreme caution, I felt the side of my head. There was a good-sized lump there. "No, it

331

can't be undone. Not that I would want to even if I could change it. Ouch. I don't suppose you have an ice pack handy?"

He shook his head, glancing briefly at me before returning his eyes to the road. "You are happy with Kristoff? I had thought that you and I had a great future before us. It seemed to me that you thought so, too."

"I don't think we were ever really meant to be," I said uncomfortably, and not just due to the headache. "I will always cherish our time together, though. And I can't believe I'm saying something so predictable and trite, but I hope that you won't allow my relationship with Kristoff to come between our friendship, or your friendship with Kristoff. Assuming, that is, that you are not really working for the Brotherhood and about to turn me over to them so they can perform insanely evil acts against my person."

Alec's lips thinned. He was, as I had had occasion to note at some length, an exceedingly handsome man. He was dark haired, like Kristoff, but where Kristoff had dark auburn curls, Alec's hair was a rich, deep, dark chocolate, straight and silky, pulled back in a ponytail. His eyes were green like a cat's, and although our physical relationship hadn't gone beyond one night together, he had enough raw magnetism that even in my somewhat muddled state I felt the impact of his nearness.

"That you can even think such a thing about me pains me deeply," Alec said, his knuckles white on the steering wheel.

"Well, you have to admit that you haven't done much for making people think you're a knight in shining armor. Where have you been? What have you been doing? And why have you kidnapped me?"

"I haven't kidnapped you; I've saved you," he said, shooting me an irritated glance. "There were reapers all around my house. I sneaked in through the attic and was going to retrieve a valuable when I heard people."

I suddenly remembered the old diary Magda and I found. I slid my hand toward my stomach, relieved to feel the stiff vellum-and-goatskin journal resting against it. Alec must have seen the movement.

"Yes, my reaper journal. It would appear I need to find a new hiding place for it. Oh, don't distress yourself, love. I didn't take it from you. In fact, you will find it most interesting reading, although I would like it back when you are through with it. You might ask Kristoff to translate parts for you."

"I'm sorry," I stammered. "I didn't know
—"

He made an abortive gesture. "It doesn't
matter. I was about to strike you down when
I saw you near the stairs, having assumed
you were a reaper — or rather, one of the
reapers who would not hesitate to kill me
— when I realized it was you. What was
Kristoff doing, leaving you alone in my
home?"

"He didn't leave me alone," I said, sick to
my stomach and confused as all get-out.

"He didn't?"

"No. He was out in the guesthouse. At
least, I thought he was, but he didn't answer
me when I tried to contact him."

Alec swore and slammed his foot on the
brake, the car fishtailing wildly to the ac-
companiment of horns from the cars behind
us as he pulled an extremely illegal U-turn
across a grass strip dividing the highway,
and headed us back in the direction we'd
just come.

"Where are we going now?" I asked.

"Back to get Kristoff. They must have
him. The place was swarming with them
when I arrived."

Fear rolled through me, leaving my hands
clammy. *Kristoff? Please answer me!*

Silence hung heavily in my head.

"He's still not answering," I said, nausea leaving me weak and shaking.

"We'll find him," Alec said, his jaw tight. He glanced in the rearview mirror. "We were not followed. With luck, they will still be searching my house and will not have removed him yet."

"I'm seriously confused, here," I said, touching the lump on the side of my head again. "Are you on our side? Or are you yanking my chain? Because, so help me God, Alec, if you've done something to Kristoff —"

"We have devoted ourselves, both of us, to defeating the reapers," he said grimly, his face set. "Such acts require much self-sacrifice, and at times have left us both in positions where we were close to destruction. I have saved his life a number of times. Do you seriously believe me capable of betraying him to the reapers? Or perhaps you think I am so desperate that I am willing to take another man's Beloved?"

Shame filled me at his accusation. "No, I don't think that of you. And I apologize for what I said. It's just that you disappeared so completely, and no one knew where you were or what happened to you. And then the vampires all seemed to lose their minds and accused him of the stupidest things ever. Alec, I have to know — did you set up Kristoff?"

He shot me a startled glance. "Set him up how?"

"Make it look like he embezzled a bunch of money, and had something to do with your disappearance, and killed Anniki."

"Oh." He looked almost amused. "No, I did not arrange for that."

"Then where did you go?"

He was silent for a moment, the streetlights as we passed under them checkering his face and making it almost impossible to read his expression. "I have been working."

"Working how? For the reapers?"

The look he gave me was pure scorn.

"Sorry. Working for whom, then?"

"I have been attempting to uncover a connection between one of the reapers and a Dark One."

"The mole, you mean?"

"You know about that?"

"Kristoff told me."

He made a face. "I should have guessed."

"I knew it!" I sat up a little straighter in the seat, ignoring the brief throb of pain in my head as pieces of the puzzle slid together. "You're pretending to be a friend of the reapers in order to find out who the mole is, aren't you?"

His smile was wry and brief. "It appears I have underestimated you. Yes, I have infiltrated the reaper organization. They believe me to be a friend."

"Oh, I can't wait to tell Kristoff!" At the mention of his name my spirits plummeted. "Assuming I can. Why did the Brotherhood go to your house?"

"I suspect that someone tipped them off to your arrival."

"That's impossible," I said, gnawing on my lower lip, stretching out my senses to find Kristoff. There was nothing but a cold abyss, empty of all warmth and sensation, that was the man with whom I was now wholly and irreversibly in love. "No one knew we were coming here but Raymond, Magda, Kristoff, and me."

"Someone must have known," he insisted, making a run off the highway and sending us speeding through the night up a winding street that I recognized.

I thought briefly of the phone calls Kristoff had made, ostensibly to friends. What if one of his buddies was the mole? What if one of them had told the Brotherhood where to find us? Had they had time to badly hurt Kristoff, or was he not answering me in a misguided attempt to protect me? "Do you think he's OK?"

"We'll know in a few minutes," he answered, and I shivered at the grim note in his voice.

There was no car in front of his house. A sudden spurt of worry hit me. "Magda and Raymond! They were here, too!"

Alec frowned for a moment.

"You remember Magda, don't you? She was with me on the tour in Iceland."

"Ah, yes. Spanish, black eyes, large . . ." He gestured toward his chest.

"No bigger than mine, thank you," I said, crossing my arms. "She and her boyfriend, Raymond, were helping us."

"They are mortals, and of no concern to the reapers," he said, surprising me by driving past his house and turning into the drive of a neighboring house. "They were probably sent on their way."

"I hope so. I don't think I could stand having any more innocent people's blood, metaphorical or otherwise, on my hands. What are we doing here?"

He stopped the car and got out, gesturing for me to follow. "There is a back way into my house, via the attic."

There was a narrow, mostly invisible break in the hedge that served as a fence around his property, and between him and his neighbors. I squeezed through the break, spitting out bits of yew leaves that poked into my mouth, following silently as Alec sneaked through the garden, past a small, dark guesthouse.

"Wait here," he whispered, pushing me against a tree trunk while he crept up to one of the windows of the guesthouse. He returned a moment later, gesturing again for me to follow. We slipped past an empty pool, the water rippling gently in the evening breeze, lit from below to make the pool a glowing teal beacon that had nothing on the clarity that was Kristoff's eyes.

"Can you climb?" Alec asked in a hushed voice as he stopped next to a large split-trunked tree.

I looked upward to where the tree's branches lay against the roof of the house. Normally, I wouldn't consider such a thing, but Kristoff's life was at stake. "I'll manage," I told him.

By the time I struggled from the leafy and branch-riddled embrace of the tree and through a window into a dark, close attic, I had come to the conclusion that climbing a tree in any apparel was hazardous, but doing so in a gauzy sundress meant to entice one particular man into a frenzy was definitely not a smart idea. More than once Alec had been forced to climb down to detach me from some particularly trouble-some branch, ultimately being forced to rip the material free.

"Note to self: Next time pack tree-climbing clothes, preferably something in the non-tear nylon family," I said as I got up from where I'd landed on the attic floor. Through the thin light streaming in from the outside house lights, I could see that the front of my dress was smudged with dirt, little leaves and twigs clinging to bits of torn fabric, long, wrinkled tears leaving the bodice more a memory than an actual garment. A faint breeze on my backside told me that the skirt was likely to be in the same condition.

"I would say you look charming, but I doubt if you would appreciate my approval of your underwear," Alec said, his eyes on the exposed portion of my bra. "This way. I feel their presence in my house, so we must go very cautiously." He started to edge his way around the boxes and discarded furniture that littered his attic, pausing a moment at the door to mutter, "That is odd. I feel . . . Hmm."

"Feel what?" I whispered as he silently opened a trapdoor in the floor, sticking his head out to examine the hallway below before he got to his feet. There was a fold-out set of narrow steps that must have been very well oiled, for he lowered them without a sound.

"Feel the presence of people I had not expected. Unfortunately, I can't tell how near they are. Come. We must be silent now."

I followed him as quietly as possible as he crept slowly down the hallway. The upper floor was dark, but lights shone up from below. I picked off twigs and leaves and a couple of bugs as we headed to the main stairs. Alec held up a hand to stop me. I stayed against the wall as he slid along it to the stairs, peeking over the edge to the floor below.

He stood up suddenly and, with an inexplicable smile at me, ran down to the floor below. I stood stunned for a moment, then followed.

I made it to the bottom of the stairs before I realized what it was that had Alec so amused. Four men and two women were arranged in various poses of bondage on the huge living room floor. The women had been propped up more or less upright, their hands bound behind them, their feet tied, with duct tape across their mouths. Two men were prone on the floor, blood around them indicating that they had been injured, although they, too, had been bound. The other two leaned drunkenly against each other, their eyes spitting fury as I slowly entered the bizarre scene.

But what had me coming to a complete halt was the sight of the two men lounging on the couch.

"Took you long enough to get back," Andreas said, looking up from where he was examining his fingernail.

Rowan, who had his feet resting on one of the prone men, stopped flipping through a magazine to glance up. "You found her, I see. We figured you must have her, since they didn't."

"Yes, and you might have told me you two were in town," Alec said, strolling over to the two men. He squatted next to them and eyed them carefully. "It would have saved me a great deal of trouble. Where is he?"

"Kristoff?" Andreas nodded his head toward me. "He's over there."

I spun around and almost choked with horror. Kristoff lay on a small honey-colored couch that sat under a huge mural of the ocean, one arm hanging lifelessly off the edge.

"You bastards!" I shrieked, running across the room to where he lay. "What have you done to him?"

"I like that," Rowan said, nudging one of the guys on the floor as he raised his head. "Did you hear her? She called us bastards."

My horror turned to sheer terror as I realized the pattern on the floor was due to blood, not the design of the carpet. "Oh, my God, you've killed him! I swear by all that is holy that you will all pay for this. I will not rest one single second until you've suffered the way you've made my poor Kristoff suffer."

I collapsed on Kristoff, sobbing into his chest as I clutched his lifeless body, my mind swimming with endless agony that threatened to burst from me in a blinding, searing light.

"Ah, nothing is sweeter than the sight of a Beloved reunited with her love," Andreas said, his voice mocking the depth of despair that filled me.

Rage unlike anything I'd felt before washed over me. I lifted my face from the empty shell that was Kristoff and focused my gaze on his brother. "You think it's sweet, do you? Let's see how sweet you think this Beloved is when she's through roasting you alive, you bastard brother killer!"

"Pia, stop," a voice murmured in my ear.

"Ooh, someone's in trouble," Rowan said

archly, pushing over the reaper on the floor.

"You're second," I told him, focusing my attention on him until light rained down from above. He yelped and leaped to the side, bouncing on the couch as he patted wildly at the sparkles of light remaining on his clothing.

"Beloved, you're pulling out my hair."

Alec crossed the room, giving the two men an irritated glance. "Mind the sofa. That's Italian leather, and it didn't come cheap."

"You're third," I growled, slamming down a wall of light between Alec and the doorway through which he was obviously about to go. "Don't give me that look, Alec. I'm sure you think I'm the worst sort of idiot for falling for your innocence act, but I assure you —"

"If you're through with my ear, I wouldn't mind if you released it. I've lost all feeling in it now."

"I assure you that I . . . I . . ." I looked down. I had been clutching Kristoff's head to my bosom as I swore eternal vengeance for his death, but somehow he'd shifted so that the fingers of one hand were gripping his hair, my other hand grasping his ear.

Eyes brighter than any gem regarded me.

"Boo?" I asked, my heart doing a backflip or two.

His face twisted into a momentary grimace as a muffled laugh, followed by, "Did she just call him 'Boo'?" made its way from the vampires. "Would you mind releasing my ear?"

I stared in stupefaction at my fingers closed around his ear. It was turning white. "But . . . you're dead."

"Not quite. Nearly, but not quite," Rowan said, vaulting the recumbent reapers as he strolled over to us. He hesitated a moment. "If I touch you, will you rain light on me again?"

"Eh?" I said, my brain finally catching up with my heart.

He gently took me by the arms and pulled me off of Kristoff. "When we found him, the reapers were in the act of hacking off his head. But he's always been a fast healer."

Kristoff sat up, rubbing first his ear, then his throat. I was aghast to see a nasty, jagged-looking welt that wrapped around the front, disappearing into his collar. "It no doubt looked worse than it really was. You could have arrived a bit earlier, however."

"Traffic," Andreas said with a shrug.

"You're not . . ." I looked from Kristoff to Rowan, who had released me, and beyond him to where Alec leaned against the wall, an odd expression on his face. Andreas got to his feet and picked his way across the bodies, stopping to peer at his brother's neck.

"You'll do," he said finally with a nod.

"You guys didn't . . ." I looked back at Kristoff. "What the hell?"

He sighed and opened his arms, grunting when I threw myself into them, clutching him and kissing every part of him my mouth could reach, babbling the whole time about all my confusion and horror and love.

It took a good ten minutes to work all of that out of my system. Kristoff just held me the whole time, stroking my back and suffering me to examine him to make sure he wasn't still in some way harmed.

"They almost cut your head off," I said, pulling down the back of his collar to look at the vile scar that remained. It was still thick, red, and ugly, but was fading with each passing moment.

" 'Almost' being the key word," he said.

I spun around, glaring at the people who lay on the floor. The vampires had pulled the two women up onto the couch. "Those . . . scum! Those evil, detestable, repulsive scum!"

The men twitched violently as I stalked toward them slowly, my hands fisted, pulling down light from the moon, which even now glowed gently above the treetops.

"I had no idea your Beloved was so blood-thirsty," Rowan said. "Are her eyes glowing?"

"Beloved, this is not —" Kristoff started to say.

"Which one did it?" I interrupted. "Which one held the knife?"

"It was a sword, actually," Rowan said, gesturing toward the man nearest me.

I slammed down a ball of light smack-dab on the man's groin. He screamed through the duct tape, his body curling into a fetal ball.

"Ooh." Rowan winced, neatly sidestepping the twitching body. "He won't be having children now."

"There's a lot more he's not going to be having by the time I get through with him," I said, stepping forward with dire intent.

Kristoff caught me around the waist and pulled me back. "No, Beloved."

"Just let me smite them, Kristoff. They all deserve it! You can't deny they deserve it," I said, squirming in his grip.

"I don't, but not this way. You are too sensitive. You will hate yourself once you've recovered from your scare, and hate me for letting you do this."

"One little smiting, that's all I ask," I said, struggling. "Just that one, just Sword Boy there."

"I think 'boy' is going to be a moot term," Andreas said, watching the reaper as he rolled around the floor.

"No," Kristoff said firmly, his frown deepening into a scowl as he suddenly pushed me to arm's length, his gaze raking me up and down. "What the hell are you wearing, woman?"

"Pia had a little contretemps with the tree while climbing into the attic," Alec explained as I hastily tried to cover all my exposed parts.

"Why did you enter that way?" Rowan asked.

Alec gave a little shrug. "I had no idea you two had arrived. My first thought was to protect Pia."

"Are you going to just stand there letting them ogle you?" Kristoff demanded of me, his eyes dark as the sea in a storm.

"Nobody's ogling me," I said, giving him a look.

Kristoff glared over my shoulder. I turned to see his brother and cousin both considering me with their heads tipped identically to the side.

"Nice legs," Rowan said.

"And ass," Andreas added. "Is that some-thing sticking out of the top of her pant-ies?"

Kristoff growled. I *eep*ed, clutched at both the tattered remains of my skirt and Alec's reaper journal, and looked wildly around the room for a blanket.

Alec sighed and detached himself from the wall. "Upstairs, second room on the right. There should be some women's things —"

I was off before he finished.

The clothing I found in a guest room closet wasn't in my size, and the only skirt I could fit into was too tight to be comfort-able. I raided the room Kristoff had said was Alec's, finally making my way down-stairs in a pair of silk lounging pants that were a bit snug around the hips, and a worn T-shirt that was also a bit tight. Retrieving my purse from where it had fallen before I fell down the stairs, I put the journal in it and took a moment to comb the twigs out of my hair.

"I have several questions, and I'd like them all answered," I announced as I finally descended the stairs into the living room. "First of all, where are Magda and Ray-mond?"

Kristoff eyed my unorthodox outfit. *That*

was the best you could find?

Don't be impertinent.

"A couple of the reapers were trying to scare them when we arrived. We scared them, instead," Andreas said with a pointed smile at the woman sitting nearest him.

Her eyes narrowed with spite.

"Your friends left. We thought it would be best if they were not in the way," Rowan explained.

"OK. They must have gone to find the hotel we were going to head to after this. I'll call later. Next question — what on earth are you two doing here, evidently rescuing Kristoff, when you were utter and complete bastards, betraying him in Vienna?"

"She likes that word 'bastard,' doesn't she?" Rowan asked Andreas.

"I suppose it's understandable, given her point of view," he answered.

"Boo?" I asked, pinning Kristoff with a gimlet eye.

He sighed as the two men snickered, gesturing me to a chair. I sat, but crossed my arms.

You just had to use that name in front of them, didn't you? They'll never let me hear the end of it.

You'll survive. Answer my question.

"They didn't betray me," he said, jumping to the side when one of the reapers got his legs around a glass coffee table and sent it tumbling toward Kristoff.

Andreas and Rowan hauled the reaper up onto the chair opposite me. I singed his toes.

"Beloved . . ."

"I'm stopping, I'm stopping. Go on."

Kristoff looked helplessly at his brother and the other two vampires. "I could use a little help."

"Oh, no," Alec said, gesturing toward me. "She's your Beloved. You can explain the pact to her."

"Pact? What pact would that be?" I asked, narrowing my eyes at the man who filled my every waking thought.

Kristoff smiled smugly in my mind.

And right now those thoughts lie heavily in the "what's going to happen if you don't stop stalling and start spilling" arena.

Kristoff glanced at the reapers, then over to Alec. "Do you mind storing them elsewhere?"

"Not at all," Alec answered, making a fancy little bow. "Might I suggest the cellar?"

It took them a few minutes to haul all the reapers downstairs. Judging by muffled thumps, I believe a couple of them were dropped on the way, but I didn't feel too bad on their account. They had come close to killing Kristoff, and probably would have harmed Magda and Raymond if the vampires hadn't stopped them.

"Proceed," I said when they had all trooped upstairs to where I sat.

"It started about fourteen months ago." Kristoff sat next to me, frowning at the tight T-shirt. "If you recall, I told you that it had become clear someone was passing information to the reapers."

"The mole," I said, nodding, my hand on his leg. Just feeling him so warm and solid next to me made me relax.

"The council tried for several months to pinpoint the leak, but was unable to. The mole knew they were looking for him, and the flow of information was temporarily halted. We eventually decided to take matters into our own hands. We decided that if one of us was marked as the traitor, it would allow the real one to relax his guard and go back to passing information."

"So you set it up to make it look like you were the traitor?" My fingers tightened on his leg. "Why you?"

Kristoff shrugged, his fingers absently toying with the tendrils of hair that had escaped from my ponytail. "Luck of the draw. It took some time, but we eventually arranged it so that the council, presented with the evidence, had no choice but to imprison me."

"But one of the charges had to do with Anniki." A horrible thought occurred to me.

"No," Kristoff said quickly. "We did not kill her. But we incorporated the mystery of her death into our plans, as we did the captive reapers. Alec went to ground, ostensibly a victim of my heinous plan, but actually to mislead the real traitor."

"So all that trying to find Alec was an act?" I asked, prepared to be annoyed by his pretense.

Alec made a face as Kristoff answered. "Not all of it. Alec disappeared as planned, but then he went completely out of contact, which was not what we intended. We really were trying to trace him, just not from the time he left Iceland, which you believed."

"It was too dangerous for me to make contact," Alec explained. "I was being watched, and suspicions were already high as to my true intentions. I knew that sooner or later our paths would cross again."

"It was very convincing," I said, giving Kristoff a little frown.

He shrugged. "It had to be. Rowan and Andreas had to appear to support the council, although Andreas couldn't quite bring himself to condemn me as easily as did Rowan."

"He was never a good actor," Rowan said, nodding toward Andreas. "I was much more convincing. I thought you were going to spit at me once or twice."

"You're damned lucky I didn't," I told him before turning back to Kristoff. "OK, I got that. You guys set up this whole big thing to flush out the mole. I'm a bit pissed that you didn't bother to tell me about it, though."

Kristoff's fingers were warm on the back of my neck. "Our plans were set into motion long before I met you, Beloved. I had no idea if you could continue to carry out your role if you knew the truth."

Relief filled me. *So that was your deep, dark secret.*

My what? He was startled, a wary feeling in his mind.

The big secret I could feel you keeping from me. The dark place in your mind, the one you always keep me from seeing. I have to admit that I'm relieved that this is what you were keeping from me, and not something a lot more . . . well, scary. I was worried.

He said nothing for a moment. No doubt he was embarrassed about the fact that I knew he was keeping something from me. It didn't matter, I told myself. We hadn't known each other long at all, and although I would have preferred Kristoff feeling as if he could trust me, I understood that he was reticent to share such involved plans until he was more comfortable with our relationship.

Don't worry, Boo. I'm not going to yell at you for not trusting me. I understand. I'm just glad that this is now out in the open. "I assume those couple of unnamed friends you kept calling were Andreas and Rowan?"

Kristoff nodded. *Pia —*

Don't apologize. Or rather, don't do it now. You can do so later, with some massage oil, perhaps. You like lemon? "I take it that you knew that Alec was pretending to be the Ilargi all along, then?"

"No." He glanced over to his friend. "That took me by surprise, as well. I had no idea that Alec had anything to do with the reapers."

"I told you I'd find a way to infiltrate them," Alec told him.

"I thought you meant to do so by the woman."

"What woman?" I asked.

"A reaper, a woman I'd met a few years ago. She proved difficult," Alec said, dismissing the subject. "I found another one, a secretary who had just joined and knew little about them. She was most informative."

"So you found a way into the reaper headquarters?" Rowan asked, suddenly interested.

Alec nodded. "I myself couldn't go inside — there were too many high-ranking reapers there who would have known me for what I am — but I did discover a way we can bypass the security."

I looked from him to Kristoff. "I hate to sound like a party pooper, but now that we found you, Alec, we don't need to break in. It's not likely your mole is going to be there, after all."

"There is still the matter of the director to be dealt with," Kristoff said, taking my hand.

I tried to pull it away. His fingers tightened.

"I am not going to be party to wholesale murder for the sake of . . . well, I don't even know what that would be, since there is no earthly reason you can have other than revenge for wanting to go after Frederic," I told him.

"There are a number of compelling reasons why we should do just that," he argued.

"Oh, yeah? Name one that doesn't involve you guys wanting to get even."

Kristoff opened his mouth, looked askance for a moment, then cast a pleading glance at his brother and cousin.

"Huh? *Huh?*" I looked at them as well.

"Well, there's . . ." Andreas stopped, his face screwing up as he thought. "There's . . . er . . ."

"I thought so."

"He poses a threat," Rowan said suddenly. The other two vampires nodded eagerly.

"A very big threat," Andreas added.

"To whom? Other than in general to you vampires, I mean."

"To Kristoff," Rowan said, pointing.

Kristoff looked as surprised as I felt.

"He doesn't even know Kristoff!" I protested. "Well, hardly knows him. He did imprison him, and tried to kill him after he couldn't make me do the job for him, but that was two months ago, and I'm sure by now he's forgotten all about Kristoff."

"Thank you," the love of my life said dryly.

You know what I mean, Boo. Besides, so long as I remember you, you have nothing to complain about, I said, blowing him a mental kiss.

His fingers tightened around mine.

"No other suggestions before I rest my case?" I asked the threesome.

The gentle whoosh of air from the air

conditioner was the only sound for a moment.

"I hate to destroy any illusions you might possess regarding the director, Pia, but I'm afraid there is one very compelling reason for us to confront him and the other reapers." Alec stood in the doorway, leaning against it with a mildly interested expression, as if he was somewhat bored.

"What would that be?" I asked.

He smiled. "You."

"Me? I don't stand in the way of anything Frederic wants."

"You are a Zorya and a Beloved. Surely you've been in the Brotherhood long enough to know how vehement they are about anything to do with us. In their eyes, you are an abomination, tainted by your relationship to Kristoff, a contradiction to everything sacred. You must, at all costs, be destroyed before you can contaminate anyone else."

I stared at him, my jaw slack, for a moment or two. "But . . . the reapers offered me a deal. They're going to execrate me once I get Ulfur."

The look he gave me was pitying. I leaned into Kristoff, needing comfort. "It says much about your purity of character that you believed what the reapers told you, but unfortunately, we know them of old. They will not honor their agreement with you."

Kristoff?

I'm afraid he's right, he said slowly.

You knew this? I asked, astonished.

I suspected that the deal the reapers made with you would not be honored, yes. But I did not know for certain, and since you wanted above all things to no longer be a Zorya, it seemed worthwhile to pursue.

You might have mentioned your suspicions to me, you know. I'm a big girl, Kristoff. I can take a little adversity.

I had no proof either way.

"I'm sorry, but a vaguely could-be-possible threat still isn't enough," I said after thinking about the matter, as well as making a mental note to have a long talk with Kristoff about my relationship expectations. Incredibly handsome and mouthwateringly sexy he might be, but he had a lot to learn about relationships. "I realize I can't stop you guys, but you won't get any help from me. My job now is to find Ulfur. The trail for the Ilargi may have run into a dead end, but I'm not giving up."

"Excellent," Alec said, striding into the center of the room, his eyes twinkling with enjoyment. "Then we can count on your assistance after all."

"Huh? I just said —"

"You said you were going to find the Ilargi. Well, my fair little Zorya, that trail ends with the director." His smile grew wider as I stared at him in incomprehension. "Oh, didn't I tell you? Frederic Robert knows who the Ilargi is."

CHAPTER 14

"So he just dropped that bombshell on you, and then went to bed?"

Magda and Raymond were seated in the chairs around a small round table in one corner of the hotel room, rapt expressions on both their faces.

"Well, it wasn't quite that quick, but yes, basically, he said he believed that Frederic knew who the Ilargi was, and was tolerating him because he eliminated the need for Zoryas."

"I'm not sure I understand your explanation of why this director fellow is doing what you say he's doing," Raymond said, his brows pulled together as he tried to puzzle out everything.

"You would not be alone in that," Kristoff said as he passed me. He was pacing the room, his face abstracted with thought, obviously thinking about the plan for the following day.

I sat on the bed, leaning against the headboard. I badly wanted to get Kristoff next to me, but knew full well that I wouldn't be able to stop touching him should I do so. I closed my eyes for a moment, the faint scent of him teasing my nose, stirring the craving I had to taste him, to feel his tongue sliding along mine, to run my fingers along the smooth, silky lines of his back and chest, to caress the muscles that lay so heavily under his skin, begging for touches and kisses and long, loving strokes of my tongue.

If you truly want me to bed you right here and now, continue with those thoughts. Particularly the one involving your tongue.

I sat upright, blinking. *Sorry. Got a little carried away there. I didn't mean for you to overhear that. Just ignore it.*

Ignore it? Ignore it? Woman, just being near you leaves me hard. I'm getting used to having a perpetual erection, but you don't have to make things worse by indulging in fantasies that almost drive me insane with need.

I said I was sorry, I answered with a little smile to myself.

"Pia?"

"Hmm?" With an effort, I dragged my mind from the contemplation of Kristoff's erection to the subject at hand.

The day my penis ceases to be the subject at hand is the day I give up living.

"Oh, sorry. Um. Oh, Frederic."

I giggled into Kristoff's mind and tried to look thoughtful, and not in the least bit like someone who was remembering that she owed the man she loved a blow job that would knock his socks off.

That's it! Kristoff marched into the bathroom and slammed shut the door.

Magda looked in surprise at the door. "What's wrong with him?"

"Er . . . nothing. He's just a bit distracted."

For which I have you to thank!

Hush. Go dip Sparky into some cold water so we can talk about what to do.

"Why doesn't he want Zoryas to be around?" Raymond asked. "The director, that is."

"He does, but only doing his bidding, not messing with something useful, like doing their original job."

"Oh." He thought about that for a moment. "I suppose that makes sense. Kind of."

"It does to me," Magda said, stretching as she smothered a yawn. "I'm just glad you guys got out of that all right. I was about to call in the police when the vampires showed up. I tell you, Pia, those reapers are just downright nasty. Ray and I ran off to get help the second we spotted the first one, but we got separated, and the reapers who grabbed me were saying all sorts of things about me having been dirtied by you and that I needed cleansing. Who knows what they might have done if your vampires hadn't shown up?"

"Only one of them is mine, and I had no idea about the others, because someone didn't tell me his super-secret plan, but that's a lecture for another day."

"Mm-hmm." Magda yawned again.

Raymond stood up. "We should get to bed, sweetheart. Sounds like tomorrow is going to be a very big day."

I slid off the bed and accompanied them to the door. "I know you said you wouldn't miss it, but this plan the vampires have is likely to be dangerous. It probably would be best —"

Magda snorted loudly, giving me a quick hug to take the sting out of the gesture. "Don't be silly. We're in this for the long haul, aren't we, punkin?"

"Oh, definitely. Only . . . well, don't you think that we need some equipment?" Raymond asked, frowning.

"What kind of equipment?" Magda asked.

"Oh, I don't know," he said, waving his

hands in a vague gesture. "High-tech stuff. You know, the sort people use to break into places. Detectors and scanners and things like that. The sort of stuff Tom Cruise would have if he were going to do the job."

Another one who watches too much television and movies. Kristoff sighed into my mind. *Is that all you mortals do? Do none of you read anymore?*

Stop eavesdropping. I'm not a radio receiver. And for the record, I have more overdue library books than anyone in my town.

"Come on, sugar pants. Let's go back to our room. I'll hum the *Mission: Impossible* theme for you while you stealth your way into bed."

The sound of Raymond's laughter trailed after them as they left.

I closed the door, leaning against it to look at Kristoff as he emerged from the bathroom. "Alone at last, I guess."

He didn't waste any time. One moment he was standing across the room; the next he was smooshing me up against the door.

"You will take off that ridiculous outfit now," he demanded, his eyes the color of lapis lazuli.

I wriggled against him, breathing in the wonderful scent that coiled around me. I tried once again to pinpoint what it was, but decided it was just Kristoff, and nothing more. "I don't know whether to be flattered that you think other men are going to ogle the amplitude that is me, or amused that you're jealous. I think I'll go with both. But before I take off my clothes and let you feed — and don't deny you need blood, because even if I couldn't feel the hunger gnawing inside you, the state of Alec's floor made it quite clear you lost a lot of blood — before I do that, I have something I want to say to you."

His lips thinned slightly. "You wish to berate me for not telling you about the pact."

"No. Well, yes, but I've moved past that," I said as I kissed the cleft in his chin before leaning into his mouth, whispering on his lips, "I love you, Kristoff. I love you passionately, happily, wholly, wonderfully. I love you despite the fact that you didn't tell me about the pact or share your concerns about Frederic. I love you even though you wouldn't haven chosen me to be your Beloved."

He started to protest. I put my fingers across his lips.

"I love you now, I'll love you half an hour from now, and, assuming I really am immortal, I'll love you a hundred years from now. Nothing will change that."

He hesitated a moment before his arms went around me, pulling my hips close to his as his mouth took charge of the little nibbling kisses I was scattering along his lips. I gave myself up to the pleasure he stirred within me, but one part of me, one tiny part of my heart, wept at his hesitation.

I could feel the emotion in him, and knew it had to be regret that he couldn't love me in return.

"Never say I would not have chosen you," he murmured into my collarbone, his lips blazing a path that left me shivering with anticipation. "You are everything a Beloved should be."

"Too much talking," I said, touched by his sweetness, and aroused at the same time, gasping when he hit the spot behind my ear that always melted me. I yanked up the tail of his shirt, sliding my hands under the fluid material to stroke his equally silky skin.

He stopped for a moment to help me rid him of his shirt before his hands returned to yank off the T-shirt, his hands immediately returning to cup my now highly sensitized breasts. I bit the heavy muscles of his shoulder, licking away the sting. *I've got no complaints about you, either. I'm another story, but you're fine.*

I do not find you anything but delectable — he started to say.

I know, I know. You like me. I appreciate that fact. But you're so incredibly handsome, Kristoff. Women stop and look at you when you walk by. I know; I've seen them. I can't help but feel that you deserve to be seen with someone who isn't quite so pudgy. Not that I'm going to give you up, but I still can't help but feel that way.

Now you have angered me, he said, and I could feel the truth behind the statement. *I deserve* you, *woman. Now stop being insecure and tell me you love me again.*

I love you — oh, dear God, yes, right there. I quivered for a moment in his arms as his mouth descended on a now bare breast, the sensation of his tongue and teeth and lips on such sensitive flesh radiating outward until I was one gigantic erogenous zone. *I'm not insecure. I'm just a realist. Oh, and stop.*

He pulled back, his eyes dark with passion, but also containing a distinctly wild look. *Stop? Now? Right now? Or later, after we're finished? I will stop later, if you like. Later is better.*

I grinned and pointed to the bed. "Stop for a moment, Boo. Take off your pants and lie down."

He narrowed his eyes. "You're not going to try to get the upper hand on me again, are you?"

"Oh, this hand is definitely upper," I answered, raising my hand before pointing to the bed again. "And you owe me. You had it your own way in the Blue Lagoon, and now I get to have my turn."

"You liked my way," he pointed out, but shucked the remainder of his clothing.

"Of course I did. Didn't you notice me walking funny? But now it's your turn, and I intend to return the compliment. Bed, please. And close your eyes."

He lay down on the bed, his arms behind his head, those lovely teal eyes of his now a glittering, rich indigo. He frowned as I started to slip out of the pants but then paused, glancing toward him.

"You're not going to start that again, are you?"

"I'm not insecure, but I might have one teensy, tiny issue with being naked," I told him, quickly removing the pants, but clutching them in front of me so he couldn't see all the bulgy parts.

"That's an understatement."

"Fine, then. It won't be nearly as much fun if you insist on keeping your eyes open, but have it your way. Turn off the light."

"No."

"Kristoff —" I started to say, but he interrupted me, sitting up on the bed.

"I want to see you."

"And I don't want you to see me. There's far too much to be seen, and frankly, I'd rather not spend the rest of eternity dieting because you want to stand around and look at my pudge."

"I'm sitting, not standing, and I like looking at you."

I clutched the pants tighter, frowning at the absurdity of the situation. "You can't look at me until I've dropped at least two dress sizes. Possibly three."

"I've seen you already," he pointed out, a hint of a smile on his lips. I was distracted for a moment by those lips, but managed to pull my mind back in the nick of time.

"Only briefly, and only because I wanted to see if you were going to run screaming from the room at the sight of my overabundance."

He rolled his eyes. "I know you don't wish to hear about my past relationships with women, but you might be interested to know that the first woman I slept with was shaped just as you're shaped. She was delicious in every way, and I lusted after her from the time my voice changed until the day I was married."

I blinked at him, not sure what to say to that. "You lusted after a fat lady?"

"No. I lusted after a wonderfully voluptuous woman, one whose curves tempted me into exploring them, a woman whose silky skin beckoned my mouth to taste the delights that only she could offer. I worshiped the breasts that were made for my hands only, paid homage to the sublime beauty of her hips and belly, and would have given up my most prized possession to caress her shapely, enticing thighs."

"Oh, wow," I breathed, my entire body tingling at the words. "Who was she?"

"The woman I lusted after all those hundreds of years ago? The wife of the lord who ruled my mother's town," he said, his eyes molten with desire.

I swallowed, my throat tight with yearning. "Lucky lady."

"The woman I was describing, however, is you." He leaned forward. "You make the lord's wife pale by comparison, Pia. The body you view as unattractive leaves me breathless with desire. The curves you dislike drive me insane with the need to touch and taste them. The softness you deplore leaves me wild with a carnal desire to bite you."

My mouth dropped open for a moment as I looked down at myself. "I know you're hungry, but —"

"Not that sort of bite," he said, an excitingly wolfish look in his eyes as he crawled across the bed toward me. "I do not need to see you to want to feed from you. But when I see your body, see those delicious curves beckon and entice me, when I feel your softness pressed against me, welcoming me, it makes me want to bite. I want to mark you as mine so that all other males will know they cannot have you. I want to possess you, Pia, in the most primitive and profound way a male can possess a female. I want to mate with you. I want to make love to you. I want you for my own, my woman, the other half of me. Would you truly deny me that pleasure?"

He had been pouring into my brain all the images and sensations and emotions that followed his words, primitive emotions, as he warned, possessive and dominating and at the same time protective, all of which swirled in and around me, leaving me keyed up like a bomb about to explode. "God, no!" I yelled, and threw the pants at the chair, all but ripping off my underwear as I flung myself onto him.

He caught me in a tangle of arms and legs

and breasts and a hard, hot penis that pressed against me as I squirmed on him, trying to kiss and caress and lick every spot of him I could reach, all while he did the same.

What followed wasn't the controlled love-making I had planned, with just enough oral sex to drive him insane, then a long, slow loving. No, this was primal and earthy, a meeting of flesh and a merging of souls, a frenzied mating of two people who knew beyond all doubt that they were intended to be together. Wild and unmindful of all inhibitions, I threw caution to the wind, and tasted and touched and licked, and allowed him to do the same. He probed and teased and tormented until I was writhing with ecstasy, trying to reciprocate, needing to drive him just as hard and furious as he was driving me.

By the time he lifted me over his poised erection, I was almost sobbing with the joy of the moment, my body singing as he plunged me downward, my muscles rippling around the hard brand of his penis as it invaded my depths, his hips thrusting it deeper than anyone had been before. He pulled me down to his chest as he bucked upward, his teeth piercing the flesh of my breast as an orgasm swept over me, catching me in its breathless grip and spiraling me out of control. His voice sounded hoarsely in my ears as he gave in to his own climax, his experience merging with mine, sending us both flying.

As I lay on his damp, panting body, one thought emerged in my rapture-numbed mind: No matter what Angelica had been to him, I knew with absolute certainty that she had never given him the ecstasy that he found in my arms.

I drifted off to sleep comforted by that idea, which was tainted only by the nagging, growing conviction that it would not be enough.

CHAPTER 15

"How long do we have to wait?"

Kristoff glanced at his watch before answering Magda. "They should be here any minute."

"You're sure they wanted to meet us here?" I asked, glancing around us. All four of us were sitting together at an outdoor café table shaded by gently swaying palm trees and exotic shrubs, surrounded on three sides by very upscale shops that hadn't yet opened.

Across the street, an innocuous building was the focus of our collective attention. It looked like the offices of some financial bigwig, with tall, tinted windows, a lot of chrome, and pale cream stone siding. On the door was a discreet sign that bore the name of the organization, along with the symbol of a crescent moon. Nothing about the building gave hint to the fact that inside it was the brains of a group that had done its best to systematically torture and murder vampires over the last five hundred years.

I shivered despite the midmorning heat.

"I'm sure." Kristoff's eyes never rested; they were constantly scanning the early-morning latte crowd as they strolled out of the café, window-shopping before eventually moving off to their respective destinations. The chatter of birds mingled with the low-level hum of conversation from various business types as they picked up their morning coffee, had a pastry, yakked with their Pilates partners, or any of the million other things people with ample free time and money did on a bright, sunny Wednesday morning.

You don't think we're too close to the building? I asked, a smidgen nervous. *What if some of the Brotherhood people get their coffee here?*

Andreas and Rowan would not have asked us to meet here if there were any danger. To be honest, I doubt if the director is allowing anyone entrance to the building.

I glanced over at it again. Although the building appeared perfectly normal, I had to admit there was an air of expectation, of subdued excitement in the air that I didn't wholly ascribe to our little group.

"I wish I'd had time to get a gun. Everyone

has guns in LA. Even the paperboys are armed," Raymond muttered.

"Don't pout, pookums. You got a Taser. That should work if someone tries to attack us."

I looked in surprise at Raymond. "You bought a Taser?"

He nodded, flipping open his jacket to show the inner pocket. A small black unit protruded an inch above the pocket. "And it's all juiced up, ready to go. It may not kill anyone, but it sure will stun the shit out of them."

"Nice," I said, doubtfully. "Er . . . we probably won't need it. I think three vampires and the three of us ought to be enough to take on the whole office."

"It can't hurt," Raymond pointed out.

"That's right. Besides, Kristoff is armed, isn't he?" Magda asked him.

"Kristoff has a knife," I said, giving in to the blush that followed the memory of me assisting him in the donning of his ankle sheath. A few hours earlier I had finally convinced him it was my turn to give him some attention. A little self-satisfied smile crept over my lips as I remembered his statement afterward that I had not only knocked his socks off; I'd lit his feet on fire, too.

"So we wait." Magda drummed her fingers on the table, watching absently as Ray double-checked his camera. "Wish I had something to read. I think I'll go see if they have any newspapers inside. Come with me, boopsie?"

"Certainly," Raymond said, magnanimously tucking away his electronic toy and following Magda as she reentered the café.

"That's what I forgot to ask you," I said, diving for my purse as Magda's words prodded my memory. "You can translate this for me."

Kristoff's eyebrows rose as I pulled out Alec's reaper notebook. Before I could offer it to him, he snatched it from my hands. "Where did you get that?"

I explained briefly how we'd found it. "But it's OK; you don't have to worry that Alec will be pissed because we swiped it — he knows I have it."

His eyebrows rose even higher. "He does?"

"Yes. In fact, he told me I'd find it interesting reading, and suggested that I have you translate it for me." I scooted my chair closer to him and opened the notebook up to the first page, pointing to the words I recognized. "It mentions you."

He froze for a moment, his muscles tense

and tight, as if he were going to pounce on it.

I glanced at him in surprise. "You don't have to read it if you feel weird about reading your friend's thoughts about you. At least, I assume that's what he's talking about in here. Did he meet you when you guys were both chasing reapers?"

"Yes," he said, but it was an afterthought. He stared down at the journal with a wooden expression for a moment; then slowly that melted into abstracted horror.

"What's it say?" I asked, peering over his arm at the text. "I don't read Latin. Is it something gruesome?"

Emotions swamped me, thick and hot, a sudden explosion that told me he'd been trying to keep them under control, anger chasing fear, followed by a deep, dark fury that had his fingers clenching around the book.

"Kristoff? What's the matter?" I asked, my skin crawling as the horrible emotions roiled around inside him. "Dear God, what does it say?"

"He was there," he managed to say, his accent more pronounced.

"Who was where? Alec? Where was he?"

He slammed closed the journal, unmindful of its age and delicate state. I flinched as his knuckles turned white, trying to make sense of the emotions that burst from him like lava, burning and searing everything in their path as they spilled out. "He was there at the beginning. At my beginning."

"At your birth? Is he an old friend of your family?" I asked, remembering that he had said Alec was something around eighty years older than Kristoff.

"No." His jaw worked for a few seconds.

"Then what . . . ?"

His eyes met mine, and I had to keep myself from flinching, so deadly were they. They were pale as an iceberg against snow, and the depth of the fury in them stripped the breath from my lungs. "He was there at my rebirth."

"Oh." Enlightenment dawned. "He was there when the vampire had you turned into one, too? He must have known him, then."

"He knew him." Kristoff's face twisted into an agonized sneer for a moment. "He knew him because he *was* him. Alec is the one who turned me, Pia. My old friend."

The last word was spit out with a venom that left me staring in horror. "Alec? You can't be serious —"

He leaped to his feet, snarling under his breath as he glared at the journal for a moment before shoving it at me. "Put that damned thing away."

Hurriedly, I shoved it in my purse, following him as he stalked off, heedless of the sunlight and what it would do to him if it caught him full in the face. "Kristoff, wait a minute! What about Magda and Raymond? Boo!"

He didn't stop; he just ran across the road, almost getting himself run down in the process. I waved an apology at the irate driver who was cursing him out as I dashed after him, confused, worried, and very, very angry at Alec.

That bastard had known what he was doing when he told me to have Kristoff translate the journal. He had to know what effect it would have. I made a few mental promises about introducing Alec to the wrath of a pissed-off Beloved as I followed Kristoff into a small, square building that sat behind the Brotherhood headquarters.

It was evidently some sort of a warehouse for paper products, huge pallets of plastic-wrapped bales of paper peppered around the nearly empty building. I trotted after Kristoff, whose long legs were making mincemeat of the distance, finally catching his hand. He didn't brush me off, but neither did his fingers stroke mine as they normally did.

"Where is he?" Kristoff bellowed, his voice echoing in a grotesque parody of his normally velvety smooth tones.

Andreas and Rowan were squatting, peering down at a square hole in the floor, a grate lying between them. It was obviously some sort of a plumbing or electrical access point to the guts of the building. They both glanced up in surprise as the last of the echo died away.

"I told you that we'd let you know once we were sure the way in is safe," Andreas said, getting to his feet. "Alec was just going to check that it was clear before we started."

"Alec is doing nothing of the kind," Kristoff said, his voice a snarl.

Rowan pursed his lips for a moment, glancing at the two brothers. "What's happened?"

"Alec gave me his reaper journal to read. Kristoff says that it proves that Alec is the one who made him into a vampire," I said quickly, tugging on Kristoff's hand. *Hello, remember me? I'm the woman who saved your soul. Stop thinking about decapitating Alec. Maybe there is a reason he did what he did.*

There is a reason, he answered, and for a moment a bleak despair filled him. He quickly pushed me out of his mind.

Both men stared at me as if I had turned into a particularly unbelievable form of kumquat.

"Alec did?" Rowan said at last, shaking his head. "You must have read it wrong. Let me see the journal."

I started to open my purse, but Kristoff grabbed my hand. "No," he snapped. "I did not misread it. Alec was there. He was responsible."

"Even if he was, there's nothing you can do about it now," I said with what I thought was a whole lot of reason. "Yes, it was nasty, and yes, you have the right to have some issues with him about it, but it really has no bearing on things now, does it? What's past is past. It's not like it's going to harm us in any way. Besides, we have bigger fish to fry."

The two men looked at Kristoff, neither of them saying anything while he struggled with his emotions.

Boo, I know it hurts. I know you feel betrayed. But really, this is not the time to be pissed at him. We need a solid force if we're going to tackle Frederic. Be-sides. I nudged his hand. *Maybe this was his way of atoning for the whole thing.*

Kristoff's gaze, which had been focused on the black hole before us, swiveled to meet mine. His eyes were still far too light for my happiness. "He is not atoning, Beloved. He is attacking. And I will not allow him to win. Too much is at stake."

He jumped down into the hole without another word.

"Well, so much for reason." I crouched down at the edge of the hole, grateful I'd chosen jeans to wear for the day's activities. I glanced up at the two men standing with identical surprised expressions on their faces. "Magda and Raymond are still at the café. Could one of you get them? It looks like Attack Plan Alpha is kicking into high gear a little early."

I didn't wait for their response, just swung my legs over the side and jumped, praying I wouldn't break a leg in the process.

Luckily, the drop was only a few feet down, the subterranean area obviously used by maintenance personnel. Dim yellow lights hung from the walls, buzzing dully in the closed, sour-smelling area. Kristoff was doubled over in the confined space, about thirty yards ahead of me, heading in the direction of the Brotherhood building.

By the time he stopped and I caught up to him, sweat was beading on my forehead, and I had a painful stitch in my side.

"Kristoff, we need to talk."

"No, we don't. Do not try to stop me,

Beloved. You have no idea what this means."

"Like hell I don't." I gasped, following him up a row of metal rungs that were embedded into a cement wall. To my intense relief, the ladder led up through another hole in the floor. I hoisted myself up, almost blind in the darkness, but I could tell from the vague black outlines visible by a faint strip of light that we must be in some sort of a storeroom.

Kristoff grabbed me under the arms, pulling me to my feet.

"Are we in the Brotherhood building?" I asked in a whisper.

He nodded. "Stay here while I look for reapers."

"Oh, no. Where goes my Dark One, so goes his Beloved," I said, grabbing on to the back of his jacket. "That's my new motto, anyway."

A noise behind me heralded the arrival of Andreas. His silhouette moved against the bulky shadows as he climbed out of the hole. "Rowan went to get the others. What do you think Alec is doing?"

"Just what he said he'd do," I said before Kristoff could answer. "He had no reason to do otherwise. The business in the journal is personal, and doesn't have anything to do with the mole you're trying to catch."

Don't be so certain of that, Kristoff thought at me.

I put his suspicions down to a normal response to the underhanded way Alec had revealed the truth, and pressed up against him when he opened the door a crack to look out.

"It's clear. The meeting room should be in the back."

"I just hope Alec knows what he's doing," I murmured, emerging from the room. "If we're wrong and there is a Zenith, she's going to view his being a decoy as the perfect opportunity to have a little vampire melting party."

"He knew the danger when he volunteered to be the one caught," Andreas said behind me.

The hallway was brightly lit, but devoid of Brotherhood folk. I glanced around, curious, as we passed a couple of closed doors, but despite my worst suspicions, no klaxons went off alerting people to our presence, and no one went screaming down the hallway yelling about vampires. There wasn't even a security camera tucked away in the corner of the hall. The only noise to be heard was our nearly silent footsteps, and the almost sibilant whoosh of air.

"Don't you think it's a little odd that there

aren't more guards around?" I whispered, the hairs on the back of my neck standing on end. "Or, rather, *any* guards?"

"If Alec has done his job, they will be swarming him," Andreas answered.

"Yes, but they'd also want to know where he came from, and be searching for any of us. You said there were a ton of Brotherhood people here, right?" I asked Kristoff.

"No. I said they were preparing for a battle. The two things are not the same," Kristoff said. "There are fewer reapers here than normal, but the ones who are here are higher in the organization. They are members of the governing board."

"Brought out the big guns, did Frederic?" I murmured.

As we approached a double door at the end of the hallway, Kristoff paused for a moment, his head tipped as he listened intently. I put my hand on his back, as much for my own comfort as to remind him he was not alone anymore, when I noticed something curious.

"Uh, guys?" I held up my wrist. A crescent moon–shaped light glowed gently as it swung from my bracelet. "There are spirits here. Do you think it's Ulfur?"

"He is a lich now, not a spirit. He wouldn't register on your stone that way."

"Oh. Good point. Well, regardless, there are some ghosties here somewhere."

"Stay behind me," Kristoff said, glancing over my shoulder at Andreas. The latter nodded at him as they exchanged some sort of macho guy look, the kind that said they had to protect the poor little feeble female in their care.

Silly vampires. I snorted to myself, flexing my fingers as I gathered a little light, preparing to halt the charge of reapers that was sure to follow when Kristoff flung open the doors to the conference room. They should know by now that this female was far from feeble.

Kristoff opened one of the doors a smidgen. Andreas and I crowded around him to peer in.

". . . tried and tried, but I just can't understand them. Maybe one of you can, but for the life of me, I can't see how I'm expected to do a job if these people can't even be bothered to speak something understandable!"

The voice that reached our ears was female, whiny, and had a faint inflection that I mentally termed "mall rat."

"Get her out of here," a low male voice said. Its sheer lack of emotion sent a little skittering of fear down my back. That and a jolt of recognition, not to mention a number of memories I'd rather do without.

"Frederic's in there," I said in an almost inaudible whisper.

Kristoff nodded.

"You were told before that the director had no time for this," a male voice said in a bossy, also familiar tone. "You must leave now."

"Great. And Mattias."

Kristoff's back twitched.

"I don't care what sort of war games you're running — how am I going to get these two to T'ien?" the whiny woman demanded to know.

"You will leave now. You never should have been allowed in. The office is closed while the board deals with some unprecedented events. You must find your spirits' destination by yourse —"

The door suddenly opened in front of us. For a moment, we stared in surprise at an equally surprised Mattias, behind whom was a petite woman holding a Chihuahua. Beyond her I could see two spirits, both male, both Chinese, dressed in identical tattered blue cloth jackets and pants. They looked like the poor immigrants forced to work on the railroad lines during one of California's many growth spurts.

Mattias was the first to recover. "Wife!" he said, his blond brows pulling together in a frown. His gaze narrowed on Kristoff and Andreas. "You've come to flaunt more lovers in my face? I will not have it! You will not —"

I flung my handful of light past Kristoff and fully into Mattias's face. He stood dazzled for a moment, the scowl fading into an expression of delight. "Pookie!"

"Oh, God," Kristoff muttered.

Andreas snickered.

"Hey! He's helping *me,*" the other Zorya said, stuffing her dog into an oversize violet bag. Light flashed in her hands as she sent it flying around Mattias's head.

He turned to her, a slightly less delighted expression on his face. "Zorya Amber."

She smirked at me for a moment before turning to him, pursing her lips, and making one of the most repulsive simpers I'd ever beheld. "Big ol' sacristan wants to help Amber get rid of these annoying ghosts, doesn't he?"

"Of course," Mattias agreed.

"What is going on?" a different male voice called out from the depths of the conference room. The door was only half-open, so we couldn't see in. "What is the holdup? We have things to do to prepare for the attack.

Remove the Zorya at once."

"Mattias?" I said, smiling as he turned back to me. I shoved a handful of light into his face.

"Pia, Pia, Pia!"

"Get rid of the chick," I said, nodding toward Amber.

She gasped and started to summon light again when I grabbed her by the strap of her purse and hauled her out into the hallway.

"Stop that!" she shrieked, slapping at my hands. "You'll stretch it! Do you have any idea how much I paid for this bag?"

"Dump her outside," I told Mattias. "And don't let her gather up light!"

He grinned and grabbed both of her hands, frog-marching her outside, her squawks of protest echoing down the empty hallway. The two ghosts followed her, neither of them looking very happy.

"I'm sorry," I told them as they left. "I hope I didn't screw anything up for you guys, but things are bound to get a bit hairy, and it really is better if you're not in the middle of it."

The door was jerked open just as I turned toward it.

"Ah. You have arrived at last," Frederic said as Kristoff tried to shove me behind himself. I poked him in the shoulder and scooted to the side. Frederic's eyes bugged out a bit at the sight of me. "Zorya Pia! You . . . er . . . are here as well?"

"As you see. Good morning, Frederic," I said brightly, clutching Kristoff's arm. I might not be a wimp, but I wasn't stupid, either. "You can stop whatever horrible plans you've set into motion with the capture of Alec, because the cavalry has, in fact, arrived."

Both his eyebrows rose in genuine surprise. "Capture of Alec? Dare I assume you mean a Dark One?"

"Don't try to be coy," I said sternly, leveling my best glare at him while keeping a firm grip on Kristoff's arm. He was as tense as a panther about to leap. "We know you know who Alec is, and we also know you captured him a few minutes ago. I'm sure, if you put your mind to it, you can figure out how —"

He stopped me with a slightly raised hand, his lips curling in a sickly approximation of amusement. "My dear Pia, I haven't the slightest idea of what you're talking about."

"You . . . er . . . don't?" I looked at Kristoff. *Is he bullshitting us?*

I don't think so. Kristoff's gaze was unwavering and intent on Frederic. A lesser man would have backed up a step, but Frederic simply maintained an expression of mild interest.

"You knew we were coming, though," Kristoff said, relaxing just a smidgen.

"Yes, of course. We were told you would be arriving to kill us."

"We're not here to kill you," I said, attempting to figure out whether he was trying to pull something over on us.

He looked just as surprised as I felt, his demeanor cracking for one second as he glanced to the side.

Kristoff pushed past him into the room. It was a standard conference room, although the long table in the center had inlaid marquetry that I wished I had time to admire. Two men and a woman stood grouped at the far end, none of them shrieking threats, performing a chant to initiate one of their ghastly ceremonies, or doing anything, really, other than looking somewhat scared and nervous.

I looked at them for a few moments, then back at Frederic. He looked even more nervous than they did. Something did *not* add up.

"All right, where are all the high-powered reapers?" I asked, putting my hands on my hips.

Frederic backed into the room when Andreas walked toward him. He waved at the group of three. "This is the governing board. Rather than let you kill innocent members, we opted to clear the building and meet you here, face-to-face, in a fervent hope that we might reason with you. In fact, I think it would be best for all of us if I might have a word alone with you. . . ."

"Oh, no, I am not so naive as to fall for that old trick," I said with a knowing look.

He glanced at the governors, and again I was struck by how nervous he was. "I feel there may be some discussions that are more suited to a private situation."

Does he seriously think he's getting me alone?

If I didn't know better, I'd say he was frightened of you.

Of me? That's silly. I'm no threat to him.

Not as such, perhaps, but I wonder if your theory about him could be correct after all. If he was withholding information from the board of governors, he might fear you would tell them the truth.

About him shooting Denise? A light dawned in the murky depths of my brain. *You are the most brilliant man ever. Of course! Rick and Janice said he told everyone a vampire shot Denise. He's afraid I'm going to spill on*

394

*him and tell everyone about his plan to get rid
of Denise by having her first kill Anniki, then
killing her before she tattled. Oh, this is sweet.
And here I was thinking he was the big bad
boss, and it turned out to be us all along. Ha!
Justice at last!*

Frederic had been making not very subtle
attempts to get me out of the room while
Kristoff and I were talking. I let him wind
down before saying firmly, "I appreciate the
offer of privacy, but right here is fine with
me. And for the record, we are more than
reasonable. It's you people who seem to be
at the other end."

I was still suspicious of some sort of trick.
But try as I might, I could detect no secret
passage through which a Brotherhood army
might flow, or axes that might come flinging
from the ceiling to chop us to bits, or even
the sound of venomous snakes that might
be released under the table, trained to attack vampires.

There was just nothing but the three of
us, the four of them, and silence.

"The Brotherhood is never unreasonable,"
one of the male governors said. "We follow
a strict canon of behavior."

I made a little face at him that had him
licking his lips nervously. "You kill vampires."

"Well, yes," he admitted, taking a step back as he glanced at the vamps present. "But we do so according to the strictest rules."

"That doesn't make it right," Andreas said, scowling at them.

"You kill us, too," the lone woman in the group piped up. The governor next to her tried to hush her up. "Well, they do," she told him before turning back to glare at Andreas.

"Only in self-defense," he answered.

"You tried to kill Kristoff and Alec," I said, pointing at Frederic.

"Of course I did. It's what we do. We're the Brotherhood of the Blessed Light," he said, just as if that explained things. "I really believe this discussion would be best held in my office —"

I rubbed my forehead where a headache was starting to form. "This is getting us nowhere. Let's start at the beginning, shall we? Who told you we were coming?"

"As a matter of fact, I did," a voice said from behind us. We swung around. It was Alec. He stood with a sword in each hand and a smile on his handsome face. He made a little salute with one of the swords, bowing toward us. "I've been waiting for this for a *very* long time."

Chapter 16

Kristoff roared in anger, throwing himself toward Alec.

No slouch on the reaction front, Alec spun around and was out the door, Kristoff in hot pursuit.

"Stay here," I told the others, dashing after him.

Andreas tried to push me aside, but I slapped at his hands, grabbing his wrists and yanking him to a stop. "You have to stay with Frederic and the gang," I told him.

His scowl was familiar, if not identical to Kristoff's. "You stay."

"That's the man I love out there!" I said, jerking him back.

"He's my brother!" He grabbed me around the waist, plopping me down in a chair before running for the door.

"Love takes precedence over blood," I said, tossing up a wall of light in front of him, keeping him from leaving the room.

His glare as I ran through the light should have dropped me dead on the spot, but I simply repeated, "Stay with Frederic!" as I ran off.

Kristoff and Alec were no longer in sight as I raced down the hallway, Andreas's frustrated curses following me. A door opened as I passed it, Rowan's eyes visible as he peeked out before fully opening the door.

"Pia? What's going on?" Magda asked as they emerged from the room. Raymond was clutching his camera in one hand, the Taser in the other. Rowan glanced up and down the hall, doing a double take at Andreas trapped behind a wall of shimmering, glittering silver light.

"Alec is here. He's betrayed us! Kristoff is after him. Reapers in the room back there with ghosts. No time to talk." I threw myself forward, slamming right into Mattias, who had evidently come back from escorting the other Zorya out.

"Pia-pooh!" he burbled happily, rubbing his mouth where my forehead had smacked into it. "Smooch?"

"Get out of my way, you giant Viking," I said, disentangling myself from him in order to run around the corner. I hesitated for a second, unsure which way to go. I was in a reception area, a flight of stairs on my left, while the space to my right was taken up with an empty curved desk, and the typical setup of chairs and small occasional tables bearing what looked like informational pamphlets. Across the wall on the far side of the room was a banner that proclaimed, THE BROTHERHOOD AND YOU! FIVE SIGNS THAT YOU MIGHT BE HAUNTED.

"Wait for us; we're coming, too," Magda said as I hurried up the stairs.

"You need me. I go with you," Mattias told me.

"No! Stay with the reapers, all of you! They could be up to something, and Andreas is alone with them!"

Rowan, who had been about to follow, nodded and disappeared back into the hallway. Magda and Raymond continued on, determined looks on their faces.

"We're your posse," Magda declared as we reached the top. I was a bit breathless, but didn't pause, just charged down the corridor that resembled the one behind us. "You need us."

"My dear, really, posse?" Raymond asked somewhat wheezily as I opened door after door, searching for the man whose life was woven into mine. "You don't think that's a bit dated?"

"I love you!" declared Mattias as he followed them. "I want to be your posse, too!"

"Do you have a better word for it?" Magda asked Raymond somewhat snappishly.

"Well . . . associates."

"Dammit, Kristoff, where are you?" I muttered, flinging open the door next to me, giving the room a quick once-over, and running to the next one. "Don't do this to me!"

"I love Kristoff, too."

"Compatriots," Raymond suggested.

"That's just being pedantic," Magda told him, following me. " 'Compatriot' is much more dated than 'posse.' "

"Supporters, then," he offered.

"We're her friends, not garter belts!"

The last door opened to reveal an empty room. I stepped inside it, looking around in bewilderment, defeat bowing my shoulders before I realized what that meant.

"Roof!" I shouted, shoving Mattias and Magda out of the way as they both tried to come into the room at the same time.

"Good God, a rooftop fight? I hope I have enough film left for this," Raymond muttered as we ran en group up the last flight of stairs.

The sunlight was blinding when we

emerged from the relative dimness of the offices, the heat already kicking into high gear. The roof held a tiny little garden on one side, with all the big cooling units and communication equipment on the other side. In the center of the small swath of green grass, two men lunged at each other, both clad in coats and hats, the blades of their swords flashing silver in the sun.

"Kristoff!" I yelled, shoving aside a lawn chair as I dashed forward.

"Stay back, Beloved," he yelled, glancing over his shoulder at me.

Alec lunged, his blade coming away dulled and wet.

"Watch out!" I bellowed, picking up the chair with the intention of throwing it at Alec.

"Perhaps I should be fighting Pia rather than you," Alec taunted him. I threw the chair, but he moved aside easily.

Kristoff snarled an invective that had Alec laughing.

"Then you would know what it's like to watch your Beloved die before your eyes."

"You *what?*" I asked, setting down the second chair I had just hefted.

Alec laughed again, dancing around Kristoff, his blade moving so fast it was just a blur. I had no idea how Kristoff parried those jabs, but he did, moving as easily as if he'd been born to it.

"Let's jump him," Magda said, prodding Raymond forward a couple of steps. "You have the Taser. Go zap Alec."

"Haven't told her yet, have you?" Alec asked Kristoff.

"Told me that you made him a vampire? Oh, yes, he told me that," I said, anger causing the light to gather in my palms.

Raymond watched the intricate dance as the two men fought, shaking his head. "I wouldn't dare. They're moving too fast."

I agreed. And they were moving fast, inhumanly fast, their faces and hands turning red as they fought. I released the light, shaking my hands free of it, looking around for something else I could use to disarm Alec.

"You'd think vampires would have had the sense to fight somewhere they couldn't get sunburned," I said, eyeing a large potted plant.

"Ray, do something!" Magda demanded. "Posses don't just stand around watching!"

"Er . . ." Ray pulled his camera out of his pocket and took a picture.

"Oh, for the love of all that is right and holy . . ." Magda snatched his camera away.

"He didn't tell you how he killed my

Beloved? How he watched her die slowly, her flesh melting off her body? He didn't tell you how I almost died that night, too?" Alec called.

My eyes widened as I looked at Kristoff. *You killed Alec's Beloved?*

No.

Then why —

My wife did. I told you she killed the mate of a Dark One.

You didn't tell me she was Alec's Beloved!

I didn't know until you showed me that damned reaper journal.

"I thought you said vamps couldn't live without their Beloveds," Magda said as Raymond pestered her for his camera back.

"They can't," Alec yelled, leaping aside as Kristoff lunged forward, simultaneously throwing a metal bench at him. Alec jumped back, then immediately started an attack on the other side.

I realized at that moment what Kristoff was doing. He was keeping himself between Alec and me. My heart warmed with love for him. He wasn't just keeping me alive for his own sake, but because he truly did have gentler emotions for me. They wouldn't ever be what he had for his late girlfriend, but I had at last resigned myself to being happy with what he could give me.

"How did you survive, then?" I asked, sending Kristoff wave after wave of love.

He glanced back at me for a split second, startled. I blew him a kiss. Mattias, next to me, blew him one as well.

"We weren't yet Joined. I had just met Eleanor when she ran into the Zorya."

The word echoed with a horrible reverberation in my head.

Kristoff stumbled.

"A Zorya?" Magda asked, just as astounded as I was. "Uh-oh."

"No!" I screamed, throwing myself forward as Alec, taking advantage of the misstep, kicked Kristoff's other leg out and was instantly upon him, the sword held at Kristoff's heart. "Nooo!"

Alec looked up from Kristoff, his green eyes like those of a cat, relish evident in them as he panted, his face and hands blistered. "Why shouldn't I kill him, Pia?"

"Because I love him," I said simply.

He hesitated, his eyes searching my face. Tears spilled over my eyelashes as I looked at Kristoff, his skin blistering as well, his gaze steadfast on mine.

Alec shook his head, his fingers tightening around the hilt of the sword. "Not good enough."

"Then . . . because I can do this." I pulled

as hard as I could on the power of the moon, pulling from it the silvery cool light that filled me with a calm sense of rightness, slamming it into Alec's chest.

He flew backward into a storage bench, knocking it over, his arms and legs tangling up in the chair cushions that spilled out from inside it.

Kristoff reached for the sword Alec had knocked out of his grip, stalking over to where the man who had once been his friend lay inert in a small stream of blood seeping from a cut on his head.

I joined Kristoff. We both stood and watched Alec for a moment.

"You didn't kill him," Kristoff said.

"No. There was only enough power in that ball of light to knock him backward and maybe singe off a little chest hair. Your wife was a Zorya?"

Pain washed through him. Pain and guilt and something that, for a moment, reminded me of fear. "Yes."

"Which means, unless things have changed over the centuries, that you were a sacristan."

Kristoff turned to me, his eyes robin's-egg blue. "I did not know the woman was his Beloved."

I touched his mind with mine. He was

reluctant to allow the intimacy, but I was insistent, and he finally let me in. The dark, stained part of his mind that I thought was due to his plans with the vampires was now lit brightly.

You thought I would hate you if I knew you were once a reaper, too?

You did not wish to be Zorya anymore.

So?

You have to be married to a sacristan to be Zorya. I could not risk giving you up. And I knew that once you were aware of what I had been, how it was my wife who had started the reapers on their path of murder, you would not wish to remain with me.

I stared at him in growing disbelief. *Do you seriously believe that I would dump you because of something you were a couple of hundred years ago?*

Other women have when they found out.

Other women like Angelica?

He turned away from me, prodding Alec with his shoe.

"Show's over, I guess," Magda said softly. "Why don't we go inside and give them a bit of privacy?"

"Probably best," Raymond said, fussing over the camera that Magda had handed back to him. "Oh, now look what you did. You had it set completely wrong for this amount of sun. . . ."

"Come on, Mattias. *Mattias.* Honey, we need to have a talk about Pia. Why don't you come with Ray and me, and I'll tell you how things stand."

The others left. I grabbed Kristoff's arm and made him turn around to me. "I know you don't want to talk about her. And I promise I will never bring up her name after this, but please, Kristoff, answer me. Did the woman you loved above all others shun you because she found out about your origins?"

His eyes narrowed. "The woman I loved above all others?"

"Angelica. Your girlfriend. The one the reapers killed," I said, in case I'd gotten her name wrong.

"I loved her, but I didn't love her above all other women," he said. "And yes, we were tracing some reapers when somehow she stumbled across information about my past. She was repulsed by what I had been, and ran away from me. It was then that the reapers caught her."

"Wait a minute," I said, waggling a finger at him. "You were mourning her when I first met you."

"No, I wasn't," he said, stroking his chin.

"But . . . you had sworn eternal vengeance

or something like that. Alec told me."

He gave a little shrug. "I had sworn to avenge her death, yes. As well as find out who had given her the information about me that sent her fleeing to that death."

"Still haven't figured it out?"

We both looked down to the source of the question, Kristoff immediately putting the sword tip to Alec's neck.

Alec waved it away, pulling himself up until he was propped up on a nearby bench. "You can drop the sword. I'm not going to kill Pia."

I widened my eyes. "Were you going to try?" I squeaked.

"Yes. It seemed only fitting to take his Beloved as he took mine." Alec winced as he felt along his head, his fingers coming away smeared with red. "And speaking of killing, why didn't you end my suffering once and for all?"

"I couldn't do that without a ceremony and a group of reapers," I said, watching him carefully. "Not that I would. You really would have killed me?"

"Yes." He looked up, his gaze meeting mine before a wry smile stole over his mouth. "No. I thought I could, but I guess I'm just too weak."

"I don't think it's weakness," I said, smiling slowly. "I think you realize that Kristoff did not kill your Beloved."

Alec leaned back against the bench, his eyes closed. "Does it matter anymore?"

"Yes, it does," Kristoff said, lowering the sword. "You told Angelica the truth."

"Yes. As I did Mabel, and Augustine, and who was that dairymaid in Alsace whom you used to visit every Sunday? Marie? I told them, just as I told every woman who ever captured your heart."

"Only one woman has captured my heart," Kristoff said, raising the sword again.

I looked at him in surprise, hope bursting into unreasonable but undeniable being deep inside my heart, growing with a desperate prayer. *I thought you just said you didn't love Angelica above all others.*

Kristoff shot me a look. *I'm a little busy. Now is not the time to discuss relationships.*

I think it's just a perfectly fine time. Who have you given your heart to? I was suddenly giddy, almost light-headed as I waited for him to answer.

"And she took me by surprise," Alec said with a rueful little laugh. "I wanted to destroy her as I've destroyed all the others, hoping each time that it would do the job, drive you beyond bearing."

Dio! *You pick now to have this conversa-*

*tion? Right now? This second? This instant?
Yes! Now! Stop stalling! Tell me!*

"But you weren't driven beyond bearing.
You never were. So I changed tactics. I
figured if I couldn't rip your heart out the
way you ripped out mine, I'd destroy the
other parts of your life."

"He didn't rip out your heart. His wife
did. He had nothing to do with it," I pointed
out.

Alec cracked open one eye and glared at
me. "Pia, you do not interrupt a man when
he is explaining his master plan after having
been soundly defeated. Don't you watch any
James Bond movies?"

"Sorry," I said contritely, with a pointed
look at Kristoff. "Go on. *Both* of you."

Alec opened his mouth to speak, checked
himself, then glanced at Kristoff. "I'm missing something, aren't I?"

"She's making me admit I love her,"
Kristoff said, his voice and face equally
pained.

"You said it!" I shrieked, clutching his
chest and kissing the pained expression
right off his face. "You can't take it back!
You said it out loud in front of a witness!
Wait — are you sure? You're not just saying
that because you have mild feelings of affection for me, and don't want to break my

heart? You're not just being nice?"

"Alec?" Kristoff asked, his hands on my butt.

"Are you daft, woman? You can't tell he's arse over heels in love with you?" Alec shook his head, winced at the movement, and slowly pulled himself onto the bench until he could slump down with a grunt. "You must be losing your touch, Kris. None of the others doubted you were anything but a devoted slave to their merest of whims."

"This is different," Kristoff said, hoisting me up so my mouth was level with his. "This is my Beloved."

Say it again, I demanded as I bit his lower lip, welcoming the lovely taste of him as he gave me what I wanted.

I love you, Pia. I don't know why you ever thought I didn't. I believed I was making myself quite obvious.

That's because you're a man, and it doesn't occur to you that other people might think you were so much in love with your dead girlfriend that you could never love anyone else.

Never is a long time.

So you really did love her?

Yes.

I thought about that for a moment. *That's OK. I've been in love before, too. You're right. What we have is totally different from that.*

411

Say it again.

I love — You've loved other men? What other men?

I giggled at his outraged tone, releasing his lip. "You knew I had been with men before you."

"Been with," he said, an irritated flare to his nostrils. " 'Been with' is completely different from 'in love with.' I will require the names and addresses of these men you were in love with."

"So then I decided, What the hell, I'll let her live. And they'll live happily ever after, while I continue to suffer untold, endless agonies because I had a Beloved once, and his first wife killed her before I could so much as bed her. This is the thanks I get for my generosity."

"Shut up, Alec," Kristoff said, scooping me up in his arms and starting toward the door that led back into the building.

"You're going to leave me here?" he called after us. I stopped licking Kristoff's ear and looked back at Alec. "I'm wounded! I let you win! I didn't kill Pia and watch you die slowly, in agony, while laughing and telling you about each exquisite moment of hell that my life has been since your first Zorya wife killed my love."

"Set me down," I told Kristoff. He did so.

I took his hand and marched back to where Alec was hunched over on the bench. "I think it's time we got this over with once and for all. Kristoff, your wife was a Zorya."

"Yes."

"Did you know she was going to kill Alec's Beloved?"

"She said her oxen ran wild and trampled the woman. I did not even know she was Moravian."

I turned to Alec. "You said your Beloved was melted. Did you see Kristoff's wife do it?"

His face twisted. "Not the actual cleansing, but I didn't need to. She was decapitated, and her body was horribly mangled, with parts of her burned away. Only the damned reaper light could do that."

"That's what she meant," Kristoff said slowly, his gaze inward.

"Your wife?" I asked.

"Ruth said she'd tried to clean away the stain of the death, but couldn't. I thought she was speaking metaphorically, but she was speaking literally instead. . . ."

"She was telling the truth about the trampling, then." More puzzle pieces were coming together. "But then she probably panicked when she saw a dead vampire, and used the light to try to get rid of the body.

Poor woman. She must have been scared to death to try to hide the whole thing. And then when Alec found out and went nuts . . ."

Alec froze for a moment before slumping back against the bench, one hand over his eyes. "An accident. It was an accident after all. All this torment, each second since that moment a unique hell of its own, and her death was due to an accident. I should have killed the oxen."

"You did. They were my best team," Kristoff said, then cleared his throat when I nudged him. "Why did you never tell me this?"

Alec sighed and looked up at him. "You were my most hated enemy. You killed the one woman who could save me. Or so I thought. I turned you, pretended I was your friend so I could shadow your every footstep, and make sure that you suffered just as I did. I drove away your women, tried to take your Beloved, and plotted with infinite detail both of your demises. Why do you *think* I didn't tell you?"

"But you're not Kristoff's enemy, are you?" I said gently, leaning against Kristoff, so happy I thought I might break into song at any moment.

"No," he said dolefully. "Sometime over

414

the last hundred years the enjoyment has gone out of watching you suffer."

"You didn't tell the reapers where to find Kristoff's girlfriend, did you?" I asked, suddenly wary.

Alec shook his head. "I told her about him. I never thought she'd run straight out into the pack of them. I did my best to save her." He looked up at Kristoff. "I was truly sorry about that."

"I know."

"Before this breaks down into a true Hallmark moment and we all start buying each other Precious Moments figurines, why don't we get you off the roof?" I said, holding out my hand for Alec. "The sun is moving and it's going to hit you soon. And although the blistering is gone off your face, you don't look like you could stand too much more."

Alec let us help him to his feet, supporting him between us as we got him back to the door. "If I said I was sorry about everything, Kris . . ." He let the sentence trail off, but looked expectantly at Kristoff.

Kristoff nodded and socked Alec on the shoulder in a guy gesture of forgiveness, but Alec was still recovering from that ball of light, and tottered into the wall. Kristoff righted him with a word of apology, dusted him off, then held open the door for him.

"Why did you tell Frederic we were coming to kill him?" I asked.

"I knew by that time that I couldn't kill you. I figured I'd have them do it for me," Alec admitted.

"But you couldn't even do that, could you, you big galoot?" I said, taking Kristoff's hand. Mattias bounded up the stairs to greet me, refusing to stop kissing my free hand until Kristoff pushed him down half the flight of stairs.

"Kristoff!" he said in a wounded little voice as he picked himself up. Magda and Ray were next to him, looking startled.

Ray snapped a quick picture as we descended to the first floor.

"He's sorry, Mattias. But no more kissing, OK?"

He sighed. "Magda says we weren't really married."

"No, we weren't, because Kristoff was a sacristan. But don't worry," I said, patting his hand. "I'll find you another Zorya, someone who will like you kissing her all the time, OK?"

"That's all we need," Alec murmured under his breath. "Another Zorya."

"Everything OK?" Magda asked, her eyes round as she looked from Alec to Kristoff.

416

"Yes. Everything is just fine now. Old wounds healed over, misunderstanding cleared up, forgiveness given. It's an Oprah kind of moment."

"I'll say. So what now?"

"Now we go tell Frederic to stop killing vampires, or else. Oh! Why did the Ilargi give a Dutch necromancer your phone number?" I asked Alec as we headed down the stairs to the main floor.

"I have no idea," he answered, seeming somewhat startled by the idea.

"Yes, you do. Or at least, you made me think you did last night, when you were rescuing me from the reapers. Remember? I asked you if you were doing undercover work for the Brotherhood, and you said yes."

"Of course I did. I was lying. I knew nothing about a necromancer and an Ilargi."

"Great. Now what am I going to do?"

Rowan was waiting for us. His eyebrows rose at the sight of Alec being supported by Kristoff.

"I missed it all, didn't I?" he asked his cousin.

"Yes. I'm sorry. Next time I'll wait for you," Kristoff told him.

"You'd better." Rowan examined Alec for a moment, then slid his shoulder under Alec's arm.

"I don't suppose anyone has any idea where I can find the Ilargi?" I asked mournfully as our little ragtag group made its way down the hall to the boardroom. No one answered. "I didn't think so. Damn."

"There's something — Gah . . . I think the shutter is jammed. . . ." Raymond stopped, fighting with something on his camera.

"The Brotherhoodians aren't going to go ballistic when they see all of the vampires, are they?" Magda asked as she walked next to me.

"I'm thinking that's not going to be a big problem," I said, smiling at the memory of the worried look worn by the governors.

Rowan opened up the door, he and Kristoff helping a still wobbly Alec to a couch. Andreas, who stood with a gun pointed at the small herd of reapers, looked utterly astonished.

"Was it bad?" he asked his brother.

"Very. Pia made me tell her I love her in front of Alec."

"Ouch."

I sent a tiny little ball of light to Andreas's feet.

He grinned at me. "I mean, congratulations."

"I'm sorry about all this," I told Frederic

as he rose slowly to his feet. "It was really just a big misunderstanding. Alec doesn't want you to kill us."

"He doesn't?" Frederic asked, his face as placid as ever.

"No. Do you, Alec?"

"Not anymore, no. Ouch. I don't suppose you have a healer handy? I think a couple of my ribs are piercing my lung."

"Suck it up, buttercup," I told him. "You have healing powers. Go to it." I turned back to the reapers. "And just in case you're still worried, I will repeat that we're not here to hurt any of you guys."

All of the reapers looked pointedly at Andreas.

He grinned sheepishly and put away the gun.

"So you see? All's well. Oh, there is just one thing," I said, biting my lip.

Boo, would you mind it if I made sure that the Brotherhood doesn't hurt any more vampires?

Kristoff sighed into my mind. *I'm becoming used to the idea that my Beloved could strike me dead with the slightest flick of her fingers. If you think that's the only way, go ahead.*

That's just one of the many reasons I love you. And it's two flicks of my fingers.

419

"What's that?" the female reaper asked when I didn't finish.

"Hmm? Oh. I understand you don't have a Zenith. I'd like the job, please."

THE NEW BEGINNING

The reapers, to a man, stared at me as if I had painted myself blue, put a moose on my head, and started dancing on their table.

"You're not serious," Frederic finally said.

"I am. Quite, as a matter of fact."

"You go, girl," Magda told me, giving me a thumbs-up.

"You are aware of the fact that you are . . ." Frederic stopped, glancing at the governors.

"A Beloved. I am Kristoff's Beloved. Yes, I'm aware of that fact," I said, ignoring the gasps of horror from the governors.

Frederic turned pleading eyes on me.

"But I'm also a Zorya, one who's seen a lot in a relatively short time. I am, however, circumspect if the situation calls for it," I told him.

He didn't have any trouble reading between my verbal lines.

"It's quite out of the question," the outspoken governor said. "The very idea of a Beloved, the mortal enemy and complete opposite of everything the Brotherhood stands for, being a Zenith? Unfathomable."

"Not quite so unlikely as you might think," I said, leaning on Kristoff as I kept my eyes on Frederic.

He looked uncomfortable, between a rock and a hard place, just where I wanted him.

"Er . . ." was all he could manage to say.

"Pia is going to find me a Zorya of my own," Mattias announced, then leaned in and said in a loud whisper, "I don't want the one over there."

"Don't worry; I'll get you one you like," I whispered back. "Why don't you sit down now?"

"All right. I will miss not having you for my wife. I will miss not kissing you, and licking you, and holding your hand," he said, looking downcast for a moment; then he suddenly brightened as he turned his gaze on Kristoff.

If he kisses me one more time —

Stop fussing. He just likes you! You should be flattered.

He likes everyone when his brain is boggled.

"Director?" All three governors were watching Frederic as intently as I was, obviously waiting for them to show us the door.

422

"You cannot be considering such a thing."

"You are aware that the Zenith is the ultimate of positions within the Brotherhood," Frederic said slowly, picking his words with care. "Only the most august and revered Zoryas have climbed to its heady heights, and only after grueling and extensive searches were conducted to find the one person who could lead the membership in pursuit of our goals. You are aware that only the brightest, the best, the most devout of women can become Zenith."

"Which is why she's so perfect for it," Magda said with a little shrug.

The reapers' expressions turned to horror.

"I may not be perfect for the job, but I *am* going to take it, and you *are* going to stop killing vampires, and in turn, they will stop killing you people, and everyone is going to live together in peace and harmony, or by God, I will let judgment roll down as the waters, and righteousness as an ever-flowing stream!"

Frederic didn't miss that threat, either. "Er . . ."

"And just how to do you expect to force us to name you as Zenith?" the woman governor asked.

I smiled. Beside me, Kristoff straightened

up and donned a menacing expression. Rowan moved into place next to him. Andreas scooted over to my other side. Magda cracked her knuckles, and stood on Andreas's far side.

With a groan, Alec got to his feet and hobbled over to take up a position next to Rowan.

Mattias made a little bleating noise of distress, and joined the group.

"Mattias!" the female Zorya gasped. "You are one of us!"

"Not at all like her," Mattias said in an undertone, frowning at the woman.

My smile grew larger. "Any further questions about my qualifications?"

"Wait a second; Ray will want to be here. Ray? *Ray!*"

Frederic glanced at the others. They were silent. Horror-struck would have been an apt description.

"There's nothing to prevent us from removing you from the position, should we accede to force now," Frederic warned.

"I know. But I'm willing to bet that I can convince more than a few reapers to see the light. So to speak."

He blanched.

"*Ray!* Oh. Sorry, everyone. I'll just see what's keeping him —"

The door opened before Magda finished, and Raymond burst in waving his Taser. "I'm here! Who needs shooting?" He skidded to a stop at the sight of the wall of vampires, glancing around the room. "What did I miss?"

"Just Pia taking over as head of the reapers. She is taking over, isn't she?" Magda asked Frederic.

He hesitated for a moment. I dropped little balls of light around him in a decorative circle.

"She is. For the moment," he agreed, jerking his arm away from where his elbow strayed into one of the beams of light.

The governors said nothing, their eyes on the light.

Mattias applauded and started to mouth, *I love you,* to me when Kristoff caught his eye. He moved around behind Magda instead.

You know they won't let you stay Zenith. Kristoff's hands were warm as they caressed my back, but his mouth on mine was positively scorching.

I know. But I can slow them down for a little bit, and maybe if we work at it, we can chip away at the members until the fanatics are outnumbered. It'll be quite a job on top of tracking down the Ilargi who has Ulfur, but I think we're up to it.

I have something else in mind I think you're up to.

"Now that really warms the cockles of your heart," I heard Magda say as Kristoff, without breaking his kiss, scooped me up and started to leave.

"I don't think it's just his cockles that are going to be warmed," Raymond said.

"Ray!"

"Sorry, honey bunny. It just seemed appropriate somehow."

I giggled into Kristoff's mouth, my happiness dimming for a moment as I thought of what remained to be done. *Ulfur.*

We'll find him, Kristoff promised.

And Mattias?

He sighed. *We'll find him a woman.*

A Zorya?

A woman.

He needs a Zorya. He's a sacristan. You have one, after all. It's only right he should have one.

We'll discuss it later.

How much later?

He let me see a picture of just what he wanted to do to me. My toes curled. *You're right. We'll talk about it later. Home?*

Home.

Say it again.

I love you.

Sounds good, but I think I need to hear it again.

I love you, Pia. I love you now. I will love you tomorrow. I will love you always. I will love you until the sun and moon fade away into nothing, and the world turns to ash. I will love you beyond that, to the ends of all time. There is no beginning or end of my love for you — it simply is, as I am, and so long as I am, so will it be.

I love you too, my adorable vampire. Oh! I know! Say it in Italian. . . .

ABOUT THE AUTHOR

Katie MacAlister lives in the Pacific Northwest with her husband and dogs, and can often be found lurking around online game sites. To contact Katie, visit www.katie macalister.com.